Ripples on the Lake

Ripples
on the
Lake

Dawn Rotarangi

HarperCollins*Publishers*

National Library of New Zealand Cataloguing-in-Publication
Data
Rotarangi, Dawn, 1950-
Ripples on the lake / Dawn Rotarangi.
ISBN 978-1-86950-639-1
1. Title.
NZ823.3—dc 22

First published 2007
HarperCollins*Publishers (New Zealand) Limited*
P.O. Box 1, Auckland

ISBN (10-digit): 1 86950 639 1
ISBN (13-digit): 978 1 86950 639 1
Cover design by Natalie Winter, HarperCollins Design Studio
Internal text design and typesetting by Springfield West
Printed by Griffin Press, Australia, on 50 gsm Bulky News

CHAPTER ONE

S AFFRON DELANEY FLEW down the deserted, darkened pavement as if a dozen pit bulls snapped one step behind. Her short, feathery blonde hair was flattened against the sides of her face, so that her wind-sculpted features were sharp and wild.

The pavement ended, but she held her line and ran straight over a ground-hugging spiky-green thing, lifting her jeans-clad legs as they stuck between unyielding branches. As she shot across Ruapehu Street a Range Rover claimed the road. She slowed for a stride at the centre line, feet planted, body swaying. A horn blared. The four-wheel-drive thundered past in a rush of lights and air and Saffron ran on through diesel fumes that lingered in a dirty grey cloud.

All it had taken was one phone call from Billy. Her brother had a problem. The two went together like a dog and fleas. Her sneakers slapped against concrete, the sound altering as each shopfront bounced the sound back.

How many times had she raced to Billy's rescue? Too many. And each time she told herself this was the last one, but it never was. Billy would phone, and she would come, as if they were dance partners who could spin out to arm's length but never quite let go.

Why hadn't he come to the shop if he wanted her? He knew that most Friday nights she'd be working late at The Dog House, sculpting one of her canine clients to show-winning perfection. He frequently stopped off, hitching his behind onto the end of the dog-grooming table for five minutes while they went through the small talk. He'd scratch the dog behind its ears, directing half his chat to the animal. Sweet-talking both of them, she sometimes thought cynically. She'd keep cutting, her blue eyes continually comparing the dog on the table with the image in her mind, as she clipped and snipped. All the time, she'd listen and talk. Then, with a flick back of that forelock, and one of his heart-melting ain't-I-awful smiles, Billy would arrive at the real reason for his visit. Money — or at least his lack of it. He never had been subtle.

She changed the length of her stride to accommodate the cracks in the pavement. 'Step on a crack, break your mother's back.' Saffron had been ten the last time she had stood on a crack, the year their mother had walked out on their father. Even at that age, seventeen years ago, Saffron could sort of understand a woman choosing to leave Lucky Del. But her five children? That she couldn't understand.

A multitude of things could bring bad luck crashing down on any of Lucky Del Delaney's kids. Stepping on a crack was as likely to be the cause as anything else. At least her mother's back had been OK the last time she heard.

She slowed for the hard right into the arcade, where the streetlights weren't so bright. Her shoulder bag knocked against her hip and the startled face of a window-dresser flashed by and was gone. Her breath came in gasps and she heard the squeal of tyres as two cars dragged away from the lights on Tongariro Street.

Up ahead, the arcade came out onto Horomatangi Street and she slowed, wanting to still be capable of speech when she got to Big Wal's. A black cat, every rib jutting through a dull coat, shot from behind a rubbish bag and across her path. Saffron threw it a venomous look and wished it a life full of fleas. If there was bad luck going down — and the undertone of panic in Billy's voice said there was — then a black cat crossing was the last thing she needed.

Five steps from the corner she reined herself in and stood with hands planted on slim hips, sucking in air. Her heart hammered so that her T-shirt quivered across her full breasts. Then she marched around the corner and turned down the street towards Big Wal's hamburger joint. The sound of a love song from the 'sixties floated up the pavement to greet her.

The counter, open to the street, ran the length of the shopfront, and Billy was slouched at one end of it with his hands stuffed in his pockets. He glanced up at her from under his hair with that intense brooding stare of his. Some people thought Billy conceited, and perhaps he was — she'd once caught him practising his look in the mirror — but even though he was almost twenty-one, sometimes he seemed heartbreakingly young and alone.

A brown-skinned, running-to-fat man, wearing a white apron over shorts, whom Saffron assumed was Big Wal, leant across the counter talking to a police officer in uniform.

Saffron sucked in her breath. Billy hadn't mentioned the police. On the other hand, he usually left out pertinent facts. She smoothed down her fringe, which had blown back from her face, and walked over in what she hoped was a reassuringly law-abiding way. At the last moment, right under the officer's nose, she spoilt the effect when her foot radar caught the presence of a crack, and she threw in a hiccuppy step to get over it — as if she didn't know whether she was coming or going.

Big Wal's assistant was in his twenties, with wiry dreadlocks that probably reached to his waist. They were twisted around his head and he looked as though a large, furry possum was squatting on him. He was frying onions and steak — the smell leapt the counter and whacked Saffron in the nostrils.

She smiled, raised her eyebrows by way of greeting to Billy, and said 'Everything OK?' to whoever felt like answering. She dragged in a deep breath; her heart quietened. She rubbed her hands up and down her bare arms and wished she hadn't left her sweater back at The Dog House. The cold wind took its temperature from the three mountains standing guard at the far end of Lake Taupo. Cool in summer, frigid in winter.

'Yes,' Billy said.

'No,' Big Wal said.

The sergeant made no attempt to disguise a loud sigh, and gazed off down the empty street for a second, blinking owlishly. He looked back at Saffron. 'Who are you?'

'I'm Billy's sister. He phoned.' She looked at each one of the men in turn, and, when no one volunteered anything, added, 'What's the problem?'

'Don't ask me. I'm just trying to buy a burger,' Billy said.

Considering that she had just shoved Prince Frederick of Moldavia into a crate with his hair sticking up every which way and looking more like a dog's dinner than the show-stopping standard poodle Mrs Edmondson was expecting, she could have shaken Billy. You *phoned* me, she wanted to hiss at him.

'Is there a problem?' Saffron asked, turning to the sergeant.

The sergeant turned to Big Wal — who wasn't very big but grew six inches because the whole town knew he kept a softball bat under the counter and felt obliged to use it at least once a year to keep it dust-free.

'*Is* there a problem?' the sergeant asked Big Wal.

'Not if someone *pays* for that ruddy burger he just ate.' Big Wal glared down the counter at Billy.

'Oh, Billy,' Saffron said. The downward inflection of her voice contained no element of surprise. Her brow creased as she turned back to him. 'You didn't try to not pay for it?'

'I *did* pay for it,' Billy flung back, keeping clear of Big Wal. He knew about the softball bat.

Big Wal nodded at the pile of coins on the counter between them. 'I don't want *those* coins, boy.'

Billy glared at Big Wal, and Saffron could almost see the smoke rise from under his cap. 'I don't *have* any more money on me! I've *paid* for the burger! Take the money or not! I don't care!'

Big Wal looked carefully at the handful of change. 'Until I accept those coins as payment, then you haven't paid.'

'Tough!' Billy said.

'I don't want those coins, boy. You take them back.'

'I don't want them either,' Billy muttered.

Saffron looked from one to the other with an exaggerated turn of her head.

The sergeant blew out a rush of air, his lips vibrating like a hard-run horse, and stared at his feet for a moment. He straightened up and demanded, 'Wal, does he owe you money or not?'

'Well, yes and no,' Big Wal said slowly.

The sergeant looked down the street again, obviously wishing he were out arresting drunks or something straightforward. Saffron took pity on him.

She unzipped her shoulder bag and pulled out a clutch purse. 'What does my brother owe you? I take it you'll accept money from *me*?'

Big Wal's smile indicated that he most certainly would.

Saffron dug in her purse and handed him a five-dollar note. Big Wal rang up the sale and gave her change.

'Right, boy, that money,' and Big Wal pointed at the coins, 'belongs to you. Take it and go.'

'Or?' Billy demanded, thrusting his chin out, but not leaving the end of the counter. Maybe he'd seen the softball bat in action.

'Sweet heaven above!' Saffron cried. 'What *is* the matter with you two?' She reached out to pick up the coins. Big Wal's arm shot out and knocked her hand away, but not before her fingers had touched the coins.

For a heartbeat, all she could see was red. No Billy, no sergeant, no Big Wal's burger bar. Just red crawling through her mind, a slow-moving river of red. Instinctively, she knew it was blood. It was sticky and coagulating, as if it had been shed a while ago. She could hear a buzzing in her ears.

The coins spun away down the counter as Big Wal knocked her hand. Billy took a rapid step backwards. Dreadlocks glanced quickly over his shoulder, then turned back to the basket of chips bubbling in the vat.

Saffron's mind slowly cleared. Red become pink, then palest pink, then nothing; faces clicked back into focus. She swallowed her stomach back down and placed one hand on the counter to steady herself.

Billy was beside her now, his hand on her arm. 'Saf? You OK, Saf?' He gave her arm a hesitant rub.

Saffron nodded slowly. 'I'm OK.' She felt as if she had missed a step in the dark — as if suddenly there was nothing where there was supposed to be solid ground.

Big Wal reached across the counter and took her hand. 'Stay out of it, girl. Those coins aren't yours.'

Saffron blinked. For some reason she'd been thinking about the day when big, gentle Paddy had turned into the rottweiler from hell and transformed her arm into a prop for a war movie. Probably the blood had triggered the memory. There'd been a lot of blood that day, all of it her own.

Her mind felt as if it was playing hopscotch, missing some squares, standing on the squares that were allowed.

The squares with blood on them, petal, a voice in her head said. *Them's the rules of the game.*

She blinked again, slowly, screwing up her eyes as if closed lids could shut out her father's voice. Lucky Del had been dead for more than ten years. Astride a racehorse, his sense of timing had been a gift from heaven — or so the country's leading trainer had said at his funeral. Not tonight.

'Umm . . .' She wanted to ask a question, but didn't know what it was.

'I'm guessing that you saw something bad,' Big Wal prompted. He sounded as if it would be OK to say yes.

Saffron nodded. 'What did I see?'

'I dunno. I haven't touched them.' Big Wal stared at her, worry lines creasing his forehead.

'What . . .' She still wasn't sure what her question was. At least with Paddy she'd known what to do. Drop the nail clippers, lie still, don't look at him. He'd gripped her arm for a few more seconds, as if trying to remember why he had it in his mouth, then he'd dropped it and licked her face, as if to apologize. He'd got off her chest, and she'd clambered to her feet, shaking. Since then she tended to muzzle anything with teeth bigger than her own when she trimmed their nails.

Big Wal gave her hand a squeeze and let it go. He picked up a cloth and began to wipe the counter.

The sergeant looked from one to the other. 'If you've been paid, Wal, I'll be off.' His brow, which had been as furrowed as Big Wal's, looked as if it had just been given a jab of Botox.

Big Wal frowned. 'But he's still littering my ruddy counter,' he complained.

'So stick the money in your till, Wal. I've never seen you reluctant to pocket someone's money before.'

'Not that money. I want the boy to take it.'

'Why?'

Big Wal shrugged. 'Burger's been paid for. The money's his.'

'Are you thinking the money's counterfeit?' the sergeant

said. He bent over the coins and examined them critically. 'Haven't heard about any funny money in town.'

'Naah.' Big Wal chuckled but without humour. 'Those coins are probably more real than any of us want. Eh, girl?' He turned to Saffron.

She knew what he meant, and wished she didn't.

The sergeant took a guess that only twenty years of living and working in a town like Taupo could inspire. 'Are they tapu?'

Big Wal didn't answer. A spot on the counter took his attention, and he rubbed at it vigorously.

The sergeant, whose face had been only centimetres from the coins as he studied them, straightened his body quickly, took a step backwards and folded his arms.

'Tapu?' Saffron echoed in a whisper. The wind that had whistled around the edges of the evening suddenly seemed to blast cold. She shivered.

Dreadlocks lifted the basket of chips draining above the vat and emptied it onto a sheet of white paper. He salted the chips, wrapped them and held them out over the counter until he caught the eye of a girl sitting in a car. She leapt out, came over and took them.

'Those coins tapu?' the sergeant queried. 'How can you tell?'

Saffron noticed the sergeant's hands were now clasped behind his back.

'I know,' Big Wal said.

Dreadlocks nodded his head vigorously and rang the girl's money into the till.

'How did our Billy get hold of tapu coins?' Saffron asked

slowly. Her gaze flicked from her brother to Big Wal and back again.

Billy shrugged. 'It's just some money I had on me.'

'It's more than that, boy.'

Billy waved his hands in what might have been meant as a conciliatory gesture. 'It was a business transaction. I wanted a burger — you sell burgers.'

'So you try to palm the ruddy things off onto me.' Big Wal's eyes narrowed, and he looked as if he was considering the wisdom of giving his softball bat its annual outing in front of the law.

'Now, now, Wal. He didn't mean any harm.' The sergeant had seen the look in Big Wal's eyes. 'A coin can't hurt anyone. Not really.'

And for some reason his words made Saffron think of the black cat that had crossed her path in the arcade — except now the cat was the size of a black panther with great white teeth curving over its bottom jaw, and, instead of crossing her path and disappearing into the shadows, it was stalking behind her. And when it grabbed her, it was going to make Paddy's bite look like an affectionate nibble. Her fingers instinctively rubbed over the thin white scars the rottweiler had left on her arm.

'Where did the coins come from, Billy?'

Billy looked away down the empty street and let the silence hang in the air along with the smell of fried onion. Eventually, he said, 'I picked them up down on the lakefront. There's a place down there, some rock, where people leave money.'

Big Wal sucked his breath in through his teeth with a hiss and shook his head. He muttered a string of words in Maori.

A prayer, thought Saffron, looking at him anxiously, and wondered if a Church of England prayer would work as well against a Maori — a Maori what? Curse? She wasn't even sure what she needed protection from.

'A stretch of rocks that reach out into the water? Big rock at the end? Looks like a fist at the end of an arm?' the sergeant asked, looking at Billy.

Billy stared defiantly back at them all and jerked his head up once in agreement.

'Tama's Rock,' Big Wal and the sergeant said together.

'It was just a pile of coins,' Billy said defensively. 'Someone told me about them.'

'You stupid, greedy little—' Saffron stopped, unable to find a word that conveyed her frustration. 'If that site is tapu, then the money will be tapu. Where are the brains that the good Lord gave you? Why didn't you come to me if you were broke? You can't take money from a place like that!'

'It was just a place.'

CHAPTER TWO

<u>1790</u>

THE GROUND IS *red with the blood of women and children. The water of the lake is stained pink as it slaps against their bodies. They lie where they were hacked down as they fled, the stench of death heavy in the air. The great Tama Ariki looks upon the scene with tearless eyes. There will be utu for this — a payment in blood. A savage, merciless revenge for the slaughter of his people.*

He prowls the beach from body to body. He turns and paces back, his head swinging from side to side, as he names each of the dead. Women, children. He searches for the body of his mokopuna, his first grandson. He walks again from body to body. So many dead. So many missing. He had thought they would be safe here beside this great lake. Utu — his lips move as he whispers the word.

He slowly circles the reddened land, his hand stretched out over the blood, listening to the voices of the dead. At last, he stops beside a rock. He takes a greenstone tiki from around his neck and places it in a hollow in a rock. The hollow is filled with blood. He looks into the blood. This is his mokopuna.

This is my rock, he says.

He steps back and each of his warriors takes a token from his person and lays it where the blood is reddest. Tama Ariki nods. This is good. Tokens to comfort the spirits of his people.

He stands with his back to the lapping waters of the lake, and his body glows as the last ray of sunlight strikes. He holds out his hands. The warriors wait. And then the blood begins to flow and drips through his fingers and joins with the blood of his people.

'Not just a place,' Big Wal echoed, and his voice could have been the night wind. 'Tama Ariki's place. Tama's Rock.'

'What happened at Tama's Rock?' Saffron asked, knowing she wouldn't like the answer.

'Death!' Dreadlocks said.

Saffron jumped. It was the first word he'd spoken.

A man walked up and placed an order. He smelt of alcohol, and swayed slightly as he watched Dreadlocks slap two halves of a bun onto the grill, then take a spring roll from a freezer and ease it into the oil.

They all stared in fascination as the man pulled a handful of coins from his pocket. Big Wal tossed them into the till with a clatter. The others — Billy's ones, Tama's coins — sat on the counter.

'Happened a couple of hundred years ago,' Big Wal began as if there hadn't been an interruption, then stopped and shook his head. 'No. Some things it's better not to talk about.'

'But if we don't know what happened, how can we know how to put things right? What do we need to do?' Saffron asked. If anyone knew, it would be Big Wal.

He gave a laugh that contained all the comfort of a razor-filled cushion. 'Simple. Have nothing whatsoever to do with the ruddy things.'

'What about Billy?'

Big Wal shrugged as if Billy wasn't his concern.

'Tell me what to do — please?' Saffron asked.

'I've told you.'

'But what does Billy need to do?'

'Keep his hands in his pockets next time.'

The sergeant gave Big Wal a nod and said, 'The burger's been paid for. I'll be off then.'

'You understand this thing better than we do,' Saffron said once the sergeant had left. 'Tapu is like a sort of curse, isn't it?'

'That's close enough. It's not something to be messed with.'

'So what do we do?'

His order wrapped, the drunk wished them all a good night several times over before swaying off down the street.

Big Wal shrugged. 'Not my problem,' he said, and he was looking at Billy as he spoke. 'Take your money and go. I want to close up.' His voice was flat and quiet as he stared down the deserted street.

'We don't want the coins,' Saffron said in a small voice.

Big Wal met her gaze. 'Too bad, little lady. Neither do I. Your brother has stepped in something bad. Now he wants to wipe his feet on my patch. Uh-uh.' He shook his head. 'Tell your brother to pick 'em up and go.'

Saffron looked at Billy.

'I don't want them. We could just leave them,' Billy said.

'Not on my ruddy counter, boy.' Big Wal's hand began to disappear below the level of the counter. His voice held an edge that hadn't been there a moment ago. 'The sergeant's gone now, boy. You take them.'

Out on the edge of the night, Saffron could see the big black panther stalking them, getting closer. She blinked — and it was gone. She wished the sergeant had stayed — Big Wal looked bigger now he was gone.

'Take them!' Big Wal ordered.

'No!' Billy took two steps back — straight into the arms of Dreadlocks.

How had he got around there, Saffron wondered.

Because he knows the moves in this game, petal, a voice in her head volunteered. *We're not playing hopscotch.*

Dreadlocks's arms clamped around Billy in a bear hug as he marched forward, and suddenly Billy was pitched right under Big Wal's nose.

Saffron looked up and down the street. No one.

'You can't do that,' she said loudly, but no one was listening.

Billy raised his hands to push himself away from the counter, and Big Wal's fingers snaked forward and grabbed Billy's wrist. 'You pick those coins up and go.'

'You can't make me.'

Saffron could hear the bluster in Billy's voice. Oh, Billy, she wanted to cry, don't be a twit. He *can* make you. That's what having a softball bat is all about. You can make people do whatever you want. We're all lucked out here, Billy. Can't you see that?

Big Wal looked up and down the street, saw nothing but the cold night wind, and pulled the softball bat from underneath the counter. 'Take them!'

'No!'

'Let him go,' Saffron demanded. The men ignored her. 'Let him go,' she repeated, and pulled at Dreadlocks's arm. She might as well have tugged at a tree.

'You *are* going to do it, boy. Give yourself a break and do it the easy way.' He waited for a moment, and when there was no response Big Wal gave a shrug and nodded to Dreadlocks, who immediately slammed his body down and bent Billy double over the counter, his arm and hand splayed out on the surface.

'No!' Billy howled, sensing what was to come.

Saffron screamed. She leapt at Dreadlocks, clambering onto his back, hanging on with one arm around his neck, her face buried in onion-smelling dreads and clawing at his face with her free hand.

'Fuck off,' he muttered, his head twisting from side to side. He sounded more annoyed than hurt. Her finger slipped into his mouth. He bit down. She yowled and snapped her teeth closed on his ear in return, her mouth full of wiry hair. She flung her other arm around his throat, gripped with her knees and began to force his head back when she saw the bat rise.

'No!' She tried to hurl herself sideways at Big Wal, landed half on the counter, but with her right leg still locked around Dreadlocks's hips she fell backwards to the ground.

The bat smashed down, and a howl of pain ripped from Billy's lips. His body jerked to rigid attention for a second, then his knees buckled, and his body slumped. He hung for long seconds, wedged between the counter and Dreadlocks's body, then slowly his knees straightened and stiffened. Dreadlocks took a step back, brawny arms reaching to the counter, imprisoning Billy inside them. Billy's face contorted with pain. Silently he eased the fingers of his right hand under his left hand and picked it up. He supported it in his right hand, rocking slightly on his feet, as if he could soothe the pain away.

Into the silence, the voice of Connie Francis began another song of love.

Saffron clambered to her feet. 'You bastard!' she said softly, punching weakly at Dreadlocks's back, tears sliding down her face. Billy's shattered left hand lay cradled in his right. She half reached out towards it and blood dripped from her own finger onto the counter.

'Oh, Billy, oh . . .'

'Take the coins, boy,' Big Wal said. 'I get no pleasure from this.' He assessed the weight of the bat in his hand. 'But I'll do it again if that's what it takes.' He sounded tired.

Saffron turned desperately. This was Friday night. Where was everyone?

Dreadlocks was indifferent to the blood trickling down his face from his ear. He yanked Billy's hand from its cradle and slapped it down onto the counter again. Billy screamed as broken bones grated together.

'No!' Saffron held up one hand in the universal stop sign. 'No! No more. Leave him! I'll take the coins.'

She ran her hand along the counter, scooped up the coins . . . and fell into a sea of blood.

Angry blood-red waves boiled all around her, and a black

sky pressed down so close she felt as if it was going to push her beneath the surface. Waves broke against her body and splattered warm drops of blood on her face. She grimaced and spat at the sharp coppery taste. Her arms flailed and the blood seemed to suck her down as the black sky lowered. Another wave broke against her and blood filled her mouth. She choked, coughed, spat. A rock jutted, flinging crimson tears to the wind as red waves smashed themselves upon it. The rock glistened with blood, but it was above the surface of this disgusting sea, so she dog-paddled towards it. She reached the rock and tried to grab hold but her fingers scraped down, and her nails filled with red slime. Gobs of it stuck to the back of her hands. She clung to the rock, her face pressed against the blood-slick surface. She tried to pull herself up, but someone was already on the rock. She saw a dark shape above and felt someone prising her fingers off the rock, trying to drown her in this terrible crimson sea.

She heard a clink, and slowly — very slowly — the blood washed away, fading in colour from blood red to the glowing pink of dawn until there was nothing.

Saffron felt as if she had been washed away. She wasn't sure if her eyes were closed and she opened them or if it was simply her vision returning, but Big Wal's burger bar floated slowly back into her awareness.

She staggered and felt someone's hand under her arm supporting her. It was Big Wal, and she guessed he had forced her fingers open and released the coins into her shoulder bag because he still held her opened hand in his. With her other hand, she pawed at her mouth.

'It was in my mouth,' she whispered. She could still feel

that warm, disgusting smoothness.

Big Wal nodded, although he couldn't know what she meant. Or maybe he did. Maybe just being close to the coins was enough for him.

'I'm sorry you got dragged into this, girl. You should have walked away.'

She pulled away, staggered across the pavement and dry-retched over the gutter, still able to taste blood in her mouth. 'You bastard!' she said weakly over her shoulder. 'What did you have to go and hurt Billy for?' She retched again and strings of saliva hung from her mouth. Groaning, she wiped her mouth on the back of her hand, then disgustedly scrubbed her hand on her jeans.

Big Wal gave her a smile laced with sadness. 'Sometimes life don't give you enough options. You make do with the best one you can find. In a week's time, perhaps you'll understand.'

She wiped at her mouth again. 'What do you mean?'

'You'll find out soon enough.'

'I won't be running around mutilating people with a softball bat.' She walked over to Billy and looked down at his hand. It was a mess.

'You'll be surprised what you'll do in the end.' With a shiver, Big Wal flipped up a section of counter and walked back through. He picked up a cloth and began to wipe a red splatter off the counter. Saffron would have laid odds it wasn't tomato sauce.

'I'll phone Heather,' she said to Billy. 'She'll know what to do.'

'I know what to do, Saf. Get me to a hospital.' Billy leant against the end wall beside a Spacies game, holding his hand.

'And call that cop back to arrest him.' He jerked his head towards Big Wal.

Hesitantly, Saffron stuck her hand into her shoulder bag. She didn't want to touch the coins again. 'Are they in here?' she asked Big Wal.

'They sure as hell aren't in my pocket.'

She looked into the bag as if she thought the coins might charge out and bite her, spied her mobile, gingerly pulled it out and punched in her home number. The three unmarried Delaney girls shared the house Lucky Del had left them, on Lake Terrace. It was going to be worth a fortune when it was the last undeveloped site on the lakefront. That's what Saffron had told them all through the lean years after their father's death. One day we'll sell, and we'll all be rich. By the time they'd paid off the mortgage and split it five ways they wouldn't be super rich, but, as Daphne kept saying, it was going to be a whole lot better than a slap in the face with a wet fish.

'It's me, petal,' Saffron said when the phone was answered. 'Can you come down to Big Wal's on Horomatangi Street? Billy and I have had a bit of a . . . mishap.'

'Mishap! You wouldn't call it that if it was your hand!'

'I don't want to alarm her,' Saffron said, moving the phone away from her mouth as she spoke. 'We've had enough accidents for one night. Just come down and pick us up,' she added into the phone. She dropped the mobile back into her bag and zipped it closed.

'The cops,' Billy reminded her.

'Damn right,' Saffron muttered, and reached for the phone again.

Big Wal leant his forearms on the counter. 'Of course you can play this however you want, but if you want my advice, it might be best to leave the police out of it.'

'You would say that.' Saffron fixed Big Wal with an unfriendly look. 'Is this an emergency?' she asked Billy. 'Do I dial the emergency number? I don't know any other.'

'Feels like an emergency to me,' Billy groaned. He squatted on the ground, his back still against the end wall, head bent over his hand, blond forelock blocking out the world. His cap had fallen to the ground.

'You were asking for my advice a little while ago,' Big Wal pointed out.

'That was before you took to Billy with a bat.'

'You should listen to him,' Dreadlocks said over his shoulder. 'He knows about this stuff.'

The mobile in her hand, Saffron looked at Billy, still squatting on the ground, out into the empty street, back at Big Wal. Dreadlocks was right. It couldn't hurt to listen to what Big Wal had to say first. She didn't want to think about the blood. Big Wal knew about this — this — whatever had happened to her with the coins — in a way that no European person could. It was hard-wired into his subconscious. It couldn't hurt to hear what he had to say.

She waggled the phone at him. 'So. Why would it be best for me not to tell the police you assaulted our Billy with a deadly weapon?'

Big Wal took a final wipe at the counter, looked at the red splotches on the cloth and threw it into the corner. 'You think you've had a bum deal tonight. But it's going to get a whole lot rougher.'

'If it gets much rougher, we'll be dead,' Saffron pointed out.

'Exactly.'

Saffron stared at him. 'What . . .' She looked around as if she wanted a witness. 'Are you threatening us?' Her voice shot up the scale. This could have been a scene out of the Tami Hoag novel she'd finished a couple of nights back.

Big Wal chuckled. 'Not me. You probably can't see it right at the moment, but I'm on your side.'

'Yeah, well you're fired. We don't need you.'

'What I meant was: Tama plays a mean game.'

'No, no, no! This has nothing to do with this Tama. *You* hit Billy. It's *you* we want to see strung up for this. I've got nothing against this Tama guy.'

'I'm thinking it's more a case of what *he* might have against *you*. He,' and Big Wal jerked his thumb at Billy, 'stole things that belong to Tama, and you,' and he fixed his gaze back on Saffron, 'have the coins in your bag. Girl, I wouldn't want to be in your shoes.'

'But that's all separate,' Saffron insisted. '*You* assaulted Billy.'

Big Wal shook his head slowly from side to side.

A red Mini nosed into a park, its exhaust fumes mingling with the smell of burgers. A tall, jeans-clad woman climbed out of the car. Her feet were bare and her fair hair hung in wet strands. Her head turned from Billy, still squatting on the ground, to Saffron.

'What's happened?'

'Billy's hand is hurt. He needs to go to hospital.'

Heather squatted in front of Billy. 'Let me see.' She didn't touch the hand. She stared at it for a moment, viewed it from all angles, then said, 'It's broken. It'll have to be set.'

'I know that. Just get me to hospital.'

'What happened?' Heather asked again, looking up at her sister.

'He,' and Saffron nodded her head towards Big Wal, 'took to Billy with a softball bat. You're the nurse. You take Billy to A&E, and I'll sort the rest of this.'

'The rest of this?' Heather queried.

'You don't want to know, petal. Believe me.'

CHAPTER THREE

NICK JONES PARKED beside the red Mini, clambered out of the *Taupo Star* runabout and stretched. It had been a long day. He stretched the knots out of his lean frame, then rubbed his fingers over hair short enough never to need combing. Saved time in the mornings. His nostrils widened appreciatively as the smell from the burger bar greeted him.

'Evening, Wal, Huamai.' He nodded at the two men behind the counter as he walked across. 'Brass monkey wind tonight,' he volunteered. 'You're lucky you're on that side of the counter.'

Big Wal made the best burgers in town, so Nick got his dinner here most nights. He figured a burger was close enough to meat and three veg to be acceptable on a daily basis. The kilojoule count hadn't caught up with him yet, but at thirty-seven he figured it had to be closing in.

Two women who looked like peas from the same pod — tall, willowy, blonde — both turned to stare at him, and Nick felt a flicker of interest. He was forever fourteen when it came to cupid-bowed lips. Jean Harlow had been his first love and she lingered still in some black-and-white corner of his mind, fully clothed, a little creased and pouting just for him.

The woman with the Jean Harlow mouth stood at the counter and looked cold. More than cold. She was bare-armed; her eyes were bigger than the other woman's, her face whiter. She looked ill and was shivering, and he wondered if he ought to offer his jacket. The other woman crouched beside a young man on the pavement. Blood dripped from his hand. That interested Nick even more. The youth was blond too.

'Mind if I take a photo?' he said to the young man, reaching into one of a dozen pockets and pulling out a camera. His jacket could support life for a week.

'You do and I'll stick that camera up your nose,' the woman by the counter threatened.

Nick gave her what he hoped was an apologetic look. 'No problem, lady. I did ask.' He stuck the camera back in his pocket. If they'd let him take a shot, he would have gone back to the car and grabbed the Nikon. This camera was fixed lens — lightweight, easy to use, nothing much to go wrong — strictly for emergencies.

The woman who had spoken shook her head as if dismissing Nick from her mind. She stared down at the youth on the pavement. Pain etched her face into something ugly. The expression in her eyes shouted mother louder than sister. Nick wanted to reassure her that a broken hand was nothing. Rwanda, Sarajevo, Baghdad — he had photographed a thousand people who would have happily swapped this kid's broken hand for their own injuries. Hell, a broken hand was getting out without a scratch.

'Your usual, bro?' Huamai asked, balancing a burger bun on his hand.

'Yep.'

Huamai slapped the two halves of the bun on the hot plate, peeled the paper from a meat patty and slapped that on too, and began to prepare the salad.

'Quiet night?' Nick asked Big Wal.

'Not quiet enough,' Big Wal answered, nodding at the boy. 'I was just going to close up. Feel as if I've had enough excitement for tonight.'

'Well, you caused most of it,' the woman volunteered, giving Big Wal a look that could scour pots.

Nick looked down at the young man. The other woman — had to be a sister — was helping him to his feet. He cradled his bloody left hand in his right, leaning over it protectively. 'You been showing that bloke how to hit a home run?'

'I don't like people bringing trouble to my door,' Big Wal grumbled.

Huamai put the burger together, bagged it and, without asking, grabbed a Coke from the bottle cabinet as he passed and placed both on the counter.

Nick tossed some coins down and watched as they all stared at them. He raised his eyebrows and looked from the woman to Big Wal to Huamai, but no one volunteered what was so interesting about a pile of money.

The sister was helping the lad into the Mini. She closed the door and looked back.

'You going to be OK, Saf?' she asked.

The other woman didn't look OK at all. When she moved out of the light, her eyes looked like big black stones in her face.

She nodded. 'I've got a dog to finish back at the shop. And

then I've got something to get rid of.'

'And phone the cops,' the boy called from inside the car. 'I want him busted.'

'You been upsetting the natives again, Wal?' Nick pulled open the white paper bag around his burger.

Big Wal grinned. 'Hey, I'm the tangata whenua here. Besides, the boy asked for it.'

Nick could guess what the boy had asked for. He knew all about Big Wal's softball bat and had seen it in action before tonight. 'So?' Big Wal said, addressing the woman. 'Are you going to phone the cops?'

'You deserve it.'

'Girl, you're gonna have your hands so full of trouble, so many balls in the air, that you're gonna wish you were Michael Jordan. You won't have *time* for the cops.'

'What do you mean?'

'I mean your brother has pissed Tama off big time. I know you gotta help him. I understand about family. But you're in deep trouble.'

'So you think I should simply ignore the fact that you took to my brother with a softball bat?'

'Girl, I—'

'Don't keep calling me that,' she snapped.

Big Wal shrugged. 'I don't know what else to call you.'

'Saffron,' she said between clenched teeth.

'That's good. The past has drawn us together tonight.' Big Wal stuck his hand across the counter. 'I'm—'

'I know who you are,' Saffron said.

Her voice was tight and prissy, as if she suspected Big Wal of hankering to stick his hand up her dress. His hand, however, was simply hanging in the air, and after ignoring it for as long as she could, Saffron finally stuck her own out and took it.

'Now, that's better, isn't it?'

'If you say so.' She didn't look convinced. 'What I don't get is how you attacking Billy and this Tama tie up. I mean *he* hasn't done anything to us. We've only got your word for it that there even is such a person.'

'Oh, there is, right enough. You'll soon believe that,' Big Wal said.

'Why should I worry about someone who died hundreds of years ago?'

Big Wal gave her a look as if he couldn't believe what he was hearing. 'You ask me that? After you've touched those coins?'

'What coins?' Nick asked. He figured he'd better try to make up for lost time on this conversation. The others seemed to be light years ahead of him.

'So you're claiming the coins are cursed?' she said.

Big Wal screwed his face up as if the description didn't quite fit. 'Sort of. The site is tapu — so sacred that the forces are extremely strong, strong enough to kill. Tama was a powerful chief — some people believed he was a god.'

'And the coins?'

'They're left as tokens of respect so that you can walk there in safety. The tokens are for Tama's people — the ones he lost. They were killed there. Bad things happen to people who mess with them.'

'Why should I believe you? I've never heard any of this before.'

'Maybe we don't advertise it. Maybe we think it's private and not for the likes of you to decide if you want to believe it or not. You come to this place, and you read a history book, and you think you know the land. You know nothing.' Big Wal hesitated, and then he said, 'But you touched those coins. You know that.'

Her voice escaped in a little whisper. 'Dear God, I do. What am I supposed to do with them?'

'What coins?' Nick asked again.

'If I was you, I'd offload them as quick as I could. Give them back to Tama and hope that he's got other fish to fry.'

She stared at Big Wal as if she was trying to extract every nuance of information from his face. 'Is Billy going to be OK?'

Big Wal shrugged. 'I'm not a fortune teller. I don't know.'

'But you won't do anything more to him?'

'All I wanted was for him to take those coins away.'

Nick didn't bother asking again about the coins. He'd pump Wal and Huamai when the girl had gone.

'Yeah, well, I'm sorry if we've contaminated your shop or something, but you could have just said. You didn't have to break every bone in his hand.'

Big Wal reached across and switched the music off. There was silence, then a horn blared and voices drifted up from Tongariro Street.

'I did. You and your brother weren't listening. You people never do. I'm closing up now.'

Saffron stepped back.

'You take care, girl,' Big Wal called.

'Yeah, yeah,' she called back and marched down the pavement, her bag hanging from her shoulder.

Big Wal watched the girl walk away and shook his head. She was too skinny by half. But that was the least of her troubles. Huamai was washing dishes out back. Soon, Nick would wander off to wherever he called home. He wanted to go home himself. Back to his family where even his five-year-old mokopuna knew you didn't mess with something like this. He never felt hungry by the time he got home, but his wife would have a bottle of cold beer in the fridge waiting for him. He needed to wash the taste of trouble from his mouth tonight.

He withdrew the softball bat from under the counter and wiped the business end with a cloth. A red streak or two — nothing much. He'd let the guy off lightly.

He felt Nick's eyes upon him.

'He asked for it,' Big Wal said. He didn't know why he was acting defensive. Nick had been here the night he'd laid out those three little thugs who thought a middle-aged burger man was fair game.

'How much trouble is he in?' Nick asked. He tipped the Coke to his mouth, drained it and placed the empty bottle on the counter.

'Don't know for sure. Wouldn't want to be in his shoes, though.' Big Wal hesitated and then added, 'Some people have died after messing with things from Tama's Rock.'

Nick looked at him with a frown and said, 'Yeah? No shit.'

Wal didn't know if Nick believed him or not, but that

didn't matter. He would soon be converted. Tama Ariki made believers of everyone in the end. He felt sorry for the girl. She'd seen the blood, Tama's blood. That wasn't good. The old people said blood had dripped from Tama's hands on the day of the massacre, and turned into red ochre. No one had ever found the vein of ochre down on the shore, but the old people said it was still there.

It was an ill omen to see the blood. Well, the girl had seen it. No doubt about that. She hadn't said as much, but he'd sensed the blood flowing through her mind like an avalanche of death, and he'd fought hard to keep it from himself. She'd bought into a power of trouble and he didn't think she had any idea yet just how much. Part of him wanted to run down the street after her and try to make her understand. But she was Pakeha, and they were so ruddy deaf sometimes. Didn't matter how many times you said some things, they just didn't hear. Ah, well, time would unzip her ears.

'See you about,' Nick called, and he headed off back to his car.

Nick was a good guy who'd put a lot of dollars in his pocket over the past year. Big Wal smiled. Might almost have a bit of Maori blood in his veins the way that man could eat. And he brought mates along. It was all good for business.

He flipped the counter section up and picked up the sandwich board out by the kerb. He shivered as he stood for a moment looking up the street. Mount Tauhara was out there in the dark, its green bush-clad slopes backing the town.

It reminded him of the farm where he'd lived as a boy. There'd been a small mountain at the back of the old house there, too, a rocky peak rising up into the sky. Below that, the mountain wore a fine green cloak of totara and rimu, matai and miro. Tree ferns cast their fronds, and the wild pigs would bed down in them when the days were wet and cold. Cabbage trees grew in the bottom of the gully, following the line of the creek that tumbled down from the heights where nobody ever went. The ancestors were buried in hidden reaches above the treeline. When the totara changed to small wind-scoured things, that was the time to stop climbing and come back down. Only the ancestors roamed the cloud-wreathed top. And whenever the wild pigs figured out that nobody would climb too high on the mountain, the ancestors would chase the pigs back down to the gentler slopes. Back to the creek and the almost orange-coloured dried fern fronds. It was good to have a mountain at your back.

He sighed. The Pakeha didn't know that. They didn't know Tauhara watched over them as they slept. But he for one rested better knowing Tauhara was there with at least one eye on the town.

Of course, Tauhara didn't give a rat's arse what happened to that boy and his sister.

CHAPTER FOUR

SAFFRON FOUND IT easy enough to hold herself to a rapid walk while she was still in sight of Big Wal's, but once she reached the corner and the smell of fried onion and burgers faded, she had to rein herself back from breaking into a jog. If she ran, it meant she believed Big Wal, and she didn't want to believe him. She was returning the coins to the lakefront because that was the sensible thing to do, the right and proper thing to do. Not because she believed him.

She wished Heather were with her. That Billy hadn't been hurt, and Heather was scurrying along beside her. She wanted company. Someone to share the worry.

She still felt queasy. Most likely the sweet and sour pork takeaway she'd had for dinner. Mrs Edmondson had just dropped Freddy off at The Dog House and had been telling her about the upcoming show. She'd left the takeaway to get cold while Freddy stood like a statue on the grooming table, and they discussed whether a Continental or a Saddle clip would suit him best when he came out of his Puppy clip in another month. So it was hardly surprising if, a few hours later, she was hanging over the kerb. In fact, the amount of dog hair she swallowed with her meals, it was a wonder she didn't come down with food poisoning every day of the week.

A tiny woman, her dress flapping, tottered along the pavement ahead of her, the blustery onshore wind holding back and then releasing her, in fits and starts. A couple of labradors trotted behind. Saffron would lay odds they weren't half as much trouble to look after as Billy. Chuck 'em a chunk of dog roll, and they were content. If only life with her brother could be that simple.

She was out on the edge of the CBD: another block and a throng of motels would elbow and jostle for position. A hundred metres ahead of her, the lake evened out into an endless grey prairie. It shone under the high-pressure sodium lights that towered as high as three-storey buildings before arcing across Lake Terrace. A bank between the lake and the Terrace remained from past centuries when the water level had been higher. The bank grew from nothing along at Hot Water Beach, slowly puffing itself up importantly to become a small cliff as it strode into town, and once past the main street quickly slumping back to nothing at the yacht club and rivermouth. Along Lake Terrace the streetlights and the reflecting lake bleached the night to perpetual twilight.

Her mind returned to the coins in her bag and the predictions Big Wal had made. Billy was in hospital. True, that was caused by Big Wal, not this Tama, but Big Wal said it was all connected.

One of the dogs suddenly bounced forward on stiff legs, thrust its nose violently into the woman's legs and backed off. She staggered and grabbed at the fence that ran beside the pavement. Saffron heard a frightened, bird-like cry.

'Hey!' Saffron yelled, and began to run towards the woman. Her bag banged against her back. 'Hey!'

The dog half-crouched, staring at the woman intently, then raced in again, its top lip curled, teeth showing, head snaking down. Saffron knew it was going to do more than bump the woman this time.

In the four strides the dog took to reach the woman, Saffron had assessed the situation. These weren't man-eaters, despite their behaviour; twelve years of handling dogs told her that. These were a couple of throw the stick and feed me dogs, the sort that run about with the kids and go to the shop with mum. Good dogs, acting bad.

She swung the bag from her shoulder and hurled it. The dog gave a startled yip as the bag hit it on the head, and spun around. An erect ridge of hair running the length of its spine hinted at a gene or two of Rhodesian ridgeback. She could hear the low reverberating growl, and saliva dripped from one corner of its jaw.

She raced up, and the two dogs backed off, reluctantly in the case of the cross-breed. It looked big and menacing as its focus changed from the woman to Saffron.

Already, the raised hackles on the other dog, a golden lab, were lowering back into a loose ripple of fur and skin. Another minute and it would be slobbering all over her and pestering her for food. She could hear the nails of one dog tip-tapping on the pavement. Needed trimming.

A frail old Maori woman clung to the picket fence. There was silence for a moment as the cross-breed swallowed and gave another low throaty growl.

'Let's just stop and think about this for a sec, eh, big fella?' she said to the dog. The sound of her voice, quiet and confident, seemed to relax the animal. 'I bet your mum'd be mortified to see you acting up like this.'

Slowly and deliberately, she walked forward until she stood between the dogs and the old woman. Moving towards them would have been a big mistake with some dogs, but not these two.

She stared at the cross-breed, deliberately holding its gaze. The dog stared back into her eyes for a few seconds, then looked away. She was top dog. She'd never had any doubt about that. Now the dog knew it.

'So how about we get on home?' she said, indicating the street ahead.

Hackles that had been raised slowly lowered so that both dogs seemed to deflate before her eyes.

'Get home,' she said again, in a voice laced with disapproval, as if she'd caught them raiding the rubbish tin. The dogs backed off a few strides and stopped. 'Get,' she warned. She walked towards them, arm raised, pointing back up the street. 'Go home.' Reluctantly, the two dogs turned and trotted away. The cross-breed stopping once to look back.

Saffron faced the old woman. A black dress reached to mid-calf on a tiny body so that she looked like a child playing dress-up, until you saw her wizened face. She pulled back as Saffron neared, clutching at the fence as if she could pull herself along it.

'It's OK,' Saffron said softly. 'The dogs have gone.' But she could see that it was she, not the dogs, who was frightening the old woman now. 'I won't hurt you.'

The old woman glanced up at her, and Saffron paused, her mouth opening slightly, her eyes narrowing. Tattooed on her companion's chin and lips was a moko.

She hadn't seen an old woman with a moko for — how many years? The blue-black lines told their ancestry and history as clearly as a genealogical chart to those who understood the subtle tribal variations in the intricate lines and whorls. Young women, caught up in the pride of Maori renaissance, were getting tattooed again, but all the old women who had worn the moko were dead.

Except for this one.

So many things tonight seemed caught in a wind that twisted separate strands together and braided them into a dark, grim rope. Billy and the coins; her drowning in a bloody sea; now this old woman with a moko. Without thinking, Saffron's fingers touched the smooth skin on her own chin. The last kuia with a moko had died maybe twenty years back. Everyone knew that. It had been in the papers, on television.

That wind-braided rope was beginning to tighten around her neck. Her fingers traced down her chin to her throat. She wished Heather were beside her.

The old woman stared at Saffron's leather shoulder bag still lying on the pavement. Saffron had forgotten about the coins but the old woman's frightened gaze brought it all back. She glanced down and thought she saw movement. Quickly, she stamped one foot down on the zipped opening. Before anything escapes, she thought, and shuddered. She stood like that, teeth clenched, pushing down hard on the neck of the bag with her foot, working hard at convincing herself she had imagined that flicker of changing light and shadow dance across the surface of the bag. Then, with a trace of self-consciousness, she grabbed the bag off the pavement, checked it was closed and anchored it under one arm. Please don't let me feel movement, she prayed. *Please.*

'Where are you headed? I'll see you to your door, just in case the dogs come back.'

The woman shook her head.

'Are you sure?'

The old woman had been heading towards the lake, but now she changed direction, pulling herself along the fence, away from Saffron and the water, her breath coming in shallow, frightened gasps.

Saffron took a step backward, and the old woman stopped.

'Put them back,' she whispered over her shoulder. 'Put them back, girl, before he hurts you.'

'Put what back?'

'They belong to Tama Ariki.' The words rolled off her tongue, each vowel rich and full-bodied.

'How do you know about the coins?' Saffron demanded, not liking the rough edge of panic she heard in her own voice.

'They're not coins.'

'What are they, then?'

'Tokens. For the babies. Put them back, girl. They don't belong to you.'

'What babies? Big Wal didn't say anything about babies.'

'The babies we lost that day.'

Even at a dozen paces, Saffron saw tears swimming in the

old woman's eyes. She retreated along the fence towards the corner, grabbing pickets for support, her voice emerging in tiny gasps of air.

'Are you OK now?' Saffron called after her. 'Can I help?'

'Put them back.' The old woman disappeared around the corner, but her voice surged back to Saffron on a trick of the wind, suddenly strong, insistent, demanding. 'Put them back.'

Saffron took a couple of steps before drifting to a stop. The old woman was gone. She had to get rid of the coins. She couldn't pretend any longer that she didn't believe what Big Wal had said. Every footstep now picked up the echo of his words like jackboots falling into step with the rhythm of war. She watched carefully as cracks in the pavement passed in ordered ranks beneath her. Maybe she had already stepped on one. Maybe that was why everything was going wrong.

CHAPTER FIVE

THE DELANEY SISTERS were on their knees digging through every handful of the sand and loose pumice pebbles that skirted the lake opposite their house. Three blonde heads bent to the task; three pairs of blue eyes searched. The only point of difference was that the third woman wore tailored trousers and a floral shirt rather than the jeans and jerseys favoured by her sisters.

Down here, you listened to the lake rather than watched it. It became something real, something alive and tactile, not just a view to be photographed and mounted in an album.

Saffron's fingers felt as if she had scoured pots with them. The night before, she had buried the coins on the beach. She didn't want them in the house or at The Dog House — not if even a fraction of what Big Wal said about Tama and the curse was true. But now she couldn't find them.

She held up her hand and inspected the finger Dreadlocks had bitten. She shook her head. She still couldn't believe someone had bitten her, or that she had bitten someone else. There were other things about the previous night she couldn't believe, but she was trying hard not to think about them.

Her mind was fuzzy from lack of sleep, and everything this morning seemed surreal.

'I still think you should get a jab for that. You can catch a dozen things from a bite,' Heather said.

'I've been bitten by bigger teeth than that.'

'But they were dogs.'

'And I never went down with galloping rabies,' Saffron continued.

'It's hepatitis I'm worried about.'

Mo pushed herself to her feet, frowning slightly as she dusted sand from her knees. 'She's right, Saf. Hepatitis isn't something you can just shrug off.'

Trust Mo to agree with Heather. Ever since Mo had married four years ago and had Lucy, she had come over all health-conscious. Obviously, it was a motherhood thing.

'I'll stop off at A&E later,' Saffron promised, knowing she wouldn't.

'So do you really think this is a curse?' Mo asked. Even though Mo was married, they still saw her almost every day. She'd pop into The Dog House if she was in town, or stop off at the house on Lake Terrace to have a cuppa and a chat. And, of course, there were the Thursday night video and MallowPuff sessions. Mo still hadn't weaned herself off those.

'I think it's something like that,' Saffron said. 'Big Wal said it wasn't something to take lightly. And look at Billy — within twelve hours of taking the coins, he's in hospital.'

'He's not any more,' Heather added. 'I phoned about an hour ago, and they said he'd discharged himself.'

Saffron groaned. 'What on earth did he do that for? So where is he?'

'Buy a paper and see where the horses are running,' Heather said in an expressionless voice.

'If he's well enough to go to the races, he's well enough to be down here helping us,' Mo grumbled.

'He shouldn't be out of hospital yet,' Heather said.

'I know. I just mean if he thinks he's well enough to go anywhere, he could help us. Why do we always end up picking up after him?'

'Because we're his ever-loving sisters, that's why,' Saffron said. 'I need him to show me exactly where he got the coins. If I'm going to replace them, I want to do it right. I don't want this Tama giving us the thumbs-down just because I've put them at the wrong rock. I'm not sure where Tama's Rock is.'

Heather looked up and down the shore, as if she thought she might see a neatly printed council sign reading 'Tama's Rock'. 'Never heard of it,' she said.

'Neither have I,' Saffron added. 'But Big Wal and the policeman knew all about it.' She didn't add, 'And so did the old woman who somehow knew I had the coins in my bag.'

She tried to ignore the sense of panic peek-a-booing on the other side of common sense. They were just coins. They could buy a couple of packets of MallowPuffs. That's all. But they were more than that, whispered the Delaney blood that flowed through her veins. Much, much more than that.

A small white poodle trotted along the lakefront towards them. Pixie was a regular at The Dog House, but Saffron's gaze slid over the dog without recognition.

Big Wal had said return the coins. It made sense. It couldn't do any harm, and it might change the Delaneys' luck.

Someone had left those coins at Tama's Rock as a token

for good fortune. Probably some elderly Maori who knew the legend of Tama, but even among a younger generation of New Zealanders there were many who wouldn't walk past without leaving a token. She hadn't known about Tama's Rock, but she'd seen other places herself, and she always left a coin. She didn't know the legends, but she knew about luck. Oh, yes, all of Lucky Del Delaney's children knew about luck.

'Where's Daphne?' Mo asked.

'Room Four is doing a class project,' Heather said. 'Wetas. She'll stop off and help us look later if we still haven't found them.'

Saffron threw herself down on her back, pushed off her sneakers and glowered up at the sky. If she glowered long and hard enough maybe she could burn away the fear.

Heather squatted beside her on her haunches. 'They're not here, Saf.'

Mo looked doubtfully at the sand before cautiously seating herself beside her sisters.

'I know that, petal,' Saffron said. 'But they have to be. I buried them right here.'

'Maybe someone picked them up,' Mo said.

'Naah. People don't pick up money nowadays. Not coins.'

'I do,' Heather said.

Saffron grinned at her sister. 'Me too! But we're not most people.' She didn't add that most people didn't know what it was like to have a father who gambled away every cent in the house, didn't know what it was like to plunge between wealth and poverty so often and so fast that you'd swear you were a-bobbing in a rowboat on the ocean. 'Most people only pick up notes.'

Mo rolled her eyes.

'It's a fact,' Saffron insisted. 'I read it somewhere.' Her finger throbbed and the plaster was wet with blood. She blinked. She'd seen too much blood recently. She slapped her thoughts away from that direction. 'I'll stick on a bigger plaster next time.'

'Next time?'

Saffron rolled over onto her belly. 'There has to be a next time, petal. You know that. We have to find those coins and return them.'

'Maybe we should just leave them lost,' Mo suggested. 'Maybe that's what fate is telling us.'

Saffron sat up. A fishing boat moved slowly across her line of vision. The wind, from the south, drove the waves ahead of it so that they lapped noisily on the shore. Fine pumice sand, forever caught in a backwash it could never quite escape, made the shoreline gritty white.

'We have to find them. You've seen what happened to Billy.'

'But the man at the burger bar did that,' Mo pointed out.

'Ye-es. But somehow it's all connected. That's what Big Wal thinks, anyway.'

'He would,' Heather said caustically. 'Maybe Mo's right. Maybe fate is telling us to leave these coins lost. That way, it isn't our problem.'

'Wishful thinking,' Saffron said. 'It's Billy's problem and that makes it ours.'

'Maybe the burger guy invented the whole story to get himself off the hook,' Heather said. 'Billy was screaming for his blood. He wanted him charged for assault.'

'I don't think he made it up,' Saffron said reluctantly. 'I wish I did. I think Big Wal did what he did to try and protect himself and his family. He wanted to distance himself from the curse.'

'So do we,' Mo said emphatically. 'This worries me, Saf. Steve and I have Lucy to think of. Why does Billy always drag us into these things?'

'He's never got tangled up in a Maori curse before,' Saffron pointed out.

'Everything else,' Heather said.

'I phoned Steve and Lucy first thing this morning. I was telling Steve about the coins,' Mo said. Her voice was noncommittal, and her sisters waited for the next bit. She picked up a piece of what looked like greenstone but was actually a wave-smoothed piece of broken glass and examined it carefully. 'He didn't think we should get involved.'

Saffron looked at her younger sister sadly. 'Billy's our brother. The only one we've got. We have to help.' Mo had stayed with her sisters overnight and Saffron knew Steve didn't like it when she did that. She fancied he was drawing a route map for Mo, and it didn't include unexpected sleepovers or Thursday night video sessions.

'I'm just telling you what Steve said,' Mo said, a touch of heat in her voice.

'And we understand where he's coming from,' Heather said. 'You and Lucy are his family. But Billy is our family. Yours too, Mo. You don't just cast aside your family when you marry.'

'I'm not doing that.' Mo threw the glass into the water

where it tossed in the backwash of swirling sand. 'Steve just thought we should be careful. That's all.'

'Has he heard things about this Tama's Rock?' Saffron asked. 'I'd never heard about it before last night, and I've lived my whole life in Taupo.'

Mo met her eyes. 'He said about five years ago they had a couple of university students working for them over the holidays. One of them picked up some money down along the lakefront, and the next day he was killed in an accident at the plant. A Maori guy who worked with them said the money must have come from Tama's Rock. Steve just remembered the name.'

'Doesn't prove anything,' Heather said.

'He might have picked the money up anywhere. Probably not the same place as Billy at all,' Saffron pointed out.

'I'm not saying it is. I'm just telling you what Steve told me. He thought we should be careful.'

'And we are being careful,' Saffron said soothingly. 'That's why we're going to find these coins, and we're going to return them to Tama's Rock. That way, if there is a curse we'll lay it to rest.'

'A sort of insurance,' Heather added.

'Exactly.'

But Mo wasn't done yet. 'Steve thought the less we had to do with it the better. He said us girls hadn't really had anything to do with the coins at all. He thought we should leave it like that.'

'You mean he thought we should hang Billy out to dry,' Saffron interpreted. She didn't add that she thought it might be a bit late for her. She'd picked the coins up, held them in her hand, seen the blood. She grimaced, an all-over shiver, and rubbed her arms briskly.

'You OK, Saf?' Heather touched her hand.

'Yeah. Just . . .' She shrugged. Better not say too much. Mo was spooked already.

'You get that bite on your finger seen to,' Heather said.

'I will.' Saffron knew that for the next two weeks Heather would link every unexpected blink or twitch she made to this bite. 'We're just making sure that the bad luck bird isn't about to crap on us.' Saffron poked her feet back into her sneakers and scrambled to her feet. 'Now, let's have breakfast.'

Saffron gave what she hoped was an encouraging smile. Heather flashed the same smile back to her, and Saffron saw how false it looked: she doesn't believe we're laying this to rest any more than I do, she thought. They both smiled at Mo.

'Well, I think Steve is right,' Mo said. The smiles hadn't worked on her either. 'Don't get me wrong, I'll help find them. But I think we're mad. Steve was *there* when that guy fell in the mincer. He said that if we'd seen him when he came out the other end, then we wouldn't be fooling about with these coins.'

'Ugh,' Heather shuddered, and Saffron was tempted to ask her if *she* felt OK.

Instead, she simply said, 'We don't know that Billy took these coins from the same place.'

They climbed the wooden steps up from the lakefront. A dozen or more ducks slept on the grass at the top, their heads folded back along their backs; they looked like brown feather dusters. Someone was setting out the signs for the Great Lake Hole-in-One Challenge. Soon, the tourists would be lining up to whack away at golf balls in the hope of getting one in the hole on the pontoon moored a hundred metres out in the lake.

Heather spoke. 'Don't look now, ladies, but here comes Gilbert.'

Saffron groaned loudly. Gilbert Williams, their neighbour, was the last person she needed right now. Not that it would be her or Heather or Mo he was looking for. It would be Daphne. He was twenty-five years her senior but worshipped her with earnest ardour.

'Shush,' Mo hissed at her. 'He'll hear you.'

A small, dark-haired man hurried across the Terrace between a logging truck and a campervan. Despite its name, Lake Terrace was part of State Highway One linking the towns north and south of Taupo. There'd been talk of building a bypass to keep the heavy vehicles out of the town centre for years. Saffron would believe it when she saw it.

'Have you seen Daphne this morning?' Gilbert called as he approached. He wrung his hands together as if her non-appearance was a matter of some concern.

'Good morning, Gilbert,' Saffron said pointedly.

'She's not at your house,' he went on. He had to look up to speak to them: the three Delaney girls all towered over him. 'I've just been there.'

'That's because she went out early,' Heather explained.

'Oh dear. I'd hoped to see her first.' He continued to wring his hands together.

Such clean-looking hands, Saffron thought. The dark hairs sprinkled across their backs always looked out of place on such pale, clean skin. Saffron glanced at her own hands and the blood beginning to crust around her fingernail, and tucked them behind her back.

'I've discovered something most interesting about the giant weta.'

Saffron's eyebrows rose. *Was* there anything of interest still left to discover about wetas? Had there *ever* been? Room Four's class project was in its second week and she and Heather knew much, *much* more than they had ever wanted to know about wetas. Saffron was looking forward immensely to the next class project.

'We'll tell her you were looking for her,' she said, looking over his head.

Gilbert looked from one sister to the next to the next. 'Where did you say she was? Perhaps I'd better tell her about this. I really do believe I might know where we could find a giant weta.'

'I'm not sure exactly where she was taking the kids this morning, Gilbert.' Saffron did know, but she figured twenty kids in tow were enough for anyone without a middle-aged, lovesick neighbour and a giant weta tagging along. 'Sorry I can't be of more help.'

He looked anxiously at Heather.

'She didn't tell me,' Heather added. 'I was in late last night.'

'Humph!' Gilbert snorted. 'Yes, indeed you were! I am aware of *exactly* what time you came home last night. And went out again. *And* returned yet again. Living next door to you girls is like trying to sleep in Grand Central Station! The muffler on that Mini needs attention, it makes a dreadful noise. You know I can't tolerate noise. You girls woke me up last night — or should I say this morning — and I was *quite* unable to fall sleep again. It wouldn't surprise me if I suffer one of my migraines later.' He eyed the red Mini parked next to Mo's Capri with vicious intent, as if he could see himself scratching a key down the length of its grinning paintwork.

'Billy had an accident last night. That was why we were coming and going so late.'

Gilbert snorted again. 'He drives too fast.' As an after-thought, he added, 'Is he all right?'

'It wasn't a car accident. But, yes, he's all right. He broke his hand.'

'Fell over, did he?'

Saffron could almost hear Gilbert's voice saying, 'Drunk, was he?'

'He had his—' Heather began.

Saffron interrupted. 'Something fell on his hand.'

'Well, I'm sorry to hear that.' Gilbert sounded far less sorry than he had been to miss seeing Daphne. 'Tell Daphne I'll pop over later when I see she's home. Tell her I think I know where we'll be able to find a giant weta. I think she'll be most surprised. We won't need to go bush at all. We could be there and back in a day.'

'I'll tell her,' Saffron said, wondering if Daphne was aware that Gilbert wanted to go bush with her.

They waited for a break in the traffic and crossed Lake Terrace together. Two houses, one brick, one white weatherboard, stood staunchly side by side, as if together they could hold back the troop of motels that marched towards town. A black cat, asleep in the middle of the brick house's driveway, rose, stretched and walked to greet them. Saffron and Heather looked warily at the animal as Mo bent over and stroked it.

'Ah, you remember Samantha then, Mrs Pearson,' Gilbert said. 'My little Sammy was sorry when you moved out. You always were the animal lover.'

Saffron pulled a face at Heather, who grinned back. What did that make them? Top of the SPCA's most wanted list? They liked cats. They *did*. It's just not easy living next door to a black cat when you're — well, not superstitious, but hey, everyone knew it was bad luck if a black cat crossed your path. And this cat teased them. It would feint one way, then suddenly dash the other. It crossed and recrossed their paths with all the skill of a soccer superstar. There were times when Saffron's progress up the garden path resembled a Scottish reel.

Now, however, after accepting Mo's homage, the cat twined itself around their neighbour's legs and looked up at them all as if butter wouldn't melt in its mouth.

'I shall come over when Daphne returns,' Gilbert said. He gave a nod and marched back up the drive to his house. The cat followed.

'I wish you wouldn't encourage that cat, Mo,' Saffron complained. 'Heather and I are the ones who have to live with it.'

'That's just superstition,' Mo said.

'What is? That cat comes into the house and breaks things. Doesn't it?' she added, looking to Heather for support. Mo hadn't been so offhand when *she* had lived next door.

'Gets on the table and leaves hair everywhere,' Heather agreed.

Mo smiled. 'I know what you three are like.'

And that just about said it all, Saffron thought sadly. It used to be us four. The four Delaney girls. And then Mo got married. Daphne would be next: lots of men lusted after Daphne. Heather was quieter, and talked about nursing overseas sometimes after some television programme had dished up one too many kid with a swollen belly and snotty nose. But one day some good man would sweep her off her feet.

And Saffron had better find a man herself before that happened, because Delaney girls didn't do alone.

Mo came to a halt beside the two cars parked in their drive. 'I've got to meet Steve and Lucy downtown. We're taking her to Cherry Island this morning. There'll be tantrums to teatime if I don't show up. But I'll come back and look some more later — if you need me to. Give me a ring.'

Saffron gave her a hug. 'See you later, petal. Give Lucy a kiss from us.'

'See you,' Heather called, as Mo got into her white Capri. 'And doesn't she hope that we find those coins without her,' Heather said as Mo drove away. 'Steve this and Steve that.'

'He *is* her husband,' Saffron pointed out, although she knew what Heather meant. Their Mo just wasn't the same any more.

It felt as if the family had come to a fork in the path. She and Heather and Daphne had gone down one path, Mo had taken the other. And, of course, Billy was headed down yet another track. The same track their daddy had galloped down.

CHAPTER SIX

NICK JONES SPUN around as he heard the sound of tyres losing rubber to tarmac. The Nikon was already at eye level as the front bumper of the car hit the girl. She flew up into the air, all pink dress and long hair, and landed on the bonnet. By the time she had gone through the front windscreen, leaving only two white-socked and pink-shoed feet outside, he had three photographs.

Nick lowered the camera from his eye and stood motionless as he listened to the silence bounce off every building. He had his shot. He didn't need to preview his picture to know that. The image was his, and whether the kid lived or died, for one moment in time she had been his too. He stood and waited, and eventually a woman began to scream. The scream went on and on, drawing pictures in blood of a hundred photographs he thought he'd forgotten. Then the stillness fled, and Tongariro Street jerked into action.

Nick looked at his feet on the pavement. Had he taken a step or two towards the child? To help. He could have sworn he had. Hadn't he been past the café? Or had he simply turned, shot the unfolding drama and captured a photo his editor would never publish?

Better not to ask himself that question.

He ran back to where the car halted. A bare-chested man was already inside the vehicle, holding his shirt against the girl's arm as a pressure pad with one hand and taking her pulse with his other hand. The pale blue of the shirt was rapidly darkening to red. He looked as if he knew what he was doing, so Nick framed in tight and took another photograph. He didn't know why.

Had he moved back to help the child when he saw she was going to be hit? Wasn't time, he argued. It was over before he could do a thing. He was halfway up the street.

He replayed the sequence of events in his head. He'd heard the squeal of the tyres — that had been the first thing. After that, it had all been automatic. He'd rolled into his shot, his eye seeing little Miss Pink Shoes framed in black tarmac, clear road all around her — the camera around his neck already in his hands and gliding towards his eye. Then the blue Nissan sliding into shot, smoke scorching up from the tyres. By that time he had framed, focused and, as the bumper hit, taken his first shot. A just-in-case reading for skin tone, taken off the palm of his hand when he had walked out of the *Star* office earlier, meant that shutter speed and f-stop would be acceptable, if not perfect.

He pulled a packet of cigarettes from his pocket, lit up, breathed in and stared down some busybody who mentioned petrol fumes. Jeez, mate, he wanted to snap. It's the kid that's broken, not the car.

He watched as an ambulance pulled up, and two St John officers took over from the man who had dived straight into the car. Nick recognized him as a local vet as he clambered out, splotched in blood.

The paramedics got the kid out of the Nissan. Pink hair ribbons, half-untied and dangling, suddenly reminded him of the pink masking tape he'd used to lattice the windows in his room just before the US started bombing Baghdad. A bright garish pink had been the only colour left as the press pack joined the residents of the city and hunkered down for war.

You'd think pink would be a safe colour.

He got a couple more shots, then ground the still-smouldering cigarette out with the toe of his shoe and turned away.

Nick jammed himself into the chair behind the computer squeezed in a tiny corner of the *Star* newsroom. He removed the memory card from the Nikon, inserted it into the card reader plugged into the computer and downloaded his images. He entered PhotoShop and went through the thumbnail images, deciding which he would use. Working on one image at a time, he cropped for maximum effect, sharpened, then played around with the levels and curves until he was satisfied. Then he printed them out. The pictures could go right through to reproduction in the paper without an actual photo being printed, but sometimes he still liked to hold the hard copy in his hand.

The editor would use the one of the local vet, which is why Nick had framed tightly enough to exclude every drop of blood. Taupo was very keen on hometown heroes.

The printouts of an airborne Miss Pink Shoes were good. He stuffed them into a drawer and wondered why he'd taken them.

Is that real blood? asked Jason, craning his neck to see as Nick slammed the drawer. He was on work experience from the local high school.

Real blood? Of course it was real blood. He was one of the best in the business at photographing real blood. He wondered where Ansel Adams would have rated blood on his Zone System.

He wasn't quite so good at preventing real blood from getting spilt.

Remind me to tell you about my wife some time. When we've got a few minutes to sit back and chew the fat. Fay spilt real blood. I couldn't stop it, but I got one hell of a photo. Could have won awards with that photo. Remind me to tell you all about it some time.

Nick was returning along Lake Terrace from the Tauhara Primary School pet day when he caught sight of the blonde from Big Wal's the night before walking across the grass. Her T-shirt looked clean this morning. The previous night, she'd looked like a dropout from a tie-dying class. A small white poodle trotted at her heels.

He pulled into the kerb and walked with studied casualness back to where the woman waited for a gap in the traffic. As a green Peugeot cruised past, its driver waved and both Nick and the woman responded. It seemed as if everyone north of Taupo was heading south this morning, all of them rubber-necking through the township on the way.

'I think I waved at your friends,' Nick said, standing with his thumbs hooked into his waistband.

She was nearly his height, looking back at him almost eye

to eye. Not quite. He liked that, he decided. She looked as if she was debating with herself whether she would reply, but good manners won in the end. It made him think of the night before when Wal had stuck his hand out, and the woman had shaken hands with him eventually, although you could see she'd rather have spat at him.

'Roy Rodgers is everybody's friend,' she said, in a voice that sounded as if she wasn't. She was talking to him, but her gaze was fixed on the flow of traffic.

'So long as you're someone,' she added. Her eyes matched the short blue scarf tied around her neck.

Nick shrugged. 'That rules me out.' He didn't quite know why he was walking his patter past this woman. She didn't like him. She was zero degrees warmer than the lake and that wasn't warm at all. Besides, he didn't usually bother. He had other priorities. 'So if it's not me, then that means *you're* someone?'

She looked at him then and smiled reluctantly, as if she admired his persistence. 'You're the curious one, but that stands to reason, I guess,' and she nodded her head in the direction of the *Star* runabout. 'We own that house over there.' She pointed across the road.

'And owning the house over the road makes you someone?' He cocked an eyebrow at her, aware that he was trying to create an impression, but not able to stop himself.

'Part-own,' she corrected, as if this was an important distinction. 'There are five of us. Roy Rodgers is in real estate. He's been trying to lay his paws on that site for years. He just about throws his cape down in the mud every time he sees me coming. I'm the eldest, you see.'

Nick pulled his eyes off the woman and turned and looked at the house. It wasn't much, an old-fashioned weatherboard cottage, gleaming with fresh white paint, but looking like a country cousin among the string of high-class motels that strutted the lakefront. A high fence woven from manuka branches shut the backyard off from the front. Next door, there was a brick house, the only other private residence left on the lakefront so close to town. A black cat sunned itself in the driveway.

'I can see what you're thinking,' she said. 'That old thing!'

'This is why I always lose at poker.'

She laughed unwillingly. 'It's the site, not the house, Roy's after. We'll sell one day, when it's the last undeveloped site along the waterfront.'

He nodded back at the steps. 'It's nice walking down by the lake this time of day.'

'I wasn't walking. I was looking for something.' Her voice had been warming, but now the chill returned.

Wal and Huamai had told him about the boy trying to offload the coins and the sister who had saved his bacon. The night before, with half a dozen whiskies under his belt, the story of some ancient Maori chief taking retribution on a light-fingered boy sounded reasonable. This morning, he'd thought about Wal's story again — and backlit by Taupo sunshine it seemed nothing more than superstition.

His day had wobbled after shooting Miss Pink Shoes. A short moment of triumph followed by doubt as his mind had wandered down a well-trodden path. Fay had been gone two years. Why did she make him feel bad? There'd been a time — the good years — when a photograph like the one of Miss Pink Shoes had filled him with pleasure. But that was before he'd taken that shot of Fay. Fay dying.

He manhandled his thoughts from Fay back to the woman in front of him. It was easier than usual. 'Anything important?'

'Not really.' She paused and ran her fingers through her hair. 'A hair slide.'

Nick cocked his head on one side. 'I could help,' he said. He couldn't. He had images to download — the cats, dogs and guinea pigs of Tauhara Primary awaited their fifteen seconds of fame — but he said it anyway. He *wanted* to help.

She looked at him carefully, and for a moment he thought he might be in with a chance. 'You at Big Wal's last night?' she asked.

So he was just some hazy recollection. He'd obviously made a real impression on her. 'Is that what this is about?'

'No. Why should it be?'

'Just asking.' She was lying, but he'd swallow the lie for the moment if that was what she wanted. There was an awkward silence, and then he said, 'Nick Jones. I'm the photographer for the *Taupo Star*.'

The coolness stayed in her voice as she responded. 'Saffron Delaney. I own The Dog House on Heu Heu Street.'

'Ah, the local poodle parlour.' He knew that was the wrong thing to say before the words were all out.

'Among fifty other breeds. Even your macho mutts need a bath every now and then. And ears cleaned. And anal glands expressed. And nails trimmed. Why do men think poodles are the only dogs that ever go to a grooming parlour?'

'Just an expression,' he said. He wasn't making much headway. 'What I—'

Nick heard the crackle from the scanner in the car. 'Back in a tick. I'll just catch that.' He thought he felt her eyes on his back as he pulled the car door open.

The scanner was set on the emergency frequency, and he caught only the last few words of the transmission, an accident out by the Napier turnoff.

Nick slid behind the wheel, keyed the engine, did a U-turn in the illusion of a gap and accelerated out of town.

Horns blared. Saffron watched the tail of the car zigzag before it straightened out. So much for *his* offer to help, she thought, her mouth set in a grim line. Thirty seconds before, he'd been trying to chat her up.

She could have told him he didn't stand a chance. He was a press photographer, that was enough. But then he would have asked why and she would have had to tell him about Daddy.

She elbowed Nick's image from her mind. Wasn't hard. He was about as memorable as she obviously was. Everything about him was average. No film star looks, not even an interesting scar. Average, average, average.

She scooped up Pixie in her arms, ran across Lake Terrace, then set the little dog down and watched as it trotted off along the pavement. Pixie would get skittled one day.

She checked the letter box for bills but there weren't any. Their luck wasn't all bad.

How come she was the only one looking for these coins? She wasn't being fair, she knew. Heather had spent almost as much time searching as she had. She was at the hairdresser's and would be back soon. And Mo, with a husband and a young child and another on the way, Mo had other priorities. She could understand that. And Daphne was working. But none of them had touched the coins and seen what she had seen. She shivered. Billy had touched the coins — he must have seen or felt something. Billy should be helping, but, as usual, he'd left his sisters to clean up after him. She supposed it was her own fault. She'd wiped his nose for him once too often when he was a bub, but she'd felt sorry for him. Little Billy dancing on Daddy's knee while the radio blared and the horses ran.

She walked up the drive and took the path that led down the side of the house. Gilbert's cat peered out at her from under an azalea bush, eyes bright and intense, as if it were planning an ambush. She pushed open a gate and went through into a yard full of apple trees. There were apples on most of them — big shiny red ones, green, russet, golden — as if someone had forgotten to take down the Christmas baubles.

Saffron stepped up onto a small veranda. Set into the back door was a leadlight rose window. It was out of character with the plainness of the house, but she'd always loved that window and the patterns it scattered across the floor inside. This morning it looked like a big red mouth, and she gave a shudder as she let herself into the house.

The coins had to be found. She didn't need to be a Delaney to know that.

CHAPTER SEVEN

IT WAS THE OLD WOMAN from the night before. The same long-sleeved black dress fluttered around her calves in the midday breeze and a black scarf covered her head. In her mouth was an unlit pipe and she leant on a stick as she shuffled along the foreshore.

'Did you get home all right?' Saffron asked.

The woman ignored her question. 'I saw you looking.' She wore her dress like a shroud above bare feet. She seemed more confident today, as if perhaps she had digested and adjusted to the events of the night.

'We lost — something,' Saffron said.

'I know you have.' The woman gazed off at the three mountains — Tongariro, Ruapehu, Ngauruhoe. 'Did you find them?'

Saffron shook her head. She suspected the old woman already knew the answer. And how did she know it was a 'them' and not an 'it'? Because she knew it was the coins that were lost.

She wished the man from the *Star* were still here. She glanced up the bank, but there was no one about. Even the tourists had left the Great Lake Hole-in-One Challenge for easier pursuits. A diver in a black wetsuit was retrieving golf balls from around the pontoon. Every now and then, his flippers broke the surface like some mythological sea creature.

She tried to tell herself this was just an old woman out for an afternoon walk. She could turn away and walk back up the steps to the house any time she wanted. Except her feet felt as rooted to the ground as the three mountains standing guard at the end of the lake.

'Tell me about Tama,' Saffron asked. 'And the coins.' She hadn't intended to say that. The words just came out. She knew everyone who walked along the foreshore — except the tourists, of course — but this old crone wasn't one of them. She'd never seen this woman before last night.

'I know Tama Ariki.'

Saffron felt her mind sidestep hastily around the present tense — as if it was a snake she'd spotted beside the path. Or Gilbert's cat. She wet her lips. 'And the coins that are left for him?'

'Now you listen to me.' The old woman removed the pipe from her mouth, cleared her throat and spat on the sand. 'They're not coins, and they're not for him.'

'What are they then?'

'They're gifts to the spirits of the people we lost.' She shook her head and wiped at her eyes. 'Oh, the tears that were shed that day.'

She makes it sound as if she was there, Saffron thought uneasily. 'Can you tell me about it? Big Wal wouldn't tell me.'

'You should listen to your ancestors, girl. They'll tell you what to do.'

Saffron thought of the voices she had begun to hear in her head. Daddy was full of advice. It was a shame that none of it was any help whatsoever. The only thing Daddy knew about was who was likely to win the last race, and even that he got wrong sometimes.

The old woman shuffled over to a driftwood stump that had washed ashore, or maybe it was the remains of a felled gum tree. Further along the shore, nearer to the yacht club and the river entrance, a handful of gums still grew. The stump was a hard skeletal white, gaunt and bony, with a green moss seat. The old woman sat, her face pinching as old bones moved beneath her skin. She patted the stump beside her.

Saffron sat. It was too close, and she could feel a bony thigh against her own, but the old woman didn't seem to notice. Above them, a sapling fluttered brilliant orange and yellow leaves in the breeze.

The old woman coughed and spat to one side again, then began. 'Now, this is how it was. Far back in the history of my people, there was a terrible wrong done. The great chief Tama Ariki left his mokopuna with the women and old people of the tribe while he and the men went to talk to the people of this lake. We were newly arrived, and there had been fighting on the coast. Treachery. Betrayal. Our people killed. We sought sanctuary.

'When Tama Ariki returned the next day, many of the women and children were dead. Our enemy had followed us here, a few warriors so drunk on blood they could not pull back when the others did. They followed and waited their chance. They slaughtered the women and children like animals. The ground was soaked with blood.' A quaver of air fluttered from the old woman's lips. 'So much blood,' she whispered.

'So what did Tama Ariki do?'

'Shush, shush, girl. I'll tell you.' The old woman rocked slowly back and forth. 'You see the blood, too, don't you?' She reached across and took Saffron's hand, and instead of feeling dry and harsh, her skin was soft and childlike. 'After a while it won't be so bad.'

Perhaps the old woman was intending to reassure Saffron, but she made it sound as if she would continue to see the blood forever.

'So many tears were shed. When Tama Ariki found his people killed, he walked back and forth in great sadness and anger, and everywhere his foot fell, the print filled with blood and the ground became tapu. Does a pretty little white girl like you know what that means?'

Saffron nodded. 'Sort of sacred and taboo all at the same time.'

'Near enough. You have to be this colour to really understand what tapu means,' and the old woman patted the skin on her own hand. 'Tama Ariki was a chief of great power. If you walk in his footprints, even to this day, you get struck down by his mere.'

Maybe the old woman sensed Saffron's doubt because she raised one hand and made a feeble club strike in the air. 'Poof! Like that. From out of the sky. You're dead.

'The people of the lake gave us sanctuary. We gathered up our dead and laid them to rest. But there were four babies missing, and we never found their bodies. Tama Ariki's own grandson was never found. Their bodies were taken — to make us suffer more.

'Tama Ariki took his revenge upon our enemy and burned them alive in their huts. Every last one of them.' The old woman spat violently on the ground. 'We moved further around the lake, and for a long while our people were forbidden to come here. Everywhere that Tama Ariki's blood fell, it had turned to red ochre.'

She cocked her head and looked at Saffron expectantly. She seemed disappointed with her lack of response.

'The sacred red ochre, girl,' the old woman prompted, holding out one hand as if it held a truth to be weighed.

'Yes,' Saffron said uncertainly.

The old woman sighed, tutted, shook her head and frowned, but took up her story again.

'Eventually, Tama Ariki took pity upon his people and allowed them to walk the path by the blood of his mokopuna in safety, but they had to leave a token.'

'A gift to placate the spirits of his people?'

The old woman patted Saffron's hand approvingly.

'And that's what the pile of coins is?'

'It can be anything that you value, but coins are what people mostly leave.'

'And if someone should take some of the coins?'

The old woman coughed, patted Saffron's hand rapidly and shook her head.

Saffron got the idea. She raised her hand and made a strike in the air. 'Poof! Tama's club.' Then her mouth opened as she saw Big Wal's softball bat hurtling towards Billy's hand. 'Oh!'

The old woman stuck her unlit pipe back in her mouth and chewed on the stem. Then she removed it and said, 'I saw Tama Ariki's mere last night. Maybe you did too, girl?'

Saffron nodded unwillingly. Had anyone *asked* her if she wanted to be the seer of ancient curses, or had she been voted in, in her absence?

Into her mind came an image of Daddy legging her up onto the pony he'd bought for them all. For her and Heather and Mo and Daphne — and Billy too, although he was still too young to ride, and the pony was long gone by the time he was old enough. *Up you go, petal*, Daddy said. Y*ou're the bravest.*

She didn't feel very brave.

The old woman got slowly to her feet, so Saffron rose too. The old woman leant upon her stick and bent over. Joints cracked and Saffron winced. The old woman breathed heavily through her mouth, making a rasping noise in her chest. Saffron fidgeted from one foot to the other, hands clenching and unclenching, unsure whether she ought to make a grab for her before she collapsed head-first into the sand. Finally, the old woman straightened.

'Give me your hand, girl.'

Saffron hesitated.

'Give me your hand,' the old woman insisted.

Slowly, Saffron held out her hand. It was clenched in a fist, and she forced herself to open it. Her eyes locked on her palm. Tama's club could have been hovering in the sky over her head yet she could not have dragged her gaze away. The old woman dropped the coins into Saffron's hand and folded her fingers over them. 'They're yours now,' she said. She took a deep breath that ended in a fit of coughing.

As the coins touched Saffron's skin, blood raced like a dark red tidal wave through her mind. Distantly, she heard the old woman choking and wondered if they were both drowning in a sea of blood. The old woman's hand locked around hers like the talons of a bird. The coins seared into her skin.

. . . *breathe, girl, breathe your way through it, it's only blood, breathe your way up.*

From somewhere she could hear the old woman crooning to her. The only word she could make out was 'breathe' so she breathed, and discovered the old woman was right. She could breathe her way through the redness until finally she was standing on the beach again with a wind cooling her sweat-slicked skin, her hair glued to her neck, and the coins burning into her hand like solder.

She blew her breath out in a series of steady controlled pants. Just like when Mo had given birth to Lucy, she thought. The breathing seemed to help with the pain in her hand. She unlocked her fingers and cautiously looked down at the coins, afraid of what gazing upon them might do. She wasn't struck blind. The skin on her palm was red.

Saffron bit her lip. 'They're burning me.'

The old woman studied Saffron's hand intently. 'I don't think they like you much, girl. You must give them back to Tama Ariki.'

Saffron's voice quivered as she spoke. 'Where do I take them?' It felt as if someone had aimed a magnifying glass at her hand. She looked down at the seven, maybe eight gold coins, heaped on her palm. The skin around them was the colour of boiled lobster. She didn't like to think what the skin underneath might look like. She panted, and the pain seemed to steady.

The old woman looked up at her, and Saffron could feel her pity. She folded Saffron's fingers over the coins and patted them, staring up into her eyes intently as she did so. Saffron's breath escaped in a drawn-out hiss as heat seared the skin on her fingers.

The old woman turned down the beach. 'I'll walk with you. I'll show you. It won't be long now, girl.'

Saffron nodded blindly. She was not going to whimper. She was not! 'Have you ever had babies?' the old woman asked.

'No,' Saffron said.

'And I see no moko.' There was disapproval in her voice.

'No.' She had once thought about getting a butterfly tattooed on her butt.

'The pain is like that. Some pain you must welcome. Let it be—'

'Saffron!'

At the sound of her name Saffron stopped. Uncertainly, she half turned. Gilbert was hurrying down the shoreline towards her.

Not now, you silly little man, she wanted to scream at him. Go away!

She held her hand to her stomach — it felt as if she was clutching a handful of live coals. Sweat trickled down her face.

'Have you seen Daphne yet?' Gilbert called, as he scurried up.

She shook her head. She wasn't sure if she could talk. If

she opened her mouth, she might scream.

He glanced at his watch. 'It's way after lunchtime. I thought she'd be home by now.'

'I couldn't say,' Saffron whispered.

Gilbert examined her as if she was an object someone had brought into his antique shop. 'You don't look very well, if you don't mind me saying.'

'I'm not. Got a bug, I think.'

'So perhaps you'd be better at home lying down rather than wandering about spreading whatever it is you have.' He took a step back.

'I will. I just have to do something first.'

He shook his head. 'Everyone thinks that their wants come before public health. I would have thought with a nurse in your family you would be a little more enlightened.'

'I'm busy right now. I can't talk. I'll tell Daphne you want her.'

'I remember last winter I caught a severe case of flu. Very nasty. Every second person who came into the shop had it. Coughing and spluttering all over the place.'

Saffron's mind seemed to be separating from her body. She felt as if she was hovering above herself, looking down. She quite liked it up here. The pain wasn't so bad. The pain was down there. Up here, there was a cool breeze that dried the sweat on her brow. Down there, there was a dark little man buzzing away like a mosquito at a tall, pain-wracked woman with one hand clutched to her stomach as if she had a bad bellyache. Maybe she was having a baby.

'. . . and it was the doctor who told me that,' Gilbert finished.

Saffron nodded. She felt like a puppeteer pulling the strings. Pull this string and the Saffron doll nods. She wished she knew where the string was to make the Gilbert doll walk.

'I have to go,' she whispered.

'You should be home in bed,' Gilbert said. 'You look as if you're burning up.'

Saffron wanted to laugh, but knew if she did she'd scream. She turned stiffly on her feet. The Saffron doll wasn't moving very well. She took a step, then remembered the old woman. Where was she?

She looked back to Gilbert and panted a couple of times. 'Did you see an old woman?'

His eyes narrowed. 'Old woman? There's no old woman.'

'She was here a moment ago,' Saffron said, with a vague wave of her other hand. 'She has a moko on her chin.'

Gilbert stared at her, then shook his head firmly. 'There are no old women with the moko left. I read in the paper many years ago when the last one died.'

'But I was talking to her.'

'I didn't see anyone.'

'I might sit down,' Saffron said. Her knees buckled and she flopped down onto the sand. His words told her what she knew already, in the deepest, darkest part of her mind. There was no old woman. There never had been. She was clutching a handful of what felt like live coals to her stomach because some figment of her imagination told her she must.

Gilbert stepped away from her. 'Have you been drinking?'

Saffron shook her head. She wished she had. 'Do you want

me to phone anyone for you?'

She shook her head again, panted several times and then flapped her free hand at him once in a wave of dismissal.

'Take an aspirin and go to bed.' He scuttled back along the beach. He clambered over the stormwater outlet, and at the foot of the steps she saw him turn and look back at her. Probably thought he was going to catch her swigging out of a bottle in a brown paper bag, she thought.

Cautiously, she moved her hand away from her stomach and looked down. She half expected to see a scorch mark on her T-shirt. When she pulled the fabric up, her stomach was pink.

She opened her fingers slightly so she could see into her hand. Blisters formed a neat circle of plump cushions around the coins. She felt her bottom lip tremble a little, but she couldn't just sit here and cry. That wouldn't solve anything. She closed her fingers and felt a tear slide down her cheek anyway. Wiping it away with her other hand, she clambered woodenly to her feet.

The old woman . . .

Who lives in your head, petal, whispered Daddy.

She stopped, circled stiffly, even though she knew the voice had echoed out of her own mind. Nobody called her 'petal'. Not since Daddy died. He used to call them 'petal': Saffron, Mimosa, Heather and Daphne. His little flowers, he used to say. But Daddy had died, and nobody had ever called her 'petal' again.

She swallowed. That wasn't important. Not now. She was getting sidetracked. The Saffron doll had the attention span of a newt.

The old woman had been showing her where Tama's Rock was. They had begun to walk in this direction, so obviously the rock was somewhere ahead. But there were dozens of rocks along the next few hundred metres before the lakefront was halted by the river entrance.

Big Wal, she thought through a haze of pain. If anyone knows which is Tama's Rock, he will.

She climbed the steps up the bank, moving with an unnatural, forced smoothness. It was only by holding in every natural instinct that she could function at all. Every fibre of her being commanded her to drop the coins, fling them away. Control she didn't know she possessed made her hold them. She passed a group of tourists coming down.

'You look unwell, dear,' said a woman with an English accent. 'Can we help?'

Saffron didn't hear. She walked on, head held high, right hand extended in front of her like a platter carrying a dreadful burden.

The pain in her hand was a living, pulsing beast. Every now and then she panted. She crossed the road, hearing the screech of brakes and the blare of horns, but not connecting the sounds with herself.

CHAPTER EIGHT

NICK JUMPED ON the brakes, threw the nose of the car to the left as the line of traffic he was travelling in suddenly concertinaed and hoped the driver in front chose the other way. He was cruising the town, camera on the seat beside him, filling in time before his next shoot. It was the fourth time he'd driven past the Delaney woman's house.

'What the . . .' he muttered, as he peered up ahead.

Saffron Delaney, drifting like a sleepwalker, emerged on the other side of Lake Terrace.

He signalled left and drew out of the traffic as it began to move again. He parked, grabbed a packet of cigarettes off the console, leapt out and sprinted across the road. A single horn tooted at him.

'Are you all right?' He grabbed her arm. She spun around to face him as if her whole body was rigid. Move one part and everything else had to move as well.

She nodded, carefully, as if she had to concentrate so that only her head would move.

He stared into her face. 'No you're not, sweetheart. Believe me. I've seen all right and I've seen not all right.' He held her rigid arm. 'What have you got?'

Saffron said nothing.

'The coins? You found them? That's—' He'd been about to say 'that's good', but looking at her halted the words in his throat.

'I have to go.' She tried to walk away from him, and it was like holding back a wind-up toy. He half-expected to see her legs walking in place beneath her. He could have held her there with one finger hooked in the scarf around her neck.

'You're in no state to be wandering about. You came this close to being roadkill a minute ago.'

'Did I?'

'And you're off in the wrong direction.'

She panted, then looked vaguely about her.

'You were heading *towards* town a minute ago,' he pointed out.

'Yes,' she agreed, and stiffly turned herself one-eighty degrees.

Nick stared into her face. The night before, she had looked cold, pale and ill. Now she was flushed, sweat beaded her face, and she looked even worse. 'You're not well, Saffron,' he said quietly.

'Have to get the coins back,' she mumbled.

'Give them to me. You're in no state for this. I'll do it.'

'Can't.'

He raised his eyebrows. 'Why not?'

'Have to go,' she said again, and her feet began to move so that she was marching in place. She looked ridiculous, but seemed unaware of the fact. It embarrassed him to make her appear so foolish.

Uncertainly, because he knew he shouldn't, Nick released his grip, and she headed off towards the town.

'Where are you going?' he called after her, but she didn't answer.

'I think it's pretty clear what's happening there,' a voice said from somewhere down by the top button on Nick's shirt.

Nick looked down on dark hair so lush it almost looked false. 'Is it?'

'Drink,' the man said. 'Brother's the same way.'

'You'd know, would you?' Nick said brusquely. He flipped open the packet of cigarettes and shook one out. His brow furrowed as he lit up, and his eyes stayed on the back of the woman gliding down the pavement as if she had a dictionary on her head.

'Gilbert Williams,' the man said. 'I've lived next door to the Delaneys for years. There's not much about that family I don't know.'

'She doesn't look like a drinker to me,' Nick said. He presented his back to the man and watched the traffic, waiting for a gap to retrieve the car and go after her. Warm air washed his face.

'Father was unstable,' Gilbert confided from behind him. 'Whole family is. Well, not all of them,' he amended. 'The youngest of the girls is a delightful young woman. She's a teacher.' He flipped the lid on his letter box and looked inside. 'And Mrs Pearson proved my predictions wrong. I think getting married and escaping from the influence of the rest of her family saved her.'

'I wouldn't know.' The traffic was bumper to bumper.

Gilbert continued. 'And now look at that one. As I said,

either drink or drugs.' He reached down and picked up a black cat. 'Blood will out.'

'What do you mean by that?' Nick glanced at him.

'Their father was a gambler. A complete waster.'

'Must have done OK to buy on the Terrace.' There was a gap coming up behind the blue Holden. Not much of a gap, but enough.

'Bought it one week and had to mortgage it the next, is how I heard it. Didn't have the brains of a pork pie when it came to money. How those children didn't all starve after their mother left, I'll never know.'

A trades van shot out from one of the motels and into the space behind the Holden. Nick swore.

'And then the father hangs himself. What sort of example is that?'

Nick swung back to stare at Saffron's neighbour. Gilbert's chin almost rested on top of the cat. Soft, pale hands, which looked as if they'd never done a day of manual work, caressed its coat.

'What?'

Gilbert smiled, as if pleased to have at last captured his audience's attention. 'Hanged himself from the grandstand overlooking the birdcage at the Ellerslie racecourse. Being a newspaper man, I'm surprised you weren't there. It was in all the Sunday papers. Not that I read those gossip sheets, but being their neighbour, I couldn't help but hear about it. About ten years back.'

Of course — Delaney! He knew all about Lucky Del Delaney. Who didn't? He just hadn't made the connection. The man had been a brilliant jockey. He hadn't been Lucky

Del then, of course, he'd been Del Delaney, the top jockey in the country for five consecutive years. He'd won three Auckland Cups, and in a lightning raid to Australia had won the Melbourne Cup by a horse hair. But he'd started to gamble and as Del Delaney galloped towards becoming Lucky Del, he'd lost first his jockey's licence, then, a year or two later, his wife. He'd hanged himself after a particularly bad losing streak — or so people said. He hadn't left a note.

By sheer chance, Nick had been in New Zealand at the time, home while an assortment of broken bones mended. He'd been returning from the massacre at Nyarubuye when his jeep had gone over sabotage spikes laid across the road. Bones broken, time off. He was due to fly out, back to Rwanda, a couple of days later. He'd been sitting around the *Herald* photographic department, chewing over old times with Matt and Doug and a few others.

He and Matt had made it to the racecourse before the police had cut Lucky Del down. He could see the image as if he had taken it yesterday: Lucky Del's head bowed as if in prayer, a forelock of blond hair over one eye. That hid the less photogenic aspects of death by strangulation, which is what hanging usually amounted to. On the ground below his dangling feet had been a handful of pink roses — they grew roses at Ellerslie around the birdcage. The man must have picked and held them, then dropped them as he died. It had seemed almost a pretty death after the atrocities of Rwanda.

Nick had taken two photographs: one shot of Lucky Del swinging in the breeze and another of the flowers scattered on the ground below him. Then he'd married the two images together in the darkroom. No one else had done that. The

Herald hadn't published it, not a suicide, but a couple of the Sunday rags fought over it. The editor at the time had always sworn that shot would have taken the Qantas Media Award that year except the judges didn't have the balls to let it win.

'Yeah. I was there,' Nick said shortly. He'd photographed a few suicides. As he told Fay once, it was what he did. He didn't have to like it. What he didn't tell Fay was, when he put the camera to his eye, they were no longer people. They were images — to be composed and gathered. But you didn't say that, even to another photographer, and you certainly didn't say it to your wife. But you did admit it to yourself. Truth was important. That was what the images were all about. He might acknowledge their pain afterwards, but at the time he didn't feel a thing. Fay had told him he was a bastard, but she'd ruffled his hair while she said it.

The traffic was bumper to bumper again. He sprinted up the street to overtake Saffron before she walked under a car.

Nick caught her just before she reached Robert Street. Luckily. She stepped off the kerb without a glance in either direction. He grabbed her and felt the heat burning from her skin. Her T-shirt was drenched, clinging to her, and he could see the outline of her bra underneath.

'Let me help,' he said. But she didn't seem to recognize him.

If she was a daughter of Lucky Del Delaney then the sort of superstitious tale Wal had retold just might affect her. Lucky Del had believed in luck and omens. It didn't take a genius to see that his kids might gobble up Wal's story about Tama and let it give them a bellyache. He took her arm and turned her up Robert Street.

She ignored him. He didn't think she knew who he was. Every now and then she panted. It was like watching one of those modern movies that show you more than you want to see about the birth process.

She wasn't drunk. There was no smell of alcohol about her, or breath-freshener. It could be drugs, of course, but he didn't think so. If this was the effect of some new party pill, he didn't think it would catch on. She was ill.

'Give the coins to me,' he said. 'Let me help.' He took her hand and felt a stab of alarm at the heat radiating from it. 'Let me help.' He forced his fingers under her clenched ones and tried to prise her hand open.

She bent over and sank her teeth into his hand.

He yelped with surprise and swore. He dropped her hand, and she walked on as if he wasn't there.

She's gone feral, he thought in astonishment, wiping at his hand where blood welled from the imprint of a perfect set of front teeth. *Was* there something in the story Wal had told? If he forced the coins from her, she might go over the edge. He'd seen women clinging to babies who were well past their use-by date, and it was usually best to leave them. Interference, however well intentioned, caused more harm than good. He pulled out his cigarettes.

Without thinking, he patted one pocket of his jacket. Emergency camera — just in case. It lived with him, as much a part of his wardrobe as his underwear.

He caught her up, grabbing her arm as they crossed streets or if she looked as though she was going to walk into someone. He took out his lighter, then stopped. What if she ignited? It was a stupid thought — more than stupid, crazy — and he knew it, but there *had* been cases of spontaneous combustion. The heat was coming off her in waves. It wasn't natural. There was something seriously weird going on. He still didn't believe this shit about Tama, but *she* did. Maybe that was all that mattered. He left his cigarette dangling unlit between his lips, and they walked up the arcade towards Horomatangi Street. She seemed to be heading for Big Wal's, but would have walked straight past if he hadn't put his hand gently on her arm.

She looked around as if unsure where she was or why she wanted to be here. Nick led her over to the counter.

Big Wal, who was slicing tomatoes, looked up, put his knife down and came over to the front counter, wiping his hands on his apron. He stared at Saffron, then muttered something in Maori. Nick didn't know if it was an oath of surprise or words for protection.

'How long has she been like this?'

'I was talking to her this morning. She was worried but — normal. She's got the coins on her,' Nick added.

Big Wal didn't quite take a step back, but you could see he wanted to. 'What's she doing?'

'I think maybe she was coming here to find out where to return them. The brother seems to have disappeared.'

'Now why doesn't that surprise me?' Big Wal said.

Nick took a couple of steps away from Saffron and lit his cigarette. 'Where is this Tama's Rock?'

'In between Ruapehu and Titiraupenga Streets. There's a line of rocks extending out into the lake. Some people call the whole thing Tama's Rock, and sometimes people leave coins at the shore end, but really it's the last rock out in the water. That's the real Tama's Rock.'

'The rest is for dudes who don't like getting their feet wet,' Huamai said. He handed a white paper bag over the counter, and a teenage girl dropped money in his hand.

'I guess we need the real McCoy,' Nick said.

Big Wal looked him straight in the eye. 'You sure as hell do. Take the coins right out to the end rock. You'll get your feet wet. Lean over the top of the rock, and on the lake side you'll see a depression in the rock. Like a bowl. Put the money in there. Say a prayer, if you like.'

The only prayer Nick knew was the Lord's Prayer, and he wasn't sure he could remember all the words to that. He knew the start of it but he wasn't convinced a prayer to a Christian God was going to cut much ice with this Tama.

Big Wal must have seen the doubt on his face. 'It don't matter who it's to.'

Huamai scooped up a couple of loose chips floating in the vat and dropped them in the pig bin. 'Didn't used to be a bowl in the rock. When I was young, my uncle told me that before the killing Tama's Rock was round. The rock sucked its breath in, see. That's what my uncle said. The rock held its breath to soften the blow. You see they bashed the mokopuna's head against the rock.' Huamai gave a swing with his arm to demonstrate. 'Then the rock stayed like that so as not to spill the mokopuna's blood. That's what my uncle said.'

Nick had known Huamai for six months. He'd never heard him make a longer statement — oh, except for Maori land issues. Then he was like a stuck record. So that little monologue had to tell him something.

Big Wal nodded. 'You were told right.' He stared hard at Nick as if challenging him to disagree.

Nick had lived in enough different cultures to allow the differences to just be. What worried him seriously was that he was beginning to believe all this himself. Something was happening. He hadn't quite got to the point where he believed that rocks sucked in their breath, but he was beginning to believe in this Tama. That the man, god — whatever he was — had power over things.

He touched Saffron on the arm. 'Let's go.' He aimed her in the right direction, and they headed on down Horomatangi Street, left onto Tongariro Street and towards the lake.

Nick steered her through the maze of tables and chairs on the corner where Tongariro met Lake Terrace, then shepherded her across the road. They walked along the cliff top towards the Great Lake Hole-in-One Challenge. At the car park, holidaymakers sat at one of the tables eating their lunch. A campervan was parked beside them, and they were serving bacon, eggs and fried potatoes out of an electric frypan on the table. On the far side of the campervan was the *Taupo Star* car. They had come full circle.

Halfway down the steps, Nick's pager went.

Damn! He pulled out his mobile and called the office.

'Hi Nick. Where you got to, good buddy?' It was Karen from the editorial desk.

'I'm on a job.'

'Is it important? There's been a head-on crash out past Huka Falls. Charlie wants photographs. He said to tell you there's lots of blood. Litres and litres of it.'

'I hope you told him I'm made of finer stuff than that.' He hesitated and then said, 'Tell him I'm on my way. I'll be there in ten.'

Saffron was walking in front of him. He put his hand on her arm. 'I've got to go.' She didn't seem to have heard him. He pulled her around to face him. 'Saffron? I have to go. OK? Do you know where you're going?'

The look in her eyes did not inspire confidence. He helped her over the stormwater outlet.

'See the rocks?' He turned her and pointed. 'See the rocks? Go right to the end of them. Out in the water. Yes?'

He nodded, as if that would somehow help her to understand. Wishful thinking. Her face was blank.

'Saffron.' He stood directly in front of her, his face only centimetres away. He moved his head from side to side, and finally saw her eyes track him. 'Ye-es. We have ignition,' he muttered to himself. 'You reading me, Saf? The rocks. See?' He pointed and went through the entire charade again. At last, she seemed to understand.

She murmured, 'The rocks. End of the rocks.'

'You'll have to get your feet wet,' he prompted.

'Feet wet.'

'Good girl. I'll be back — soon.' It sounded a bit lame even to his ears. But what was he supposed to do? He had to think about who paid his salary, didn't he? He liked the woman, he really did — and he hadn't said that since Fay was killed — but he wasn't her baby-sitter. He owed the *Star* his loyalty. Didn't he?

He gave her a little push to set her off in the right direction, then hurdled the stormwater outlet and raced back up the steps. He stopped at the top and looked back for a moment. She'll be fine, he thought. She'll be fine.

CHAPTER NINE

HAVE TO GET my feet wet, Saffron thought, as she paddled along the lake edge. Tiny wavelets broke gently against her ankles. The bottoms of her jeans were wet to the knees. Water squelched in her sneakers. Someone had been with her, but he'd gone now. She'd been floating along above her own head like a child's balloon. It was nice being a balloon. Balloons didn't feel pain. Not much, anyway. The man had known where they were going, but now she had to decide.

She could no longer feel her hand as a separate part of her body. She occupied a universe of pain in which everything was agony.

Get my feet wet. There had to be more to it than that. She wished the man was still here because he had seemed to know what they were doing. She splashed along and came to some rocks that stretched out into the lake like an outflung arm. Something resonated in her brain. The end of the rocks? Had he said something about the end of the rocks? She clambered along them until she came to a big black water-slick rock at the end. As she climbed around the rock, wonderfully cold water crept up her legs, over her knees, her thighs, till it lapped around her waist.

Well, her feet were wet. So far, so good. She put one hand out onto the rock, then looked at her other hand, which was clutching something. An idea floating just out of her reach told her this was important.

She opened her hand. The palm was a mess of broken blisters leaking a colourless fluid. A wet and sticky pile of coins sat like an island in the centre. This was what it was about. The coins. Returning the coins. Getting her feet wet was just a step on the journey. This was the destination.

She reached out her hand and tipped the coins into a bowl-shaped depression in the rock. Then she sank her hand beneath the water, her breath hissing in over her teeth as the liquid bit. Oh, dear God, but that hurt! She hadn't thought anything could hurt more, but it did. She raised her face to the sky, lips parted, eyes closed, and waited for the agony to subside.

And at last it did. Sort of. Her whole body felt numb and when she lifted her hand the palm was raw and weeping.

Slowly the day came into focus. The monotone of grey that had made up her world for the past hour began to change. And then her senses exploded, bombarding her with colour. The lake was so blue it dazzled. The blackberry and scrubby bushes that clung to the bank were vivid green, apart from the occasional slash of vermilion and butter yellow. An early autumn-coloured tree hurt her eyes in orange and gold.

She looked up again. It was as if the air had taken on a special quality. She watched a bird wheel overhead, black against the sky, circling once, twice, three times. Was fate pointing its bony finger at her? Was Lady Luck making sure that every god in the universe knew she was the stealer of the coins? Telling Tama?

Maybe the bird is Tama Ariki, girl, the old woman whispered in her head.

The bird shrieked then, flapping strongly as it peeled off towards the three mountains at the far end of the lake. She stared after it, her mouth dry.

Well, if the bird was Tama, she thought grimly, as she worked her way back around the rock, then he would know she was *not* the stealer of the coins. She had returned them.

Hey, fate, she wanted to yell, I'm the good guy!

She remembered how her daddy had liked the old westerns where the baddies wore black hats and the hero had a white hat, before Clint Eastwood came along and muddled the whole thing up.

She was cold; her wet clothes clung to her, and she knew she would catch her death if she danced too many reels with Tama. Earlier, her body had been on fire. Now, she felt chilled and sick. She reached out with her good hand and touched the rock, an acknowledgment of paths that had crossed, a farewell.

But the old woman wasn't done with her. *Put your hand in the bowl, girl.*

She moved back and put her good hand towards the bowl.

The other one.

Hesitantly, she moved her burnt hand towards the bowl. Inside she could see the coins and some drops of liquid.

Red liquid.

Not blood! She didn't want it to be blood!

It had to be water. From the lake.

But it was blood, and it rose slowly up the sides of the bowl, covering first one coin and then another until only one remained like an island in a sea of blood, before it too disappeared.

And then blood began to drip from the wound in her hand. Slowly, one drop at a time; and as each drop fell, rings spread from the centre. She watched in horrified fascination, feeling a whimper whispering in her throat.

The blood dripped from her hand to the bowl, and the concentric ripples spread out and out, moving and distorting and changing, until she finally realized that the bowl was as big as the world, and she was slipping between two spreading ripples.

Through the ripples, on a wide sunny shore far away, sat a group of women and young children. There were babies too — fat, placid babies. Some lay on mats, sleeping; others were suckling. Some giggled and gurgled in their mothers' arms. A tiny newborn with a fluff of dark hair like duckling feathers lay against his mother's breast, a bone tiki around his neck. The woman's eyes were closed, and Saffron could see the smile that hovered on her lips. Children played. Women talked and laughed.

Saffron sat among them. She could smell the familiar aroma of food cooking in the earth oven and feel the coarse pumice sand against the back of her legs. A stiff breeze off the lake wrapped her hair across her face. When she pushed a strand of thick black hair away from her eyes she saw that her skin was brown.

Out on the water thousands of ducks and grebes swam and dived for food. There was safety and plenty after the desolation of manuka and tussock they had wandered through. Their great chief, Tama Ariki, had led them here. He knew these people — Taupo was their lake, Tongariro was their mountain. Hadn't these people welcomed them with a stirring challenge, good food and stories? The men would talk, a strategic marriage or two would be arranged, and somewhere around this lake would be a place for them. A place where they could be safe.

And so the women waited for the men to return.

The breeze became a cold, gusty wind and it brought death. Saffron heard the birds take flight. She saw the canoe scrape silently up on the beach, felt herself rise with the other women, watching, wondering and at last understanding. She heard the first hesitant call of alarm, then the desperate grabbing up of babies and children as the enemy they had fled attacked them again. Running, running, running, with children on backs and babies in arms. Saffron ran with them as women grabbed desperately at little ones too young to run, frightened children herded before them. The slow were clubbed down.

She watched as a mother fell to her knees with a tiny baby in her arms. The newborn. Saffron started to run back, but it was too late. A club jabbed out, the mother screamed, slumped, and the newborn spewed from her arms. Saffron ran faster, flying against the tide of terrified children. The mother crawled towards the baby, but the club came down again. And again. She stopped running. It was too late. A scar-faced man walked to the infant. Two tiny fists rose as if the baby wanted to be picked up. Saffron turned her head. She couldn't bear to see what must happen next. Blood thundered in her ears and something inside felt as if it was tearing.

After an eternity, sure the blow must have fallen, she looked back with tear-filled eyes. A line of rocks running out from the cliffs into the water drew her gaze along it, as if it was a path. The scar-faced man stood upon the furthest rock, where the lake splashed up around him. Except for some greenery around his waist, he was naked. His long black hair was twisted up into a topknot and skewered by a bone. He held the baby by one leg. Its head dangled above the lake, and it was crying, screaming. Occasionally, the water broke over the child's head, and the cry became a splutter.

A woman cried out in a voice ragged with pain, and the man looked up at the cliff. He laughed, holding the baby aloft and shook it at her. The woman screamed, her voice a knife that split that sun-filled day in two. And then the man cracked the baby's head open on the rock.

He swung the body around his head once, twice, and blood sprayed the rocks, and then he released his grip, and the baby flew out over the water until Saffron thought it was going to fly forever, before it fell and disappeared beneath the rippling waves.

High above, a woman's voice lifted into a high harsh keen that swept down the cliff and rode the wind over the lake to the furthest shore.

Saffron listened to the voice until the sound was the only thing left in the world.

CHAPTER TEN

SOMEONE WAS SHAKING HER, and Saffron struck at him, thinking it was the man on the rock — the baby killer. When she saw it was Nick, she stopped and started to cry.

'Are you OK?' he demanded. 'Jeez, you scared the shit out of me!'

She stopped crying and looked around at the empty beach. Nothing. All gone.

'Leave me alone.' She pushed him away.

He retreated but immediately flowed back, like a river momentarily diverted but ultimately unchanged by the current of a merging stream. 'I don't think so, sweetheart. You're not safe to be out without your mother.'

Nick's arms folded around her. Her head was bowed so that her face was close to his pale green shirt, and woven into the fabric was the image of the baby, as if he had stamped his mark on her forever.

Closing her eyes, feeling tears bead on her lashes, she laid her cheek against Nick and let him hold her. She breathed in a blend of aftershave and smoke — a smell that reminded her of Daddy. Nick's fingers gently stroked her back, his murmured words caressed her mind, the anger that had briefly enflamed him gone. Slowly his presence pushed the image away, so that when she opened her eyes all she saw was the warp and weft of linen.

She raised her chin. Nick's face was centimetres from hers, his camera a lump between their bodies. She stared at him, trying to read what she saw. He kissed her tears away, the pressure of his lips firm and sure, and she wanted to let him make everything safe. She wanted to feel better, except she couldn't let herself — not after what she'd just seen. It felt too much like betrayal.

Nick's hands cupped her shoulders. He held her away from him, studying her mouth, and the look in her eyes changed. His head dipped towards her.

Quickly she pushed him away again, wriggling out from under his grip, hating the way her fingertips identified the bulge of muscle beneath them and identified it as toned and male. She hurried over to a rock and sat down, knees clenched primly together. He was a press photographer, for heaven's sake. Had the water washed away any common sense she'd had?

Nick followed. He was wet to his belt, and water dripped from his trousers. 'I raced back as quickly as I could, and you were standing out there up to your waist in the water wailing like a banshee. Scared the shit out of me.'

'Sorry.'

He crouched in front of her, his hands resting gently on her legs. 'Don't be sorry.' He shook his head. 'You scared me. I was scared for you. Are you all right?'

'I think so.' She held out her hand to him, palm up, like a

small child. She was acutely aware of his fingers massaging her thighs. Something had started — in his mind at least — and she had to shut it down.

He swore. 'The coins did that?'

She was grateful when his kneading fingers left her legs to hold her injured hand.

'You idiot,' he said softly. 'Why didn't you drop them?'

'I had to return them. You know that.'

'Yes, but . . .' He held his breath, lips still slightly parted, as he stared at her. She pulled her hand away roughly, and he said 'Yes' again, as if it meant something, and reached into his pocket for his cigarettes. 'What are you?' he said finally.

'An idiot.'

'You got that right.' He stood up and held out his hand to her. 'I'm taking you home before you freeze. You need to do something with that hand.'

She breathed out shakily. The moment had passed, so she let him help her off the rock. 'Heather will know what to do. She's a nurse. I don't think she'll have left for work yet.'

When they walked into the kitchen, Heather's eyes widened in shock. She'd been sprawled in a big old armchair in the corner, her feet dangling over the arm rest, sun spilling through the open window, but she dropped the paperback she'd been reading, leapt to her feet and pushed her sister into a chair at the table. 'You're soaked to the skin. What on earth happened?'

'Have you got a heater?' Nick asked.

'Cupboard down the hall.' Heather pulled Saffron's wet jeans off.

'You'd better take a look at her hand,' Nick called, as he

manhandled a large electric heater down the hallway and into the kitchen. He placed it in front of Saffron, plugged it into the outlet on the stove and switched it to high.

'Saf! What happened? That's a nasty burn.' Heather carefully felt the skin. 'Still some heat in it.' She led Saffron over to the kitchen sink and turned the cold tap onto the hand, ignoring her sister's yelp of pain. 'What happened to her?' Heather asked Nick, who was repositioning the chair behind Saffron.

'She found the coins.'

'The coins did this?' Heather said in disbelief.

'It appears so.' He pulled the heater close again.

'How? Were they in a fire? What happened?'

'They burnt me,' Saffron said quietly. The water was making the burn feel worse, not better. There was a faint smell from the layer of summer-gathered dust on the heater element.

'Who did? Who burnt you?'

'The coins. This water isn't making it feel better.'

'That's not what it's for. How did the coins burn you?' Heather pressed her fingers to Saffron's pulse.

Saffron gave a shiver. 'The old woman found them and gave them to me, and the minute they touched my hand, I could feel them beginning to burn.'

'What old woman?' Heather asked. She peered into Saffron's eyes with the clinical detachment of the medically literate.

'Last night, when I touched the coins I saw blood. And I did at first when she gave them to me this morning. But somehow I controlled that, and then they started to burn.'

Saffron almost wished she'd stuck with the blood. At least once it had gone, it had gone. The pain in her hand had not.

'Do you know anything about all this?' Heather asked, glancing at Nick.

'Not much. She was wandering about with the coins when I found her, sort of confused. I took her to Big Wal's to find out where Tama's Rock was. And then . . .' he hesitated. 'That's what she did,' he finished.

He stood behind Saffron's chair, holding out the cloth of his sodden trousers, trying to dry them in the warmth radiating from the heater.

Heather stared at him. 'You didn't think it might be a good idea to take the coins off her? She's got a second-degree burn to her hand. Luckily, it covers only a small area. A burn like this, to enough of your body, kills you.'

'She wouldn't give the coins up,' Nick said, looking around for an ashtray.

'And that stopped you? A big fellow like you?'

'What did you want me to do? Knock her to the ground? Break her fingers? She didn't want to give them to me.'

Heather looked up from Saffron's hand to Nick. 'Sorry. I know what Saf's like once she gets the bit between her teeth. Still, she's returned the coins. Surely that has to be an end to it all?'

'Does it?' Saffron knew, logically, that what Heather said should be right — but was it? Did logic matter to this Tama?

Does he play by the rules of the game, petal? That's what you need to know. She gave a start. She didn't like the way voices were popping into her head.

99

'What?' Heather said, staring at her.

Nick picked up an apple from the bowl and examined it with distaste, as if he expected it to be full of worms. Saffron looked between his face and her sister's. Neither looked reassured, and she didn't blame them, because Tama and his club were hovering in the sky above their little world.

Tama's club. The words popped into her mind as if they'd always been there. But until the previous night she'd never heard of Tama, and she was sure — *quite sure* — that no one last night had mentioned his club. So where had the words sprung from?

From the old woman, of course, petal, a voice whispered in her head.

She looked across at Nick and found him staring at her. There was something in his eyes that she didn't like. OK, he might have nice muscly arms and strong hands but she had to remember how they got like that. Toned from years of lugging all that photographic gear about. He was blood brother to the ghouls who had swooped in at Daddy's death. She had to remember that.

She looked like a drowned rat. Nick suspected she was a beautiful woman — that mouth certainly gave her a head-start — but every time he saw her, she looked awful.

'Are you OK now?' he asked. 'I'm going to have to shoot off. I've got an assignment this afternoon.'

Saffron looked up at him. 'I'm OK. No need for you to hang around.'

He felt himself dismissed. She'd clung to him down by the lake. Now, she couldn't wait for him to go. He jammed a cigarette in his mouth. 'I'll see you ladies later.'

There was a sharp noise outside. The two Delaney girls jumped as if they'd just sat on whoopee cushions. Even Nick flinched, then grimaced at his own response.

Saffron lurched from her seat and peered out the window. He saw the tension flow from her so that her body appeared almost to deflate as she settled back into her chair.

'I thought—' she said, but she didn't say what she'd thought.

The back door was flung open, and a young woman raced in. Blonde, blue eyes, tanned legs zooming up from sneakers to disappear under denim shorts. Had to be another Delaney girl.

'What a day!' she said, dumping down a large canvas bag and throwing car keys onto the table and herself into the armchair. 'Kids! Whatever you do, don't have any. Or at least don't have twenty of them. Are there any MallowPuffs left? Golly, it's hot in here.' She fanned herself with her hand.

Her eyes slid over to Nick as if she'd only just noticed him, and Nick felt male hormones kick-start his Harley. A vision of himself swanning into somewhere posh with the three Delaney girls hanging off his arms enriched the fuel mix tenfold.

'Daphne, this is Nick Jones. Nick, our sister Daphne.' It was Saffron who took care of the introduction, one hand still dangling under the flow of water. 'Nick's a photographer with the *Taupo Star*.'

He saw the gleam in Daphne's eye die, and she ended up looking at him the way Fay used to look at a sponge mix that failed to clear the top of the tin. 'Oh.'

Saffron and Heather gave her polite smiles as if they understood exactly what she meant. Nick's Harley spluttered to a halt. 'Nice meeting you, Daphne.'

He walked down the garden path and through the manuka gate, wondering if the Delaney girls were talking about him. Sadly, he thought they weren't. He hadn't impressed them, and wondered why that should matter.

Hot air slapped him in the face when he opened the car door. It carried with it the smell of the overflowing ashtray. He kept forgetting to empty it. He almost tipped it onto the road, but at the last minute, and with a not very confident hope that maybe the Delaney girls were spying on him out their front window, he carried it across to the litter bin.

He got into the car, swore when he almost cooked his back on the seat, and headed off around the lake to meet some guy at an archaeological dig.

Chapter Eleven

'D O WE NEED that heater going?' Daphne asked. She wriggled uncomfortably on the armchair and finally pulled a paperback from under her behind. She flipped it over to read the title, declared, 'Tami Hoag. Read it', and tossed it on the floor.

'Don't lose my place,' Heather said sharply. She inclined her head towards Saffron. 'She's been in the lake.'

'Why?' Daphne jumped out of the chair, yanked open the pantry door. She found the last MallowPuff from their Thursday video night and bit into it. Chocolate crumbs sprinkled her top.

'It's a long story,' Saffron said. 'But I've returned the coins.'

'Well, that's OK then.' Daphne's cheeks bulged, her words almost unintelligible.

'Is it?' Saffron began to turn the tap off. The coldness of the water was hurting more than the burn.

Heather pulled her nose out of Daphne's canvas holdall and pushed Saffron's hand away. She carried a clear plastic container in one hand, and Saffron looked without interest at the long-horned, brown insect inside.

'So why does she need more water?' Daphne asked. 'I'd have thought she'd had enough for one day.'

Heather clasped Saffron's wrist and held her palm towards Daphne.

Daphne winced. 'Youch! How did you do that?'

'Long story,' Saffron said again.

'The coins burnt her. Don't ask how — we don't know.'

There was a knock on the back door, and the three sisters looked at each other.

'If they're selling religion or vacuum cleaners, they're dead,' Heather said. She dropped the plastic container back in the bag and went to the back door.

'Hoy! Be nice to my wetas,' Daphne called after her. 'It took me *weeks* to get the permit to collect these,' she explained to Saffron. 'I don't want them scared to death now that I've got them.'

'Gilbert has been looking for you,' Saffron said. 'Grab me that towel, will you.'

Daphne pulled a face. 'Have I time to make an escape?' she asked, as she spread the towel over Saffron's bare legs and panties.

She hadn't. Heather returned almost immediately with Gilbert at her heels. He halted at the doorway, his face flushing as Daphne came into view.

'You're home at last,' he said.

Daphne forced a smile. 'Home at last.'

Gilbert's cat appeared behind him, twining around the little man's legs as if it wanted to darn them together.

'I was researching our project on the internet, and I found

out some very interesting facts,' Gilbert said. The flush had moved down to his neck.

'Really.' Daphne met Saffron's eye, then looked away.

'There's an area over by Mahoenui where a new species of giant weta has been discovered.'

Daphne was silent.

'Never heard of the place,' Heather said, filling the void.

'North of Taumarunui,' Gilbert added.

Daphne looked as if she was trying to find a word other than 'really'. Saffron sympathized with her sister — it couldn't be much fun being the object of Gilbert's affection, particularly when Daphne was a good head taller than he was. Gilbert Williams had known Daphne for most of her life, but six months ago she had become a Greek goddess in his eyes.

'That's certainly very interesting,' Daphne said. She fiddled with the friendship ring that she wore, twisting it around and around on her finger.

'I could take you over there tomorrow,' he offered.

'The kids caught quite a few wetas today. I'm rather up to my eyeballs in wetas at the moment.'

'Giant wetas?' he asked.

The note of pride in his voice would have been ludicrous if it wasn't so pathetic. 'No giant wetas,' Daphne admitted.

'I looked in your sample jars,' Heather said. 'I thought some of the wetas looked quite big.'

Gilbert tutted quietly. 'The giant weta is a separate species. Not simply a large weta.' He shook his head and smiled at Daphne again, as if to say, *You and I are the only two educated ones here*.

'I think I'd need another permit for the giant weta,' Daphne said. 'Because they're a separate species.'

Saffron was wondering if Gilbert was about to whip a permit out of his back pocket when the telephone rang. Heather was closest and answered. 'It's Mo,' she mouthed to the others. Her face slowly dropped. 'Saffy and Daph will come over. They'll be there as soon as they can.'

'What?' Saffron and Daphne said together.

'Lucy's been hurt. They've taken her to Rotorua hospital. Mo and Steve are there. I said you and Daph would go. I want to come, but I daren't. Half the nursing staff is away with some bug that's doing the rounds.'

'Lucy?' Saffron realized she had half-expected to hear that something bad had happened to Billy. As she stood up, the towel covering her legs slipped to the floor.

Gilbert's face turned bright red. 'I'd better go.' He fled the kitchen, and a moment later they heard the back door close.

Daphne ran down the passage to Saffron's room and came back carrying a dry pair of jeans. 'Come on, shove your bum into these. You OK?'

'I'm fine.' She stared at Daphne for a moment and then said vehemently, 'It was supposed to stop. I returned the coins. That should be an end to it. Why Lucy?'

'It's probably a coincidence. Lucy hasn't had anything to do with the coins.'

'Maybe,' Saffron said. 'But why Rotorua? Why not the local hospital? Does that mean it's serious?'

'Taupo don't have the facilities for children, kids are always taken to Rotorua. Standard procedure. It doesn't mean anything at all,' Heather said reassuringly. 'But sit down. I've got to dress your hand first.'

'But Lucy —'

'She'll keep. She's in good hands. There's nothing you can do.'

'But Mo —'

Heather placed her hands on Saffron's shoulders and pushed her back into the chair. 'This will only take five minutes, but if that wound gets infected you're going to be one sorry lady. Now sit down and stay down. The sooner I dress your hand, the sooner you two can leave.'

Saffron and Daphne stood outside a locked security door and pushed a buzzer to gain access to the children's ward. They walked past the nurses' station and down a corridor with brightly coloured, giant paper flowers stuck to the walls, peering in each door they passed.

'There they are,' Daphne said suddenly, and pointed.

They turned into the room, unconsciously in step, and closed in on Mo and Steve. Mo was in a chair, gazing at their daughter; Steve was perched on the bed.

Three beds lined up on each side of the room, but only two were occupied. Lucy's was beside a window through which Saffron could see Lake Rotorua. Not her lake, she thought. An old steam boat, undoubtedly full of tourists, cut across the water.

'Hello, sweetheart. How's my best girl?' She bent over and kissed her niece, who was tucked under a quilt adorned with teddy bears.

Lucy smiled back at her, but in a sleepy, uninterested manner. Her eyes closed and long lashes lay dark on pale cheeks.

'She's been asleep,' Mo said. 'They said she'll probably sleep a lot.'

A doll with pigtails made out of yellow wool shared the pillow with Lucy's silky blonde hair. On the wall above the bed were shiny, complicated-looking medical things — things that only a really sick kid would need. Thankfully, none of them were being used on Lucy.

'How badly is she hurt?' Saffron asked, looking at Mo.

'Fractured right radius, lacerations and concussion,' Mo said. She sounded as if she was quoting.

Didn't sound *too* bad, Saffron thought. Not good, but not life-threatening. And kids' bones mended fast.

'What happened?'

'Steve and Lucy went shopping while they were waiting for me this morning. Lucy got hit by a car.' Mo didn't look at Steve as she spoke, but her hand extended across the bed to rub her husband's arm.

Saffron guessed Steve was blaming himself, taking it hard. Mo had miscarried twice before they had had Lucy. She was the sun in his universe — she and Mo.

Mo stood up and patted her empty chair for Saffron, then sat on the bed beside Steve.

'What have you done to yourself?' Mo asked, staring across the bed at Saffron's bandaged right hand.

Saffron shook her head. 'It's nothing. Just a burn.'

'There's a hole almost right through her hand,' Daphne said brightly.

'There is not. Don't be such a drama queen. Lucy's the injured one.'

'I should never have helped look for those coins this

morning,' Mo said. 'If I hadn't been doing that, then Steve and Lucy wouldn't have been shopping. They were filling in time waiting for me.'

'That doesn't make it your fault, petal,' Saffron said, as she settled herself in the chair. She could feel the warmth left from Mo's body, and it radiated into her own like heat from a stove. The lake had left a chill that she couldn't shake.

Steve picked up his wife's hand. 'We both feel bad. Mo's blaming herself for not being there, and I'm blaming myself for taking my eyes off Lucy. One minute she was walking beside me holding my hand, and the next, she just took off.'

'Saw something, I expect,' Daphne said.

'Doesn't make me feel any better.'

'It's nobody's fault,' Saffron said. 'The family is just all lucked-out at the moment.'

'You can say that again,' Daphne said. 'With Billy, and Lucy, and Saf's hand, the Delaneys' luck has disappeared up Lady Luck's ar —'

'Daphne! Not in front of Lucy!'

'She can't hear me. She's asleep.'

'I read somewhere people can hear even when they're asleep.' Saffron appealed to Mo for confirmation.

'That's right.'

There was a bag of mixed sweets on the locker beside the bed, and Steve helped himself to a spearmint leaf. 'Mo told me about these coins that Billy took last night,' he said.

Saffron waited. Even Steve was making the logical connection.

'I've heard about that rock before. They say it's some kind of curse.'

'I'm not sure exactly what it is — just that Billy should never have taken them. The site's tapu, according to Big Wal. But I've returned the coins so that should be an end to the matter.'

Steve stared fixedly at his daughter for a moment. One of Lucy's hands wandered onto the quilt. He leant forward and gently tucked it back in. 'So how do you explain this?'

'Perhaps Lucy's accident happened before I'd returned the coins. Maybe it was just plain bad luck. Billy's the one who's offended. Why should Tama hurt Lucy?'

'Look, I don't personally believe in all this Maori superstition,' Steve replied, 'but I knew someone who was killed after meddling with coins from Tama's Rock.'

'Steve and I have been talking. We don't believe in it. We just think that it's something better left alone,' Mo added.

'That's what I'm trying to do,' Saffron said. Did they think she had burnt her hand to a crisp for the fun of it? 'But I had to return the coins first. Didn't I? *Now* we can leave it alone.'

'So long as we're all agreed on that,' Mo said.

'Pass us one of those sweets, will you, Steve,' Daphne said.

'I haven't exactly been having a barrel-load of laughs with this thing,' Saffron complained.

'I know,' Steve admitted, 'but just remember you have a business to run.'

'Meaning mind my own business. Is that what you're telling me?'

'Look, Saffron, this is Billy's problem. Leave it like that. I don't want you girls getting involved. Billy's a big boy. He can sort his own problems.'

'Do you think Lucy's accident was my fault? Because I helped Billy?' It was a thought that had trashed its way through Saffron's mind a hundred times since the phone call.

'I'm not blaming you,' Steve said. 'I'm just saying leave it alone.'

'I think what he's trying to say is: if the bad luck bird is about to have a major crap, let's make sure we're not sitting directly below,' Daphne said, firing her Mintie wrapper towards the wastepaper bin.

'I'm glad to see all that time at university wasn't wasted,' Saffron said.

'It's teaching ten-year-olds,' Daphne shrugged. She picked up a Dr Seuss book and began to flick through it.

'I'm going to go and see the ward sister,' Mo said. 'Find out when the doctor will look at Lucy again.'

Steve looked across at Saffron as Mo left the room. He jerked his head as he stood up and walked over to the far window. 'Saf.'

Reluctantly, she joined him.

Tiredness lodged behind her eyeballs like grains of sand, and she wished she were down in the car park, dozing inside the Echo.

Steve spoke. 'I was there when this guy went through a mincer that had come in for repair. Big industrial thing. It's not a sight you forget in a hurry. And all the guys — OK, all the Maori guys — said it was because of the money he'd nicked from Tama's Rock.' Steve tapped out a tattoo on the window ledge. 'I'm not saying that's what it was. I don't believe it. I don't want to believe it. But that's what he done, and twenty-four hours later he was one big red smear. That's a fact.'

Saffron screwed up her face. 'So maybe Billy got off lightly?'

'Exactly.'

There was a long silence. Steve's face was expressionless when he continued. 'I never had much of a family 'til I met Mo.'

There'd been no lack of people on Steve's side of the church when he and Mo married, but they'd looked more like workmates than family. Young men with a suspicion of grease under their fingernails — no doting mum, no grey-haired aunties or nanas.

'Now I've got Mo. I've got a little girl. And so many unattached sisters-in-law I could start a dating agency.' He paused, and then added, 'Have you got any idea how many guys at work want me to fix them up on a date with one of you girls?' He shook his head and gave a twisted smile. 'I tell them — you'll never use your own phone again. They don't care.'

'There's not a man alive who doesn't fall for Daphne,' Saffron said fondly, glancing across at her sister.

'Not just Daphne,' Steve said. 'There're a couple of guys at work who are always trying to twist my arm into setting them up with you.'

'Me!' For some reason she thought of the man from the *Star* with his average everything. A nice sort of average, she admitted.

'What I'm trying to tell you, Saf, is that I worry about all of you. Not just Mo. So let this thing be. Billy's all grown up now. Let him fight his own battles.'

CHAPTER TWELVE

NICK BUMPED ALONG the farm track towards the vehicles and tent, hoping the suspension had sufficient clearance. The lake hung like a brilliant blue backdrop behind green paddocks and black-faced sheep. He went over a bump that snapped his teeth together hard. A molar gave a sharp savage stab of pain that drew saliva to his mouth.

He parked and walked around string lines that criss-crossed the dig like a chessboard. Two men squatting beside the mesh glanced at him and continued sorting through a pile of dirt.

A young woman stuck her head out of a tent and said, 'You're here, then. You're late.'

'Sorry,' Nick replied unapologetically. 'Something came up.'

'Professor Farrell is a busy man.' She emerged from the tent and stuck out a grubby hand. 'Sheila. I'm one of Andy's graduates.'

A man with a beard and enough woolly hair to single-handedly revive the carpet trade emerged from the tent. Sheila waved a hand towards Nick and said, 'This is the photographer, Professor Farrell.'

'Andy,' the man said. 'I'm trying not to be anybody's professor for a while.'

'What do you need?' Sheila asked. 'We had a reporter out here the other day.'

'Chrissie asked me to take a shot or two to support her article. In particular,' Nick pulled a notepad from his pocket and glanced at it, 'Professor Farrell holding an eggshell, and the skull.'

'Ahh, the moa eggshell.'

'I guess.' Personally, Nick thought the skull sounded more interesting.

The professor wiped his hands down the front of his T-shirt before picking up a section of broken cream-coloured shell.

'Hold it up a bit more,' Nick said, altering the settings on his flash. 'Closer to your face. Closer. Hope it doesn't smell.'

After Nick had taken his shot, Andy held out the eggshell for inspection. 'If you examine the edge of this fragment closely, you can see that the egg was probably perforated.'

'Are you saying the hole was deliberately drilled? Manmade?'

'Oh yes. Many of the well-known burial sites have drilled moa eggs present. I hope that's what I have here. A burial site.'

'Why do they have drilled moa eggs?'

'They're possibly associated with the burial of a person of rank. We can't be one hundred per cent certain, of course, but current thinking — and I'd go along with it — is that perforated moa eggshells were used to transport water. The shell is extremely strong — and large. An egg of *Dinornis giganteus*, the giant moa, was the equivalent of about sixty hen eggs.'

'An egg that size would make quite an omelette,' Sheila chipped in.

Nick had the feeling she'd made the statement many times before.

'We think that food and water were left as part of what a chief or high-ranking person would be provided with for their journey after death,' Andy continued. 'I'm hoping to find evidence of early Maori settlement.'

'If Andy can find evidence under the ignimbrite level, it would take the dates back by a thousand years,' Sheila said.

Nick tried to remember what he'd learnt about geology from his school days. 'Am I right in thinking that anything beneath the ignimbrite level is back before the Taupo eruption?'

'That's right,' Sheila said. 'The professor can explain it better than I can.'

Andy glanced up. 'Oh. Right.' He cleared his throat and fell into what sounded like a familiar lecture. 'As you doubtless know, Lake Taupo is actually a volcano and . . .'

Nick's eyes glazed over when Andy tossed 'phreato-magmatic' and 'pyroclastic' into the same sentence. Instead he thought about Saffron, with her Jean Harlow mouth. Sheila clearing her throat loudly brought him back to the dig — just when Saffron's lips were getting tantalizingly close to his.

'The last major eruption of Lake Taupo was approximately two thousand years ago. So anything beneath the ignimbrite layer would take dates for Maori habitation back considerably,' Andy concluded.

'And if we'd been sitting here when Taupo's big bang occurred?' Sheila asked.

'We'd be barbecued,' Andy said.

Sheila smiled at him as if he was a particularly apt student, then glanced at Nick to be sure he'd caught the one-liner. Nick wondered if she sat in the front row of Andy's lectures and fed him lines. He guessed she was in love with the professor.

'Lucky Taupo's already gone and done it, then,' Nick said.

'Taupo has been active for three hundred thousand years, so I think we can safely say it'll do it again one day.'

'So when should I vacate my flat?'

Andy laughed. 'When you see me packing my bags.' He shrugged. 'That's the thing: no one knows. Taupo's history of eruption has been erratic.'

He shepherded Nick into the tent where artefacts sat on a trestle table, pointing out adzes, flakes of obsidian, fish hooks — minnow style, Andy emphasized, so Nick jotted that down — and some bones.

'This site could become the next Wairau Bar, although I doubt I'll have the time to establish that this year. I'll only be here for a few more weeks. But I'll be back next season — if I obtain funding.'

'Wairau Bar?' Nick queried. 'What's that?'

'Not your normal cocktail bar,' Andy said, and Sheila laughed as if it was the first time she'd heard the joke. The woman was a gem. 'Wairau Bar is one of the earliest known sites of Maori habitation. Discovered in 1939 when a school boy dug up a skeleton. Radiocarbon-dating has put the human bone from Wairau Bar at around the end of the twelfth century. There's been nothing quite like that discovered in the North Island.'

'Next stop: *Oprah*,' Nick said.

Sheila's snort left no doubt as to what she thought about that. 'Professor Farrell has already been interviewed by numerous international scientific periodicals.'

'You're nobody in the States until you've appeared on *Oprah*, Sheila,' said Andy.

'Americans! What would they know? You're probably not aware but it was Andy who discovered the Stoney Bay bones. You might have heard of them?'

Nick had to confess his ignorance and realized that he'd slipped to the same level as the Americans in Sheila's estimation.

Andy made a dismissive gesture. 'It's not important, Sheila. Water under the bridge.'

'What do you mean?' Nick asked.

The professor shook his head. 'Least said. Now, take a look at this. This is interesting.' He moved down the trestle table.

Sheila tweaked Nick's shirt sleeve as he moved away. 'Andy discovered those bones at Stoney Bay, but Professor —'

'Sheila! No!' Andy held up his hand. 'You'll get sued if you go around saying that. He's a reporter.'

'Photographer,' Nick amended.

'All the same. Press. Give them a whiff of a story and they're onto it faster than a pig to the trough. No offence,' he added.

Nick wondered if Sheila had said any of this in front of

Chrissie. There was a bigger story here than old bones. 'And what about the skull? Chrissie wanted a photo of that too.'

'I don't know why,' Andy said in a baffled tone. 'I told her it wasn't old. It really isn't relevant to what we're doing here.'

Nick shrugged. 'That's what she wants.' It wasn't his job to second-guess the reporter. If Chrissie wanted a photo of the skull, then that's what he'd give her. Andy pointed to a skull on the end of the table.

'We're going to return it to the local people,' Sheila said. 'It isn't of an age that interests the professor.'

'It's not more than a hundred years old,' Andy said.

Nick took several photos. 'Well, I guess that's about it. I might just take one or two shots of the general site before I go.'

'Like a drink before you head back?' Andy asked.

Sheila frowned. 'Nick won't want to drink and drive,' she said.

'One won't hurt,' Andy said rebelliously.

Nick guessed it wasn't coffee he was being offered, so he said, 'A drink sounds good.'

Andy smiled at him. Sheila didn't.

Half an hour later Nick sat with his back against a sun-warmed rock and sipped slowly from a tumbler that looked as if it might have started life as a Marmite jar. The two men didn't talk much. Nick didn't understand Andy's enthusiasm for inanimate things hundreds of years old, and he guessed Andy didn't understand his need to show body parts redistributed over too much ground. Perhaps Andy was right. Because the wars kept happening. No photograph had stopped a single war.

The whisky sat between them, and every now and then Andy would refill his glass and wave the bottle hospitably at Nick. The level was steadily lowering. Every now and then, Nick's tooth reminded him of its existence. Andy poured himself another drink — more of a severe mauling than a nip, Nick thought. He was taking it slowly himself. As Sheila had said, he didn't want to be caught on a drink-driving charge.

Sheila was helping the two students on the dig. Every now and then, she looked across and frowned at Nick. When Andy disappeared behind the tent for a few moments, she strode across.

'You shouldn't encourage him,' she said without preamble. She stood in front of Nick, her arms folded across an uninteresting-looking chest, and stared down at him.

'I'm not twisting his arm. Besides, one or two drinks won't hurt him.'

'Andy has a job to do out here. It's important.'

Nick shrugged. He figured that Andy was old enough not to need a wet nurse. 'His choice.'

'I don't think you realize how important Andy's work is. If he's correct in his hypothesis this could be the biggest thing to hit the academic world for a long time.'

'I'm not stopping him.'

Sheila waved a grubby hand towards the bottle. 'No, but this is.'

'His problem. Not mine. Or yours,' he added.

'He didn't used to drink. Not before Stoney Bay.'

'What happened at Stoney Bay?'

Sheila glanced over her shoulder. 'Andy found bones there that have been dated to the thirteenth century. He'd spent years researching the Stoney Bay area. He was working on a dig there with a colleague from his uni days. They found the bones and Professor G — Andy's colleague — said he would submit their findings, and the next thing Andy knows, everyone's patting his colleague on the back, and people are commiserating with *him* about how he'd had to pull out. Andy *had* left the dig for a couple of weeks. He'd got a cut on his hand. Blood poisoning. But it was Andy's research that led them to the burial site and he was there when the remains were found. By the time Andy's *friend*,' Sheila emphasized the word scathingly, 'had told the story, you couldn't blame people for thinking Andy just popped in occasionally for a cup of tea and a chat.'

'He told you this?'

'No. He never talks about it.' She stared across at the whisky, frowning. 'But he drinks.'

'A man can drink without it having an impact on his work.' Nick said this with some certainty. It was important for him that it be so.

'Maybe. Some men.'

'But not Andy?'

'I don't know. He's never drunk this much before. I was with him last summer. It wasn't so bad then. This summer — he's a mess. He drinks every evening, and he's hung-over every morning.' She bit her lip. 'He needs this dig to be a major success. I'm not sure how many more chances there'll be. People are losing confidence in him. New Zealand isn't big enough to support too many people at the top of the tree. And New Zealand history is what interests Andy.'

Andy returned, scowling at Sheila's back as she marched back to the dig.

'Don't you listen to that woman,' he warned Nick, as he refilled his empty glass.

'Maybe she has a point. If you had something stolen from you then you should—'

'Should what? Report it to the police? Complain to the university?'

Nick shrugged. 'Why not?'

'I'll tell you why not. Because I can't prove it. I have no evidence that proves it was my research that led to us finding the Stoney Bay bones. It's a question of integrity. If I lodge a complaint, then all I do is give myself a reputation for being difficult.'

Nick stared at Andy's glass for a good ten seconds before he spoke. 'So you just have to swallow it.' His eyes rose to the professor's face, but the implication had been lost on Andy.

'I wouldn't mind if it had been a dig like this.' Andy indicated the excavations behind him. 'We pool ideas, work together, and whatever we find will be jointly acknowledged. We won't exclude anyone if they happen to be in the little boys' room when we strike something.' He tossed back his full glass and reached for the bottle. 'But Stoney Bay wasn't like that.'

He gave a savage bark of laughter and amber liquid swirled perilously close to the top of the glass. Sheila looked across.

'And the bones you found turned out to be something special?'

'Oldest bones discovered in the North Island.'

Nick took a sip from his glass. 'And what about here?'

Andy beamed at him. 'If my research on this area proves accurate, then somewhere about here I'm going to find bones that will make the Stoney Bay inhabitants look like kids from the local crèche.' He chortled to himself happily until Sheila's glaring eyes silenced him.

The sun was low in the sky when Nick left. He watched his shadow jab ahead of him like a spear as he walked across to the car. A rubbish sack full of bottles leaning against a fencepost proclaimed Andy's long engagement to the beautiful whisky. He and Andy had arranged to meet later at a bar and continue their melancholy dance with whisky. Sheila could learn a thing or two from her.

CHAPTER THIRTEEN

BILLY DELANEY LOWERED his glass of beer and wondered why life was treating him so badly. First, that psychopath at the burger bar had broken his hand, and then he'd lost a bundle of money at the races on Lucky Lizard. His landlord wasn't going to be impressed.

The live band sent music pulsing through him. He took another mouthful. He could get the money for his rent from Saf — or one of the others, if Saf was going through one of her 'it's for your own good that I don't, Billy' moods and wouldn't play ball. Why did sisters always want to do things for your own good?

And to top it all off, he'd sideswiped a car while he was parking. He'd had his good hand off the wheel while he put the automatic transmission from neutral into reverse and the car must have gone over something and it had sort of jumped into the vehicle alongside. He was all lucked out and that was a fact.

Saffron had phoned him on his way back from the races to tell him about Lucy's accident. She'd hinted that it might be a good idea if he came to the hospital. He supposed he should, but it had been a bad day. Besides, he'd just left Rotorua. He didn't want to turn around and drive back. And the kid was concussed. Sleeping mostly, Saf said. She wouldn't know if he was there or not. Kids were resilient. Everyone knew that. She'd wake up right as rain tomorrow, and that would be time for Uncle Billy to make an appearance. He'd take her a bag of sweets. His sisters would all be there, crowded around the bedside. They'd be talking to each other, but they could do that just as well at home. And anyway, had anyone come to see him in hospital? Huh? Sure, Heather had sat there half the night until he was out of surgery, but she worked there. She'd probably spent the time sitting down the nurses' station eating chocolate biscuits with her buddies. Big sacrifice! Daphne had been out on a date, and Saffron had raced off, presumably back to finish tarting up some pampered pooch. So he came in second behind a dog.

Billy drained his glass and fished in his pocket before heading up to the bar again. He could see the guy who'd wanted to take his photo at the burger bar sitting at a table with a fellow with a beard. They were putting away shots. Lucky bastards. One day he'd be able to afford top-shelf.

Billy raised his eyebrows by way of acknowledgement as he walked past.

'How's the hand?' the photographer shouted at him. He had to shout to be heard above the band.

'Good,' Billy called back and walked on.

He was cautious about pushing into the crowd at the bar so accepted the photographer's offer to buy him a drink. When he went to pay, the guy gave him a funny look and said, 'No, my shout.' Maybe he thought Billy still had some of those coins in his pocket. If so, he didn't blame him for refusing. There'd been something seriously weird about those coins. Every time he'd touched them, they felt as if they nipped at his fingers. They didn't, of course, but that was how it felt. And all that blood. Gross! He'd been very glad to ditch them.

He raised his glass to the two guys at the table. They saluted him back.

Billy waited until the guy with the beard was up at the bar, then approached again. This time, though, the man took his money. Cheapskate!

Billy cradled his drink in his good hand and nodded his head in time to the heavy bass. A nice-looking girl in a lacy black dress caught his eye now and then, but if he went over he'd have to buy her a drink, and his money wasn't going to stretch that far.

He wanted a cigarette so he went outside, lit up and walked across the road. He could relieve his bladder without any eyes curious to see how well he would manage one-handed. He was OK, thank you very much, but if he was going to piss on his foot or catch himself in the zipper, he'd prefer to do it without an audience.

He walked down Ferry Road where the big old gums had been cut down to ground-level so as to not block the view of the lake. The trees there now all grew from the foot of the cliff and would one day be found tourist-unfriendly too. A faint smell of eucalypt scented the air.

He walked up to the chain-link fence but didn't climb through. Only the tourists who flooded into Taupo at Christmas did that. They would tire of waiting for a free toilet at one of the bars and decide to have a leak in private.

Invariably one of them would walk too close to the edge. In the dark, the bushes clothing the cliff face made it look as if the ground extended further out than it did. So the council had put up a chain-link fence, but the tourists still toppled off. Now someone wanted to put up a more secure fence, but you could wall it off like Alcatraz and some noodle would still climb over.

When Ferry Road was deserted, Billy emptied his bladder against a fencepost, then tucked himself away. It was a little bit harder than getting the lad out, but, hey, there'd been a kid at college with one arm. Billy had never given a moment's thought to how the boy had managed to pee.

The wind suddenly picked up, flip-flopping a few pieces of rubbish — the sort of things you always find near the takeaway joints. White paper bags stained with tomato sauce and egg, an empty KFC box, a banknote—

A banknote?

His heart gave a sudden extra thump, the way it did as the horses rounded the home turn, jostling for position for the run up the straight.

It was almost full moon, but the gums absorbed the light so he couldn't see the denomination. He squeezed between the middle two chains on the fence and reached for the note. Nuts from the trees rolled under his foot.

The wind flicked the banknote away from him, the way a fisherman might tease a trout with the lure. Billy let his breath out cautiously. Didn't want to spook it. He almost thought it might be a hundred-dollar note. Maybe Lady Luck was swinging back to dance with him. Lucky Del always said that luck came in cycles. And when your luck was in, you had to go wherever the lady wanted to take you — whether it was a luxury holiday or a dirty weekend.

He reached out again, and his fingers touched the money. Billy could swear it was a hundred. Hundred-dollar notes had an electricity all their own. He felt a flutter of excitement. He would go back to the bar and chat up that girl, the one with the boobs in the lacy black dress. She'd ask him how he'd hurt his hand, and he'd tell her that he was a rally driver or a television stuntman. All part of the job — just another day at the office, babe. And she would be soo-oo sympathetic.

The wind tweaked the money from him. It came to rest upon the ground by the sawn-off stump of an old gum. He was close to the edge of the cliff now, but he wasn't some tourist. He knew the dangers. Carefully, Billy reached out again, and his fingers closed firmly around the banknote.

For one moment, Billy felt the joy of financial solvency. Then he felt something else, and looked down. There was a tree root around his ankle.

At some time in the past the cliff must have crumbled back, leaving silver-grey gum roots exposed, because some of them now circled right out over the edge into the dark, before diving back into the ground below his feet.

He tried to step out of the circling root, but his foot wouldn't budge. He hung onto the banknote and gave his foot a jerk. He felt the tree root tighten.

Billy licked his lips and tried to back away, but his foot wouldn't come with him. He stuffed the banknote into his pocket and reached down with his good hand to force his trapped foot through the gap. He felt the root move against his fingers, and jerked his hand back.

He yanked his foot up and back, but the root held on. His shirt felt wet under his arms. He looked down and examined the situation carefully. It felt as the root had moved, but that couldn't be right. He must have stepped into a loop, and his foot had stuck. It shouldn't be too difficult to pull his foot out. He just had to not make an ass of himself in the process.

A couple walked past, so he shuffled around and looked out over the lake as if he was soaking up the dark tranquillity. They had their hands all over each other, and he didn't think they even noticed him. He cautiously bent over again, using his fingers to try and prise the roots open, but nothing happened. He sat down and began to lever his trapped foot back and forward.

Another root slithered towards him. He scrambled quickly back to his feet. It wrapped itself around his ankle above the first root, just like that damn cat of Gilbert's. Billy tried to kick at it with his other foot, but his ankle was secured. All he succeeded in doing was kicking himself in the ankle.

This couldn't be happening. He must have drunk too much and passed out because things like this just didn't happen. He cranked the volume right up on that last thought. Nothing changed.

He gave a wobbly laugh. Maybe someone had spiked his drink. If he was lucky — and he knew that he wasn't — it would be that girl. If he was unlucky, it would be the bartender with the overfriendly smile.

At the edge of vision, he saw movement in the dark. Another root slithered towards him like a snake. It circled his ankle, looping up over the other roots, then it began to tug him towards the cliff edge.

Billy's mind screamed.

One of the roots already around his ankle took a fresh grip and began to tug. More roots snaked towards him. Desperately, Billy tried to reach the fence with his good hand, but he was too far away. His feet scrabbled in the dirt as he began to slide.

'No!' he whimpered. 'No.'

The largest root gave a jerk, and he fell to his knees. When he reached out and grabbed at a secure-looking root, it crumbled to dust in his hand. He fell forward and tried to swim his way along the ground, but the roots dragged him closer and closer to the cliff. He clawed at the ground as gum nuts rolled under him like ball bearings. His broken hand was under his body, but he didn't feel any pain. Then he felt nothing — nothing at all — beneath one ankle.

He jerked his leg up. His three limbs worked frantically like a soldier under the net on an assault course. His breath came in terrified grunts as his legs sank into the void. Clawing at the ground with his hand, he left a trail of gouge marks in his wake. He lowered his face to the ground and tried to dig his chin in.

But the roots kept pulling. His body jack-knifed at the waist, and he felt his centre of gravity change. Now his own weight was pulling him down. He screamed.

There was a bush at the edge of the cliff, and he grasped it with his hand. The roots tugged at his legs. There were dozens of them circling him now.

And then there was a shadow above him.

'Thank Christ, mate! Help me!'

He would never do another bad thing in his life. He

would go to church, never steal from honesty boxes, never lie and—

He gasped as a heel stamped down on his hand. He looked up, but could see only a black shadow.

'Help me! I'm falling! Help me!' Didn't they understand? He was going to die.

All his weight hung on one arm. He tried to dig his toes into the cliff, but the roots kept tugging. His arm felt as if it was being pulled out of its socket as his fingers locked around the bush.

The ground resonated, and he felt a pain that took his mind back to the burger bar. For a moment he thought Big Wal had returned to finish the job he'd started the night before.

But this wasn't Big Wal. Billy's head went back, his mouth open, as he stared up at a tall, muscular figure. The man's hand went up, and the club he held barrelled down. Billy felt a hundred spears of pain stab down his arm from the hand to the shoulder. Again and again, the man struck.

Billy stopped screaming.

He hung there, every fibre of his being concentrated on the grip in the fingers of his right hand. He no longer felt pain. Blood ran down his arm and dripped onto his face. He clung on for what seemed a very long time.

Then he dropped.

Billy opened his eyes to the night sky above him. There were stars, lots of stars, and a big moon.

It had never looked so beautiful.

He would lie here and someone would find him. It might be morning before they did, but it would happen, and then his sisters would be sitting beside his bed.

Someone was coming.

Over here, mate, Billy tried to call, but the words wouldn't come out. Never mind. He could hear footsteps so they would find him even if they tripped over him.

A shadow fell across him and he knew, with a terrible certainty, that this person hadn't come to rescue him but had followed him down from the top of the cliff. Come to see if he'd survived. Come to finish him off.

Why? Billy tried to say, but the word didn't come out. Blood trickled from the corner of his mouth.

Billy sensed rather than saw the club rise in the air. He didn't cry out. He wasn't sure if he was watching the club or the shadow of the club; but it reached full height, froze there for an eternity, and then he saw it falling towards him. It took a very long time to fall, and when it split his head open Billy decided it wasn't a club at all but a shitload of falling stars.

CHAPTER FOURTEEN

'COME ON — BOBO,' Alex wheedled. 'We're only just getting started.' He stretched his arm across the front seat of the Sigma and tried to reel her back in. Long blonde hair fell over his arm; short green highlights framed Bobo's face in a spiky fringe that defied gravity. The windows were beginning to steam up; the air was ripe with adolescent hormones. Mostly his, Alex guessed.

He still hesitated each time he said her name. He'd known her for three years, and for two years and eleven months she'd been Kylie. Now, she wanted to be called Bobo.

What sort of name was that? Sounded like a mutt. Here, Bobo! Good girl, Bobo!

Alex hoped Bobo was going to be a good girl — good to him. She hadn't looked twice at him through college. He knew this sudden interest in him was a direct result of his having got wheels. Sweet as. He could live with that. That was why he'd bought the car.

'Let's walk,' Bobo said as she twisted out from under his arm.

Alex's arm was around Bobo's shoulders as they walked

along Ferry Road, cut down beside the yacht club and onto the shore. She had her arm around his waist. Long silky hair tickled his arm until he could scarcely think, and the sound of his own pulse hammered in his ears like a drum. They walked along the foreshore, passed where the willow grew almost in the lake, and when the moon slipped behind a cloud and the music from the hotels and bars was just a distant bass, Alex stopped and pulled Bobo towards him.

By the way Bobo's tongue shot into his mouth when he kissed her, he guessed she wasn't as virginal as she made out. So far, so good.

'Let's lie down, babe,' he murmured. He knelt in the sand and tugged her down beside him, then infiltrated a bewildering maze of layered clothing until he reached bare skin. Hot, smooth, bare skin. He reconnoitred the fence of her panty line and slipped a couple of fingers under the elastic.

'No, Alex,' she said, pushing down on his hand and struggling to sit up. Reluctantly, Alex rolled to one side and Bobo clambered to her feet.

'Let's walk,' she said.

He caught her up and slipped his arm around her shoulders again. God, he loved that hair. There should be a law forbidding women to cut their hair. Patience, he told himself. All good things come to those that wait.

'Let's—' he started to say, when Bobo grabbed him. She was pulling him towards the ground. At last, he thought gratefully, and then he realized she was falling.

He kept her on her feet, but by then Bobo had begun to scream. And when Alex looked down at his feet, he could see why. There was a body on the ground. The head was smashed in and one hand was a bloody stump.

Nick and Andy had just crossed the street outside the bar, walking back to their cars, when two teenagers shot around the corner of Ferry Road and nearly knocked them over.

'Whoa there!' Nick said, grabbing a girl with green highlights in her hair as she slammed into him and bounced back.

The girl clutched him by the sleeve and yelled into his face. 'There's a body down there! Dead!'

'Down where?'

'On the shore.' The boy's face glowed with excitement like a kid at a birthday party. 'He's dead. All bashed up. We're going for the cops.'

Nick released his hold on the girl. 'Where exactly?'

'Go down by the yacht club and then come back this way. You can't miss it.' The youth took it for fact that Nick and Andy would want to see the body.

He was right about that, Nick thought.

'He must have fallen over the cliff. We walked on him,' the boy said. He edged along the pavement, then jerked back, as if torn between his duty to tell the police and his desire to give all the gory details.

'Almost walked on him,' the girl qualified.

'Almost walked on him,' the boy agreed reluctantly.

'You tell the police,' Nick called over his shoulder. He was moving away already. 'Let's get down there,' he called to Andy.

He unlocked the car, grabbed his jacket off the back seat

and struggled into it, the pockets bulging with lenses and filters, batteries and memory cards. He grabbed two cameras from his bag, slung them around his neck and crossed Ferry Road. Moonlight filtered through the leaves overhead as he jogged down the pavement, Andy behind him. As he ran, Nick checked how much storage he had left. He wanted to see the body before the police arrived — some cops wouldn't let you within spitting distance of a body.

A hundred and fifty metres down Ferry Road, Nick did a sharp left and walked carefully down the slope beside the yacht club building, then jogged back along the shore. Out on the lake, he thought he saw a wash of movement.

He turned his head abruptly, felt his pulse accelerate. A voice in his head yelled, 'Incoming! Incoming!', but this was Taupo. One day, he would stop hearing those words each time he saw a flash of unidentified movement.

Gum trees grew from the base of the cliff, and in a gap between them, he saw what looked like a log lying on the ground. Moonlight flooded the shore. A handful of rocks lay scattered about like a half-played game of marbles. He walked over, crouched down and the log became a body.

'Shit!'

Andy stopped half a dozen paces away and craned forward to see.

'It's Billy Delaney,' Nick said, looking up. 'You know. The guy with his arm in a sling. The one Big Wal fell out with over the coins.'

Andy edged a couple of steps closer, took another look and turned away. Even in the moonlight that coloured his blood black, it was obvious Billy's head was cracked open.

Nick rummaged through one of his jacket pockets and pulled out a small torch.

'I take it those kids did check that he's actually dead,' he said, reaching out and feeling for a pulse. 'Because he hasn't been dead long. Blood's still wet.'

Andy didn't say anything.

'He got his hand broken yesterday,' Nick said. 'But look at this other hand.' He positioned the circle of light on Billy's right hand. A rock the size of a cricket ball lay against the bloody pulp that was all that remained.

Andy risked a quick glance, then looked away again. His face was pale.

Nick stood up. He hadn't quite got his head around the fact that this was the same young guy he'd bought a drink for, an hour or two back. He'd had a similar experience a few years ago — shouted a guy a beer and an hour later watched him step on a landmine. 'They're not having much luck,' he said slowly. 'I stopped off at the sisters' place this evening, and the neighbour told me they'd all raced off to Rotorua. Their niece is hurt.'

Should he say anything to the police when they arrived? Tell them the story Big Wal had told him last night? *Excuse me, Sarge, I think the family is being victimized by some guy who died a couple of hundred years ago.* Perhaps not. He'd worked hard to earn a good relationship with the local cops. He didn't want them thinking he was a nutcase.

'I saw him leave the bar,' Nick said slowly, more to himself than to Andy. Damn! Double damn! He'd seen Billy leave. His mind followed its own path. He should have left when he saw Billy leave. If he'd followed him, he would have seen him go over. He would have got a shot of him falling.

That sense of movement again. He glanced out over the dark lake. To his right, where lake and river met, two navigational lights flashed: one blue, one red. They relentlessly caught his gaze each time he turned in their direction, but there was something else out there. Something that didn't blink and flash — something soft and subtle.

He turned his back on the lake, his gaze returning to Billy. He just hadn't thought that anything else would happen to the boy. The Delaney girls were all hyped up about it, but an afternoon away with Andy and Sheila had given him distance — perspective. The result of that complacency was that he'd missed this shot. The loss felt almost like a physical pain. He'd been so close to nailing a shot like that, and he'd missed it.

'What a horrible way to die,' Andy said beside him, and Nick froze in his musings. 'I wonder what was going through his mind as he fell.'

'Not a good way to die,' Nick agreed.

Jeez! He had a mind like a sewer rat. He didn't want to think like that. He considered himself a nice guy but the thoughts sneaked into his mind before he could censor them. Maybe he was just being honest, maybe everybody thought like that. Maybe it was a photographer's thing. Or maybe he'd seen too many wars.

He walked over to where the lake wet his shoes and stared out into the night. The wind blew in to the shore, fresh and clean against his face; waves lapped noisily against the land. He breathed in. Again, his mind registered something. He stared for a long while, his eyes half-closed as he concentrated.

Somewhere back in the town, a police siren started up. The kids had finally made it to the cop shop.

At last, the half-hidden movement on the lake snapped into focus. It was Fay, standing above the waves, her long hair blowing in the wind so that it covered her face. She'd been dead for two years. He didn't think about Fay so much now — the whisky took care of that — but tonight she was walking on water and she was judging him. Yep, Fay would certainly be doing that. She'd warned him that sometimes he was too keen to get the shot, that one day he would pay the price. She probably hadn't imagined it would be her.

He jerked his head away from the image of Fay that filled his mind. Fay, bleeding from the stump that was left of her arm. And charging through the door into that hellhole was some gung-ho photographer, clicking like crazy, and then he could see that the photographer was himself. And he needed time to stop and back up a little, to give him another chance — a chance to do it right. But it was too late. Fay had had nothing more to give. Her blood was spent, and he'd walked through it to reach her and cradled her in his arms until they'd dragged him away. One day, when he'd got his head around the fact that he'd photographed his wife while her lifeblood spurted away, he'd start worrying whether it would have been OK if she'd been someone else's wife. So, yeah, he didn't think that this little nightmare of the Delaneys was going to psych him out. He had enough nightmares of his own.

He returned to the body, put the camera to his eye and took a close-up of Billy's bloody, broken head — a photo no one would ever publish.

He let the camera hang around his neck while he lit a cigarette. When would Fay give him peace? Perhaps she didn't think he'd earned it yet. She was probably right.

'Do you think it's the curse?' Andy asked from over his shoulder. 'If this is the young man who took those coins. Or is it foul play?'

'Damned if I know what to think. I'd rather it was murder than some ancient curse run amok.'

'When you told me about it this afternoon, it sounded like a legend, a myth. But actually seeing him with his head bashed in certainly makes you think,' Andy said.

'Know what you mean.'

Nick swung around as he heard a cry. It was a sound he had heard many times before. He saw a woman running along the shore, and he knew who it was. He spat the cigarette out and had the camera ready as she closed on him.

CHAPTER FIFTEEN

A LIGHT AS BRIGHT as the sun exploded in front of her. Saffron staggered as if she'd been shot, and raced on.

There was a body lying on the shoreline. So still. She felt a cold rush of terror swoop down off the cliff top, wrap her in its arms and squeeze her until she couldn't move.

She stopped twenty paces from the body. Nick and another man hung over it like gulls that had found something tasty.

'Who is it?' She knew the harsh, broken sound she heard had come from her own throat.

There was a silence that told her everything. Finally, Nick said, 'I'm sorry, Saffron. I'm so sorry.'

Slowly she walked forward. Nick had made a mistake. In a few seconds, this nightmare that had started when she met two kids haring along the pavement towards the police station would be over.

'I'm sorry,' Nick said again.

'No.' She reached the body. Except it wasn't a body any more, it was Billy. Her face twisted in anguish. Billy. Her Billy. Lying dead at her feet. This wasn't supposed to be how it was.

Oh, but she had known. The moment those two youngsters had yelled at her that there was someone dead down on the lakefront, she'd known it was Billy. She started to kneel beside him, and Nick grabbed her arm. She pulled away, slapping at his hand. 'Let me go. I'm all right. I need to see him.'

'It's not very nice.'

'Doesn't matter. I need to see him.'

Nick released her arm, and slowly she knelt in the sand beside Billy's body. Silent tears slid down her cheeks. She reached out one hand and touched his face. Inside of her felt like a vast, empty cavern. Something cold and shrivelled sat where her heart used to be. 'What happened?' she asked. Her voice sounded as if it came from a million miles away, from another lifetime.

'Seems he fell over the cliff.'

'Billy knew the dangers. He wouldn't have got too close to the edge.'

'Seems he did.'

'Billy wouldn't have,' she insisted, as if her denial could somehow change everything. 'He used to talk about how stupid the tourists were.'

'He's not the first,' Andy added. 'He won't be the last. It's easy to misjudge the edge in the dark.'

'I should have stayed with him,' she said, looking up to Nick and shaking her head. 'I shouldn't have let him out of my sight. Not once I knew about Tama.' She ran a hand over her face.

Nick shook his head. 'What could you have done?'

'I could have stopped this.'

'I don't think so, Saf.'

She sat on the sand, her knees drawn up in front of her

and her chin resting on them, and stared at her brother. His face was a mess, all bloody, and she wanted to wash it. His poor broken hand had come out of the sling, which hung like a dirty ruffle around his neck, and his other hand looked as if Big Wal had taken to it too.

She wiped at her cheeks, and her hand came away wet. Why did Billy's other hand look so bad? Was it because he'd fallen over a cliff or—

Was it because Tama had been playing pit-a-pat with that one too?

That was Daddy's voice. She was getting used to him popping into her head. She wondered if she would start to hear Billy's voice soon. She'd like that.

The flash from Nick's camera went again.

'Why do you keep doing that?' Saffron said, anguish making her voice as thin as a reed. 'Haven't you got anything better to do?'

Nick shrugged. 'This is what I do.'

'Leave him be.' A lank of bloody hair hung over Billy's face, and she pushed it back out of his eyes. 'I should have stuck with him. I'd come downtown to see him tonight. Thought I'd just wander into a bar or two and find him — check that everything was OK. I kept thinking about what Big Wal said.'

Nick cleared his throat and reviewed the images he'd taken.

'The police are here,' Andy said.

Nick and Andy turned and watched as a light bobbed its way along the shoreline towards them. Saffron stared at Billy.

Nick walked across and held out his hand. 'Come on,' he said gently. 'Up you come.'

'Why?'

'They'll want to look at him, examine the scene. To make sure it was an accident.'

'Of course it wasn't an accident. We both know who did this.'

'Tama? They'll probably want a more scientific reason. Up you come.'

She let Nick help her to her feet.

Two police officers approached the body.

'Evening, Sergeant,' Nick called. 'His name is Billy Delaney and this is his sister.'

'We'll need to talk to you later, Miss.'

Nick led Saffron by the hand to where a fallen tree limb lay propped on the beach, its bleached, broken branches like the white stalk legs of an insect. He checked the top of the branch and then pushed her down onto it. Obediently, she sat.

'Will they take him away?'

'They'll have to.'

Of course they'd have to take him somewhere. 'Can I go with him?'

'I'll take you,' Nick said. 'When the time comes. They'll be a while looking around.'

'Isn't it obvious what happened?'

'They have to make sure it was an accident.'

'Is this my fault?' she asked Nick, the words scratching their way out. The wind skipped in across the moon-touched lake and dimpled her skin. She should have felt cold. She felt nothing.

'It's no one's fault.'

'Must be someone's. Nothing just happens.'

'If anyone was to blame, then it was Billy himself.'

'Don't you try and blame him,' she said, jerking to her feet and pulling away.

'You asked me,' Nick pointed out patiently.

'Doesn't mean you can blame him. He's the victim.'

'It's possible it's a coincidence.'

Saffron looked him in the eye. 'Do you believe that?'

'No. Not now. I think there couldn't be an end until . . . this.'

'That's not fair.'

'No.' Nick looked out over her shoulder at the water, then added, 'Life isn't.'

'A life is too big a price for what he did.'

'I would have thought so, but it isn't our opinion that counts. We didn't make the rules.'

He's right, petal, there's rules to every game.

One of the policemen walked over to them. 'I'm Senior Sergeant Barker. You've positively identified the body as your brother?'

Saffron nodded. 'It's Billy.'

'And you're . . .'

'Saffron Delaney. Billy's sister.'

Barker jotted her name in a notebook. 'Do you know what this is?' he asked, holding a slip of paper aloft between two fingers.

Saffron looked at it. Even in the light of the moon, she knew what it was. Where other kids had used Monopoly money to play shopkeepers, the Delaney kids had used tote tickets. 'A betting slip.' She held out her hand, and the sergeant gave it to her. 'From the races today at Rotorua. Two hundred to win on number seven.'

'Did your brother bet? Would this be his?'

Saffron laughed harshly. 'You have to ask? The son of Lucky Del Delaney?'

Barker looked at her closely. 'I didn't know Lucky Del was your father.' He glanced at the constable. 'Who won the sixth race at Rotorua?'

The constable thought for only the briefest of moments. 'The sixth? The top weight — Brighteyes. She was number one.'

Barker looked impressed. 'Number seven?' he asked hopefully.

'That was Lucky Lizard. He broke down and bled. He'll be out for a couple of months. Probably would have won otherwise.'

'So this is a losing ticket.' Barker turned to Saffron. 'Was your brother at the races today?'

'Yes.'

'Would he have been depressed about losing so much money?'

'Not half as much as his landlord.'

Barker leapt upon her words like a terrier upon a rat. 'So he was in financial difficulties?

Out of the corner of her eye, she could see two people approaching with a stretcher.

'Billy was always in financial difficulties. It didn't bother him much. That was the trouble.'

'Big sum of money to lose.' Barker was reluctant to let his theory go.

'Not to a Delaney.'

They placed the stretcher on the ground and lifted Billy onto it. They must have had something on the stretcher because next she heard the sound of a zip. She cried out. Nick took her hand, moving his body between her and the stretcher, blocking the sight of Billy — Billy who slept with his windows wide open all summer — locked in a body bag.

Her body began to shake, arms and hands trembling as if the wind that rustled through the gum trees above had now turned to play with her. Nick pulled her into his arms and held her until the trembling passed.

The stretcher bearers started back along the beach. A black hearse waited down below the yacht club. Nick led her by one hand behind the stretcher.

'Any possibility Billy might have jumped?' Barker continued, as he paced beside her. 'Another suicide, like your dad?'

'That was different,' Saffron said. 'Leave us alone,' she added quickly. 'None of this matters. He didn't fall, and he didn't jump.'

'Which leaves us with what?' Barker said quietly, staring across at her.

'He was pushed. That's what I think. Are you happy now?' Saffron's voice was high and sharp.

Nick tightened his grip on her hand. 'Are you familiar with Tama's Rock, Sergeant?'

'What's that got to do with this?'

'Seems young Billy took some coins from there.'

Senior Sergeant Barker blew a noisy rush of air through his nose. 'No shit!'

Big Wal switched off the electric beater he was using to make batter for the fish and listened to the police siren come out of Story Place and head towards the lakefront. Drips from the beater left dark concentric rings in the pale yellow mixture. He'd been restless all night. Something was wrong.

'I'm going down to the lake,' he told Huamai. 'You can manage?'

'Manage? The girls flock in when you're not here to scare 'em off.'

'Only the blind ones, boy.' Big Wal flipped the counter top up and walked through to the pavement.

Huamai huffed indignantly. 'I'm a babe magnet, I am.'

'Yeah, well, I think the instructions for assembling you must have been in ruddy Chinese. Someone stuck your bum fluff on your head!' Big Wal smiled as he walked away, listening to Huamai cackling in his wake.

He crossed Tongariro Street and cut across the park beside the Super Loo. The beige-pink building had a rounded roof so that it squatted just to one side of the main street like a large mushroom. There'd been quite a hoo-hah when the council had built it. There was already a free public toilet on Tongariro Street, two hundred metres away, but by all accounts, this one was popular. He'd never used it.

It was dark, and the grass cushioned his footfalls so that he walked in silence. He heard a Colonel Bogey horn back on Tongariro Street but the sound was faint. He gave each shrub a wide berth, feeling as if he walked within a spotlight — there for all to see.

And on the edge where light meets darkness and strange things can happen, he could see people walking with him. His father was there, wearing his old bush jacket, a knife on his belt and an old army .303 in one hand, a dog padding silently behind him. Aw shit, it was Flint, the old fleabag, dead maybe twenty years, but his dad had never had another pig dog like him. Wal's grandfather was there too. And his great-grandfather with a woollen blanket around his shoulders. And other men walked with them — men he knew without knowing. Men with tattoos on their faces, weapons in their hands. Some wore trousers, there were a couple of old fellows with hats, more still with bone ornaments or feathers in their hair. Two wore feather cloaks. Some were old and walked with slow dignity; some were young and walked with the arrogance of youth. But every last one of them was dead.

Big Wal knew that. The hair on the back of his neck prickled. He didn't like seeing the dead, but these men were his ancestors. They had guided him with their wisdom all his life. One day they would welcome him.

So he walked through the park and kept his eyes to the front so that no one could catch his eye, and his ancestors walked on each side of him. Perhaps they had come to guard him, or give him strength, or simply to remind him of who he was.

Ahead, he could see the flashing light of the police car. When he crossed Ferry Road his companions melted back into the shadows of the park. He walked down the track beside the yacht club and waited as a stretcher was carried past him.

Nick walked behind the stretcher with his arm around the girl.

He extended his hand to Nick and greeted him formally. If the man was surprised, he didn't show it — perhaps he could feel it was a night for formality. If Nick had been Maori, the handshake would have been a hongi, but Big Wal knew most Pakeha broke into a cold sweat at the thought of pressing noses. The girl was untouchable. She'd claw him to bits if he went near her.

'Are you happy now?' Her voice was as hard and sharp as any weapon. Did she think anger would shield her from her grief?

Big Wal flinched. 'You read me wrong, girl. I never wanted this.'

'You said Tama would hurt him. This proves you were right, doesn't it?'

'I knew what I said was right. I didn't need your boy to die to know that. I'm truly sorry.'

She walked on, yanking Nick after her. He'd stopped to stare out over the water. Big Wal followed his gaze, then jerked his eyes away. There was a Pakeha woman with long hair blowing in a wind Big Wal couldn't feel, and she was walking on top of the waves. Nick stumbled, then walked on. Big Wal fell into step behind them.

What he'd said was the truth: he'd never wished the boy harm. He'd tried to warn the boy, warn both of them, but Billy hadn't heeded his words. The young ones don't.

'This shouldn't have happened.' Saffron threw the words over her shoulder to him as if he was in some way responsible. 'I returned the coins. You said that would make it all right.'

'I said it was the best thing you could do. I didn't promise you it would fix anything. I hoped it would but I think it was already too late.'

Ahead of them, the body was being laid in the hearse,

its doors wide open as if it was waiting to swallow all the dead they could throw at it. Saffron hurried forward. Big Wal tapped Nick on the shoulder.

'Did you see the boy's body?'

'Yep.'

'Did he look like he just fell over?'

'Do you mean did he look as if someone threw him over?'

'Something like that.'

'I photographed that young fella who went over last Christmas. Billy was certainly knocked about a whole lot more. There were a lot of rocks around him as if he'd brought a bit of a landslide down with him. His head was caved in, and his hands were all beaten up. Not just the one you home-runned on — the other hand too.'

'Like maybe Tama decided to use his mere?'

Nick shrugged. 'Or sat up the top and fired rocks at him.'

'The police make anything of it?'

'They were more interested in a betting slip he had on him. Seemed to think he might have committed suicide.'

'His father did. Like father, like son.' As he spoke, Big Wal stared out into the whispering black shadows of the park.

'Saffron didn't think that likely.'

'Guess she should know.' He extended his hand to Nick. 'You take care now. And look after her.'

They shook hands again and Wal walked off. He decided to go up and around by Tongariro Street rather than back across the park. They might be his ancestors, but they were still spirits. It paid to walk softly around spirits.

On the far side of the road, he looked back. Nick was standing with one arm around the girl's shoulder. She might have been crying. And off in the shadows he could see a man patiently waiting. He wore the paintbox colours of a jockey, and he absently tapped his whip against one boot. Lucky Del Delaney was waiting for his boy.

CHAPTER SIXTEEN

SAFFRON, HEATHER AND DAPHNE stood outside the house on Lake Terrace as the sun rose, flushing the lake pink and colouring the sky. In the west, the full moon showed as a pale orb. Moment by moment it faded, like a guest who had blundered into the wrong room and was hastily trying to excuse itself.

They stood side by side, arms linked, and watched in silence. Saffron had never felt so alone. Billy, her little Billy, was gone. Stealing the coins was wrong, but *this* wrong? Wrong enough to lose his life? The world was an alien place when someone could die for so little. Like one of those foreign countries where you're knifed for the change in your pocket. A few coins. Loose change in Tama's pocket.

While she should have felt warmth from her sisters' bodies she felt cold and alone.

It wasn't like this when their father had died. She remembered the five of them around the kitchen table, talking and crying, together — a family. Death had visited them, but there had still been warmth. With Billy's death, that was gone, all gone.

Daphne shivered, and Saffron turned to her, wanting to say something to make things right, but finding no words.

'Everything red reminds me of blood right now,' Heather said, loosening her grip on Saffron's arm and clutching her jacket close.

'I know what you mean.'

And Heather hadn't seen the blood she'd seen, Saffron thought, then mentally kicked herself for being selfish. I'm translating everything back to me. Their loss is as great as mine. Being a nurse doesn't immunize you against the effect of blood — not when it's your brother's splattered over the sand. She gave Heather's arm a squeeze.

'Let's go in,' Daphne said, turning away from the lake with another shiver. 'It's cold.'

'I'll put the jug on,' Heather said.

'We're out of milk,' Saffron said. Always the mother, she thought. Even at a time like this.

'The dairy will be open,' Heather said, glancing at her watch. 'I could do with a walk.'

'Let's go down to the rock,' Saffron said. The words took her by surprise as much as they obviously did her sisters.

Heather stared at her. 'Tama's Rock?'

Saffron nodded.

'So we can sit on it while he takes pot shots at us?' Daphne frowned at her.

'I just mean . . .'

And that was the point. She didn't know what she meant. The words had just popped out of her mouth. Daphne was right. Why would they want to go anywhere near Tama's Rock? Maybe he still had the Delaneys lined up in his sights.

'Billy's death is an end to it,' Saffron said in a decisive no-nonsense voice that was supposed to signal certainty. This was the thought that rose to the surface of her mind, but beneath it were a hundred conflicting thoughts, each insisting it was the one she should trust.

'You hope,' Daphne muttered.

'You get some milk,' Saffron said, 'and I'll pop down to the rock for a moment.'

'Why?' Daphne said.

'There was an old woman who knows about the curse. She might be there.'

Daphne shrugged. 'If that's what you want to do.'

It wasn't. She wanted to huddle in close with her sisters as if they were a shoal of fish. Anyone on the outer might be the next one picked off by a sharp-toothed Tama Ariki. But she knew that was why she had to work out what happened to Billy. Find out if this was an end to it, so she could protect them.

That's what big sisters are for, petal.

Daphne started towards the house. 'Don't be long.'

'Get a Sunday paper,' Saffron called as Heather set off. 'See how the horses ran,' she added quietly.

Heather nodded. 'Of course.'

They looked at each other for a moment. None of them cared how the horses ran, but today, at least, they needed to talk weights and barrier draws and track conditions. Things they'd learnt at Daddy's knee. It was important — a requiem for Billy.

The Delaney girls — that was how people referred to them, and it had nothing to do with age. In fifty years' time they would be shuffling down the street on their walking frames and people would still say, 'There's one of the Delaney girls.' They were never seen as individuals — and how she'd chafed and fretted at that — but as four quarters of something else. Something Daddy had cherished and made flower that was now withering. Dying.

Just like Billy.

She crossed the road, then squeezed her eyes shut for the time it took a logging truck to grind past. Diesel fumes soured the air. She walked down the grass slope to the steps, then along the shore towards Tama's Rock. Before she reached it, she sat on the shore, where the rock was still cold from the night, wondering where she'd gone wrong. She picked up a pebble and threw it into the lake. It wasn't fair. She'd done the only thing she believed might make amends, but Tama had still exacted his revenge. Damn it all! How could a young man die because of a mistake over some coins?

As she pushed herself up off the rock she gave a yip of pain. She'd forgotten about her hand. Billy was dead, the family was disintegrating, her hand burnt to a crisp. Tama hadn't played by the rules.

She ran out onto the rocks, arms outstretched for balance on the uneven slippery surface, splashing through water that swirled over her feet. At the end she put one hand on Tama's Rock and leant over. The coins lay dull and wet in the bowl.

She scooped them up. 'Take your coins then!' she screamed, and raised her hand to throw them.

A noise behind her made her freeze. Even her heartbeat stopped. She turned slowly.

A large white bird was perched on a rock between her and the shore. She'd never seen a heron here before, if that was what it was. Weren't white herons extremely rare? Didn't they only nest down the West Coast somewhere? Her heart hit its rhythm again and she lowered her hand, felt heat from the coins warm against her skin.

She took a step forward, but the bird didn't fly off. A sense of uneasiness flowed through her. She took another step and made a shooing motion with her hands.

The bird had a long yellow spear-like beak, and it stared at her. Cruel black eyes glinted with awareness, as if it knew who she was. As if it knew what she clutched in her getting-hotter-by-the-moment little hand. This is your lucky day, girl, said those black eyes, because if you were smaller or I was bigger, I would pick you up in my beak and rip the flesh from your bones.

'Get!' she said. 'Shoo!' Her magic touch with dogs didn't extend to herons.

The white feathers of the bird glowed flamingo pink in the early morning light. It was beautiful, if you didn't look into those cold, black, staring eyes.

Slowly, never taking her gaze from the bird, she reached out behind her and tipped the coins back into the hollow in Tama's Rock.

Almost lazily, the bird extended its wings, flapped them and slowly took flight. As it circled overhead she ducked when its trailing black legs looked as if they would catch in her hair. She spun around as it flew, feeling a rush of fear, as if a shadow had passed over her.

Saffron stood staring after it until the bird was a speck in the distance, then ran back along the line of rocks, past the sign warning people in big red letters 'Please Do Not Touch The Golfballs', jumping onto and then off the stormwater outlet.

Someone sat on the sandbags the council had packed underneath the wooden steps to stop the bank eroding. It was the old woman. She clutched at a blanket around her shoulders. 'I saw Tama Ariki's mere fall last night. For that brother of yours.'

Saffron nodded. She didn't trust her voice.

'I warned you,' the old woman said.

'I did put them back, but he took Billy anyway. It isn't fair.'

'Fair! You think Tama Ariki cares whether you think it's fair? There are consequences to everything. I told you, girl. I warned you.'

'And I put them back.'

'Utu must be paid.'

'Is it over now?' Saffron asked. She stared, as if the force of her gaze could make the old woman give her the answer she wanted.

But the old woman stared back, and it was Saffron who averted her head and looked out over the lake, where cloud smudged the far end of the lake and the mountains to a featureless grey.

'It's not over until Tama Ariki decides it's over.'

'When will that be?' Saffron asked.

The old woman shrugged her tiny shoulders, and the blanket slipped down one arm. She dragged it back. 'It might be now, or it might be tomorrow, or next week, next year. It's over when Tama Ariki decides it's over,' she repeated.

'You must have some idea,' Saffron said stubbornly.

'It will be over when someone else tramples on his mana and draws his attention away from you.'

'You mean he's going to keep hurting us until someone else steals some of the coins?'

The old woman laughed, but her voice was bitter. 'Tama Ariki has far more things to oversee than the coins. Your family is not important to him.'

'Good. Tell him the Delaneys are unimportant people. Tell him we're . . .' She thought of one of Daphne's expressions. 'Tell Tama Ariki we're no more important than a pimple on a frog's arse.'

'I'll tell him, but he doesn't take any notice of me. I'm not important either.'

'Why do you help me when Tama is doing these terrible things to my family?'

'You helped me.'

'The dogs, you mean?'

The old woman glanced over her shoulder. 'Dogs frighten me. Mostly, they run from me with their tail between their legs. But a few, they attack me if they can.' The old woman held out her arm, pulled the blanket back and pushed up the sleeve of her dress. Saffron could see a thick red scar pulling the skin into a rope. It looked raw and new.

In reply, Saffron held out her own arm, where the scars from her encounter with Paddy the rottweiler were thin, white lines. The difference was what came from having a wound stitched.

'Tama Ariki doesn't understand. He tells me to yell at

them, hit them with my stick. The dogs all run from him.'

I just bet they do, Saffron thought grimly.

'He doesn't understand. I am old. The dogs know I am not of this time. I frighten them — so they attack. You helped me when many people would have walked past. So now, I try to help you. Try to make you see the error of your ways.'

'But I haven't erred,' Saffron protested. 'I did exactly what you told me to do. I returned the coins. So Bi—' She stopped, waved her hand in the air, the words 'Billy's death' stuck in her throat. 'This . . . this must be an end to it.'

'I hope so, girl, I really do. But Tama Ariki has a mind of his own.'

'He's done his worst,' Saffron said bitterly. 'What more can he do?'

The old woman rearranged the folds of the blanket. 'Perhaps he is just getting started.'

'What do you mean? He *killed* Billy.'

'Utu,' the old woman said, her chin jutting forward, as if Saffron's words hadn't adequately described what had happened.

'But what more could he do?'

'He could kill you. He could kill your sisters. Now, you listen to me, girl.' She shook her finger at Saffron. 'Tama Ariki can do anything. You must remember that.'

Saffron stared at her helplessly. The pink glow of morning had gone. 'How do I stop him? What more can I do?'

'I showed you a vision.'

Saffron swallowed. That wasn't something she wanted to remember. So much blood; so much death — and now Billy's blood had soaked into that same shore. 'Yes. The babies. I tried to help.' She shook her head in confusion. 'I tried to run back. But I was too late.'

'We were all too late for the newborn, Tama Ariki's first grandson. There were too many babies and little ones to gather up. We tried. And when I took you back there, you tried too. We saw that. That is why we try to help you.'

'We?' Saffron said in confusion. 'You mean you and Tama?'

The old woman snorted. 'Your brother insulted Tama Ariki's mana. He doesn't like you at all. I mean the women, the mothers of the babies. From time to time over the centuries, I have shown other women the vision of that day. It lives with me always. It is one I find easy to pull from the past into the present.'

'And what happens?'

'They run.'

'I ran too,' Saffron pointed out.

'But you stopped and turned back for the newborn. It was more than most do. The women saw that.'

Saffron remembered the fluffy duckling head of dark hair. 'I was too late.' Her voice broke as she saw again the tiny body soaring out over the lake. And that made her think of Billy — no soft watery landing for him. She stifled a sound. Her gaze dropped to where the lake water ran up towards her feet.

'We were all too late,' said the old woman.

She meant the newborn. Tama and his people would lose no sleep over Billy.

'But you listen to me,' the old woman continued. 'If he does not forget you as quickly as you would like, then—'

'You can do something?' Saffron interrupted. She stared at the old woman, a shiver of excitement sweeping over her as if ice-cold lemonade fizzed through her veins. 'Whatever it is, do it *now*. Make him forget us *now*. The coins are returned. We're sorry for what Billy did. Can you ask him to forget us?'

'I can do nothing. I am an old woman. I am not important.'

'But you're the one Tama chooses to send back. You must be important.'

'I am old and no threat to anyone. People will talk to me. I am family. I can be trusted. That is why he chooses me.'

'So you don't have any power?'

The old woman smiled. Cautiously, she slid off the sandbags and took Saffron's hand. 'I am no more important than a pimple on a frog's arse.'

'Help us, please, if you can.' Saffron searched desperately for the right words. 'Is there something you and the women want? I'll help you if I can. Help us, and I'll do whatever I can for you.'

'Be careful, girl. Don't make promises before you know what it is we ask.'

'It doesn't matter what it is. I'll do whatever you want. I give you my word.' Saffron spoke the words slowly so the old woman heard the intent in her voice. 'If Tama Ariki will turn his eyes from my family, I will do whatever you want, whatever *he* wants. It doesn't matter what it is.'

The old woman nodded her head. 'I know you will, girl. That is why we chose you. You are young, and very foolish, but you have a kind heart.'

She raised her voice and cried out in Maori.

CHAPTER SEVENTEEN

A SUDDEN GUST WHIPPED white-topped waves to the shore where they surged up the sand. Suddenly Saffron and the old woman were standing in knee-deep water. As she felt the tug of it against her legs, Saffron clutched the old woman with both hands. Then the water was gone as quickly as it had come.

A black, heavy stone settled in Saffron's stomach. The bottom of her jeans were wet against her legs, and the old woman's dress clung to her skinny stick-like shanks. What had she just promised to do? The old woman was smiling up at her like a snake-oil merchant who'd just made a sale. Slowly, Saffron released her grip. For someone who professed to be nothing more than a harmless old woman, that had been an amazing weather change.

'What did you just do?'

'I called upon the wind and waves to carry your words to Tama Ariki, so he will think it is his own idea. He doesn't listen to me.'

'Think what is his own idea?'

'That you will do whatever he wants.'

'Within reason,' Saffron added.

'I don't think he heard that bit.'

'If you have a good idea, then why don't we just do it? As you said, women understand each other. Why do we—'

'Because it isn't a good idea, not for you, girl. Maybe something will happen that draws Tama Ariki's gaze and he will forget you. That is a good idea. And because you stopped the dogs from biting, that is what I want for you. Because it is the safest way and because I like you.' She smiled at Saffron. 'But if he does not forget you, if the losses become too great, come back down here to his rock. The women will be watching. We will find you. And maybe Tama Ariki will think that girl will do whatever I want, and he will remember the four babies we never found.'

Saffron shivered at the memory of the bloody massacre.

'I must go.' The old woman started to turn away.

Saffron heard a sound. She stopped, glanced back. The old woman's back was to her, but even so, it was clear something was wrong. She seemed to have frozen solid, poised inelegantly, her bare left foot on the ground, her right foot still anchored by only a toe, exposing the thick dead skin on her heel. Saffron took a step towards her, uncertainly. The old woman's eyes were wide open, and the pupils were dilating and contracting — rippling, Saffron thought with a shudder, like the blood in the bowl on Tama's Rock.

For a moment, her hands hovered uselessly in the air. Get Heather, she thought decisively. She's having a fit. Heather will know what to do. But before she could take another step, the old woman spoke.

'Tama Ariki's mere. I see his mere. Falling from the sky.

163

Down, down, down.' The last word was a whisper. Her eyes flickered rapidly, then she squeezed them shut, licked at her lips and ran her hand across her mouth as if removing a foul-tasting scum. She opened her eyes suddenly and stared at Saffron.

'No,' Saffron said, backing slowly away. 'No!'

The old woman pawed at her mouth again. 'I'm so sorry, girl,' she whispered, shaking her head sadly. 'So sorry.'

'No!' Saffron screamed. She spun around, hurled herself up the steps two at a time and sprinted up the grass slope towards the Terrace. Her mouth was dry, her eyes wide and staring, her mind a blank except for that one word that smashed against her skull with every step. A small word in a raging world. *No!*

Daphne watched Saffron and Heather walk away, then hurried through into the house. Billy was gone. Dead. She still couldn't believe it.

The light in the kitchen was still on, so she switched it off. Unwelcome grey shadow crept into each corner, looked out at her from behind the chair, so she turned the light back on.

The bag with the wetas still sat on the floor where she'd dropped it on Saturday. There were a dozen wetas, each in its own plastic container with air holes punched in the top. She felt sorry for them. Her class had prepared a cage for them, and they would release them at the end of their studies, but for now each one scurried about its lonely prison. Alone, just like her. She wished Saffron had stayed. Saf knew she didn't do alone. None of them did.

She didn't feel hungry, but she opened the pantry to see if

there were any MallowPuffs left. MallowPuffs tasted of good times, laughter, a family united. There was an empty wrapper and she remembered that she'd already eaten the last one.

She decided to find a box to release the wetas into, while she waited for the others to return.

Gilbert's cat followed her down the brick path through the apple trees to the shed. She hoped its owner wasn't looking out his kitchen window, or he'd be over like a shot. His infatuation was embarrassing — more than embarrassing: mortifying. He'd even turned up at school a couple of times.

She opened the door to the shed at the far end of the garden, where the only things that grew were the apple trees. They should have called it the orchard, but they never did. Everything about the place was mismatched — an orchard where there should have been flowers; a brick path with bits of old mortar still stuck to some of them although the house was built of weatherboard; a beautiful leadlight window at the back of the house, plain glass at the front; a garden shed when there wasn't a garden. Nothing matched — but it had matched Lucky Del.

It was dark inside the shed, so she pushed the door wide open. The only time she ever came in here was when it was her turn to mow the grass under the apple trees. A few tools lay on a bench, the lawnmower parked to one side, red plastic container of fuel beside it, a few pots left over from someone's attempt at gardening on the back porch. Some half-used tins of paint sat on a high shelf from when Saf and Heather had painted the house last summer.

'Do you believe in this Tama Ariki?' she asked the cat, just to hear the sound of a voice. It didn't make her feel better.

Maybe she should just leave the wetas as they were. She imagined wetas were among the great survivors — like rats and cockroaches. She could take them around to the school later, or release them back where they'd caught them. The kids would be happy to catch another lot. She'd be taking a few days off work, so releasing them might be the best solution, but then she'd need to get another permit.

She wondered why, when her brother had just died, she was worrying about a bunch of wetas. At least they were something safe to worry about, which is what she needed right now.

A small black spider dangled on a line of web in front of her. She moved carefully around it, then picked up the cat and held it close. Its black shiny fur felt soft and almost sensual against her neck.

The door blew shut and it was as if someone had blown out a candle — black as three feet up the devil's bum. She took a step towards the door, hoping she would miss the spider. The cat struggled in her arms, claws extended, and she put it down.

When she turned the handle and pulled nothing happened. She yanked. Nothing. She turned, leant her back against the door and looked about. She could see nothing.

'Don't like this much, cat.' Her voice was too loud for the small shed. She heard a sudden movement and had an image of the cat going berserk in the dark and springing at her. She turned her back on the cat — or at least where she thought the cat was — and faced the door.

She twisted the handle each way but there was no movement. OK, she could handle this. No need to panic. In a few minutes, one of her sisters would be back. She'd make a noise and they'd find her. And there were tools on the bench. She could get something and prise the door open, or make a hole in it, or something. Delaney girls were nothing if not resourceful, as Saf always said. She didn't want to be shut in a dark shed — not today. Not after what had happened to Billy. She wanted light.

She felt along the bench, found a hammer.

A faint glimmer of light showed around the door as she faced it again — her eyes were adjusting to the dark. She could see the cat as a black hunched shape in the far corner.

She felt the weight of the hammer in her hand. This situation was going to look a whole lot better when it dried, she decided. The old family joke brought a twist of a smile to her lips. She stood back, raised the hammer over her shoulder and brought it down on the wood panelling of the door.

A tremendous pain exploded in her head. She staggered, then stood with her head lowered, shaking it slightly, like a Spanish bull with a neck full of spears. For a second or two, she didn't know where she was.

She raised the hammer and brought it down again. The white light burst in her head again, and the jangle of messages racing up and down her brain stem brought her to her knees. She could feel something running down her face, and went to wipe it away, but her hand didn't respond. Finally, it floated up to her head and swiped at the wetness. She guessed it was her hand because she could see her ring — the stone sparkled, which was strange because the shed was dark. Perhaps that was where the bright light had come from, she thought vaguely. But where was this wet stuff running down her face coming from? She would just sit down for a while and figure this out, but when she tried to move she fell forward. She would just lie here. Heather would tell her to lie down. Heather knew about things like that.

The white light was back. She whimpered quietly, waiting for the pain, but it didn't come. Saffy and Heather and Mo were here with her, so it wasn't so bad. She'd known they wouldn't be long. They sat in a row on the floor beside her. Her big sisters wouldn't let anything bad happen to her — they never had. And the white light didn't hurt now. It was friendly, welcoming and peaceful.

At exactly two minutes past seven, Gilbert Williams knocked as quietly and reverently as he could on the Delaneys' back door. He'd been waiting for the past hour for what he considered a reasonable time to visit. He knew Daphne was at home. The Mini was in the drive; the Echo, for some reason, was parked across the road — as if the Delaney sisters had decided to take over the entire neighbourhood with their vehicles. He'd seen them go out earlier, and only Daphne had returned. Whenever he glanced at their windows — not that he was snooping, but his kitchen window faced theirs: he couldn't help but see in — he saw only Daphne. At a time like this, the family should be gathered together, comforting each other. Instead, they'd left Daphne alone. Well, no one could accuse him of being unneighbourly.

His heart rate increased as he imagined Daphne opening the door. It didn't matter how many times he saw her, each time was like the first. The flawlessness of her skin, the absolute perfection of it, astounded him.

Daphne was like a beautiful china figurine — Meissen, early 1700s. Nothing could match what they produced in those first fifty years. The skin around her eyes was so delicate he could never decide if she used the merest touch of blue eye shadow or if her skin there was translucent. Each time he met her, his gaze was drawn to that faint blueness.

He couldn't hear her approaching so he knocked again. She might have gone back to bed, and he didn't wish to wake her. He considered that unlikely: his sleep had been disturbed for weeks after his mother died. Daphne was a sensitive young woman. She would be tossing and turning, her mind a battlefield of emotion. Gilbert took a step back — people didn't want you in their face when they opened the door — and looked out at the apple trees in the Delaneys' backyard. He frowned. There were standards to uphold on the Terrace. One or two apple trees were acceptable — he grew a triple graft with two dessert apples and a cooker down by the back fence — but no one needed two dozen.

'What an eyesore,' he muttered. 'Someone should report that girl to the council.' He meant Saffron, of course. This tangled forest would be nothing to do with Daphne. He jerked his head around at the sound of something falling. He cocked his head and listened. A cat meowed.

'Samantha?'

Hearing a familiar voice, the cat answered.

'Where are you, Sammy?'

The cat yowled loudly.

Gilbert walked down the brick path and heard her meow again. The sound came from the shed. When he turned the handle and pushed the door open, Sammy shot out like a black bullet as soon as the gap was wide enough. The door half-opened before running into something. Gilbert poked his head around the edge.

A thin, quiet cry escaped him.

'Daphne!'

He stood on the doorstep, his hands fluttering with indecision. She lay there, his Daphne, his beautiful Meissen china doll. Broken.

He knelt down and peered around the door. Blood congealed down one side of her face, the other was stark glossy white. A tin of paint lay on its side. Daphne had the face of a clown, a caricature of red and white — blood and paint.

Carefully, he reached out and felt for her pulse. Nothing.

A hammer lay on the floor beside her. He cried out again, a quiet, frightened sound, then clambered to his feet and began to run back down the path.

CHAPTER EIGHTEEN

S AFFRON RACED ACROSS Lake Terrace, tarmac disappearing silently beneath her feet, as if she ran above a molten stream, and flew up the drive. A black tail shot under the azalea bush and was gone. She threw the gate open so that it bounced off the fence and slammed behind her. She was on the back porch, reaching for the door handle, when Heather came stumbling down the brick path from the garden shed.

For a moment, Saffron was happy. A witless smile half-formed. Heather was OK. She'd thought, for the eternity it had taken to run home, that the old woman had seen something happen to her family.

Heather's white face and wet cheeks registered.

Saffron's hand fell away from the door handle. The leadlight window leered at her in a bloody smile. 'What's the matter?'

And she couldn't make out what Heather was trying to say, because she was crying and not making sense. She seemed to be saying something about Daphne. That Daphne was . . .

But that wasn't possible, she'd returned the coins. This

couldn't happen. It wouldn't be fair. She'd returned the coins.

There had to be some mistake. Heather had somehow made a mistake, got things wrong. It was Billy who was dead. Daphne had never touched the coins. Not once. She couldn't be . . . She *wasn't*. If any one deserved to be struck down by Tama, it was her. She'd touched the coins — more than once. She'd tasted the bloody sea in her mouth. *She* was the one he should be aiming for. Not Daphne.

Please, God, not Daphne.

'No,' she told Heather, smiling with a terrible forced brightness, 'you've made a mistake. Show me.'

But Heather was a nurse, and she hadn't made a mistake.

Daphne was dead.

Her eyes felt parched, as if, since Billy's death, they'd broiled under a desert sun, and now there wasn't a single tear left for Daphne.

And while they sat in the doorway of the shed with Daphne, so she wouldn't be alone, a policeman walked down the brick path and told them they'd have to move because this was a crime scene.

The sisters sat on the edge of the back porch and watched as a flock of policemen prowled the garden, pecked away at the garden shed, turning over and sorting through the debris of their life.

Saffron phoned Mo. She and Steve were in Taupo getting fresh clothes. Steve would bring Mo around.

The dressing had come off her burnt hand, so Heather bandaged it again. She didn't care. Her hand didn't hurt. Nothing did. Just this terrible, empty feeling inside. But

Heather needed to do something, and dressing her hand was as good as anything.

Senior Sergeant Barker arrived. He looked around, anywhere but at the sisters, and finally expressed his condolences to the rose-coloured leadlight window. Saffron guessed the police manual didn't cover what to say when two members of one family die in separate accidents within twelve hours. Except she knew they weren't separate. Tama Ariki was grinding them up and spitting them out.

Metal scrunched in the drive. The garden gate flew open, and Mo raced down the path, as if even yet there might be something she could do.

'Where is she?' she cried, and they pointed wordlessly to the shed. Two policemen and the black cat looked back at them as if the Delaneys were intruders in their own garden. Steve slipped his arms around Mo and pulled her close. Saffron wished she had someone to hold her. She remembered Nick embracing her after Billy's death, and wished he were here with her now.

The police eventually took Daphne away, the black cat marching down the path in front of them like the leader of the band. Then Saffron and Heather showed Mo the outside of the garden shed, the broken panel in the middle of the door. The police had gone, but they'd sealed the shed.

The black cat sat on the fence and stared at them. Curtains twitched at Gilbert's kitchen window.

'Why is it a crime scene?' Mo asked, her voice cracking. 'How did it happen?'

Saffron wet her lips and started an explanation she didn't fully understand herself. 'She was hit on the head. They're not sure if it was the paint tins falling off the shelf or the hammer. She has wounds from both.'

'Why would she hit herself?' Mo cried. 'I mean she was upset about Billy's death, we all were, but she wouldn't have killed herself. Not with a hammer.'

'They think she might have been hammering, and the hammer slipped.'

'That's possible,' Steve said. 'I had the head fly off an axe once.'

'None of it's possible,' Saffron whispered.

'If the paint tins hit her and she got a fright and moved forward, she might have misjudged the back swing.'

'Doesn't sound like Daphne,' Mo said. 'She didn't take fright easily. And why was she hammering? When was the last time Daphne picked up a hammer?'

'The door's broken,' Steve pointed out.

'We wondered if someone locked her in,' Saffron said.

'Yeah, Tama,' Heather said, a vicious bite to her voice.

'Who found her?'

Saffron jerked her head towards the twitching curtains next door. 'He was running down the drive when Heather returned from the dairy. She'd gone to get milk.'

'So how do we know it wasn't him?' Mo said, staring over the fence at curtains that now hung motionless.

'If I had to lay money between Gilbert and Tama, I'd bet on Tama,' Saffron said. 'He's already killed Billy and Gilbert wouldn't hurt a fly. He loved her. Daphne was always polite to him, but if he'd ever seriously hassled her, she would have made mincemeat out of him. Daphne didn't take prisoners. You know that.'

'Did you say anything to the police about Tama?' Steve asked.

Saffron shook her head. 'We'd only make ourselves sound crazy. Heather and I have to go down to the station and have our fingerprints taken.'

Mo grabbed her arm. 'They don't think one of—'

'They *say* it's to eliminate legitimate fingerprints but who knows what they think.'

Mo started to cry, and Steve slipped his arm around her again. The sound of Mo crying seemed to come into Saffron's head from some distant place, as if she was here by herself, the last Delaney on the planet. She wished Nick was with her.

They walked back up to the porch and sat, looking at the shed, each alone with their thoughts.

Saffron could see Daphne, aged five or six, playing down on the foreshore. The lake was the glorious intense blue that probably exists only in memory, and the air was heavy with the sweet honey smell of the buddleia that grew wild in backyards. It wasn't long after their mother had run off. There'd been tears for a while, but kids were resilient, and Daphne looked so happy. Her eyes shone with excitement, and she flashed her big sister a sideways grin as she ran past as if to say: I can't stop now, I'm having too much fun. Saffron hoped she was somewhere like that, and her eyes were sparkling. Surely heaven had to be some place that made your eyes sparkle?

'Are you two going to be OK? We have to get back to Lucy. She's too young to understand what's going on,' Mo said in a lifeless voice. But she continued to sit there staring at the apple trees with haunted eyes.

'How can this be happening?' Heather asked, her elbows on her knees. She had both hands cupped over her mouth and nose, and removed them just long enough to speak.

'I don't know. Why would Daph have been in the shed?'

'Getting something? Putting something away? The wetas, maybe.'

'I suppose so,' Saffron said.

'I'll make us coffee,' Steve said. 'Then we'll have to go.'

Saffron moved slightly as Steve slipped past her and into the house. Mo retrieved the plastic bottle of milk that was lying beside the path where Heather had dropped it, and followed him.

'Maybe it *was* just bad luck,' Heather said hopefully. 'An act of God.' There was a lengthy silence before she added, 'Where do we go from here?'

'I don't know. It's as if part of me doesn't believe this has all happened. I keep thinking I'm going to wake up, or . . .' Saffron hesitated and then the rest of her words slid out on a long sigh, 'There aren't any other options, are there? Either this is a ghastly dream or it's happening.'

Steve and Mo appeared back on the porch with four cups of coffee between them.

'Do you think this is to do with Tama?' Heather asked, looking up at Steve.

'Has to be.' He handed out the cups of coffee.

'We wondered if it could be a coincidence,' Heather said, her voice hopeful.

'There are no coincidences when it comes to tapu. First Lucy was injured — she could have been killed. And then Billy's death and now Daphne. We're being picked off like flies.'

Heather grimaced. 'Do you think so?'

Steve laughed bitterly, and he didn't sound like Steve at all. 'Work it out, Heather. Tama's working his way up from the youngest. That makes you next.'

'Me!' Heather's gaze flicked from Steve to Saffron in horror.

'Don't say that!' Saffron snapped.

'Prove I'm wrong, then. Because if Tama is working through us by age, then Mo comes after Heather. Or maybe he'll twig that Lucy is getting better and pump a super bug into her. Maybe he looks at her hospital chart each morning.'

Saffron shook her head vehemently. 'Surely he'd target the people he had the biggest grudge against?'

'Who knows how he works it out? I'm simply stating the facts. Lucy was injured first, then Billy and now Daphne. What other conclusion is there?'

'Lucy wasn't killed, she was injured. I don't think her accident was related to this.'

'Since when did a Delaney believe in coincidence? I thought it was all good luck, bad luck and polishing your four-leaf clovers. And what about Billy?'

'Billy's death was definitely related to the coins,' Saffron replied slowly. 'Daphne — I just don't know.'

'I don't agree.' Steve placed his cup on the porch so sharply that a tide of coffee slopped over. 'Tama caused all of this. And anyway, how come Daphne was alone? I know Heather was getting milk, but where were you, Saf? Where were *you*?' he insisted.

She felt them all staring at her.

'Down at Tama's Rock.'

'Why?' Steve asked quietly.

She shrugged. 'I thought I might find some answers.'

'If this is his answer, I don't think you should visit him again.'

Saffron saw herself standing on the rocks threatening to throw Tama's precious coins into the lake, and winced at Steve's words.

'Why are you blaming Saf?' Heather demanded, her face even paler than it had been.

Mo clung to her cup, as if the painted flowers encircling the rim were a hedge that could shield her from the angry words.

'Because if she hadn't touched the coins, it would have been Billy punished for what Billy did. Fair cop, I say. But no — Saf gets involved, and now we're all paying.' Steve stood in front of them, two dots of red colouring his cheeks.

'I was trying to help Billy.'

'I know what you were trying to do, and I know if it was Lucy I would have done exactly the same thing. But I'm Lucy's father. Billy is — was — your brother. There's a difference.'

Saffron got to her feet. 'It's all family, the way I see it.'

'When that guy from work went through the mincer, nobody did a damn thing. No one tried to put the coins back, no one sat on the rock contemplating their navel. Nothing. And nothing more happened. Leave it alone. That's what I'm saying. You're making things worse.'

Saffron turned her back on Steve. 'Am I? Is that how *you* see it?' she asked Heather, trying to read what she could see in her eyes.

Steve continued as if she hadn't spoken. 'Why didn't you just leave the coins on the bloody counter? That's what Billy wanted to do.'

'Big Wal wanted them moved.'

'Who gives a whore's twat what Big Wal wanted?'

'Steve!' Mo cried.

'You weren't there. You didn't see what he was doing to Billy,' Saffron said.

'I saw Billy's hand. I know what happened, but it was between them. And Tama. You should have turned your back and walked away.'

'I couldn't do that,' Saffron said. 'I had to help him.'

'Stay out of it, Saf. You're not helping. Let me look after you all.'

Steve plucked an apple from one of the trees and sent it spinning down the garden. It smacked into the back fence and disintegrated to mush.

'Steady on, Steve,' Heather's voice was getting louder. 'You can't blame Saf for Lucy's accident.'

'Can't I? Who picked the coins up?'

'But only to return them,' Saffron insisted. 'I thought it might heal things with Tama.'

Steve looked at her narrowly. 'I think we can safely say it hasn't.'

'Stop it, you two!' Mo cried out. 'Daphne is dead and you're standing here arguing! Just stop it!' She put her hands over her face.

Saffron sat down again, slipped her arm around Mo's shoulder and gave her a squeeze. 'We're all upset,' she said quietly. 'We're saying things we don't mean.'

'I meant what I said,' Steve insisted, grabbing at a slender branch and pulling his hand down it, stripping the leaves. 'Leave it alone.'

Mo looked at her, her eyes shiny with unshed tears. 'Let's not fight.'

'We're not. We won't. We're just voicing opinions.'

Tama was ripping through their lives like a cyclone, Saffron thought. And they were snapping and uprooting before his fury. She'd bought a little kowhai tree from a plant nursery once, from the bargain bin. She'd planted it and spent a couple of months watering and manuring it, even talking to it. When it blew over, she'd discovered its poor little roots had been growing around and around as if they hadn't realized they'd been released from the pot. Despite her best intentions, it hadn't been anchored at all. Just like the Delaneys.

Chapter Nineteen

BIG WAL WALKED carefully down the wooden steps onto the lakefront. At the bottom of the steps, he pulled a small switch off the wild broom that grew against the cliff and placed it upon the sand. He stood and whispered a few words before he continued. He hadn't been down here for a long time, but there was something he needed to do before he opened the burger bar.

There were boats out on the lake, tourists and fishermen, and not one of them cared what had happened to young Billy Delaney. He didn't care that much himself; he hadn't liked the lad. What he cared about was the forces the boy had stirred up. There hadn't been any trouble with Tama since that fool fell into Zippy Dogs' mincer and came out packaged into thirty-two individually wrapped, three-kilogram dog rolls, by all accounts.

And, although she wouldn't believe it, he cared about the boy's sister. She was trying to do what was right; she'd tried to look out for the boy. Of course nothing she had done would have impressed Tama half as much as if the boy had taken the coins back. Tama had been a great warrior: he expected a man to act like a man, not hide behind his sister's skirts.

It wouldn't have saved him — utu must be paid, no two ways about that — but Tama might have made it quick and clean. Wal didn't imagine falling over a cliff was either.

Wal reached the rocks, but first turned towards the bank and snapped another leaflet from a bush. A man couldn't be careful enough when it came to something like this. He climbed out to the end of the rocks, swearing under his breath when his foot twisted and his shoe filled with water. When he came to the last rock, he leant against it, then looked down into the bowl. Seven or eight coins covered the bottom. He placed the leaflet in the bowl, dropped a gold coin among the others, then murmured a karakia before retracing his steps.

He stood on the shore with water wetting his shoes and hoped he had done all he needed to do.

Huamai walked down the foreshore towards him. 'Morning,' Big Wal said.

'Morning,' Huamai answered.

'I missed the Warriors' game last night. Did you catch it?'

Huamai raised his eyebrows and jerked his head in a single flick of agreement. 'They won. Forty-eight to twenty-two. Beat the crap outta the Bulldogs.'

'That's good. I think that new winger's gonna make a big difference. I'll see you in a while, eh boy?'

'Yeah.'

Big Wal knew where Huamai was going and what he was going to do. The dreads and the dope hadn't cooked all his brains.

The Dog House felt cold when Saffron unlocked the door and

walked in. She dropped the bundle of things she carried and rubbed her arms briskly. The smell of Asuntol assaulted her nose, but, after almost twelve years of ensuring that every dog was flealess when it left, she was used to that. There was no security alarm: she didn't have what thieves wanted. The top half of a stable door was fastened back, so she pushed open the bottom half, walked through into the grooming room and switched on both dryers. She stood for a moment in the blast of hot air, listening to the familiar sound.

A two-tier row of cages filled both side walls and deep wash sinks lined the back. Part of the front wall opened into reception; a bench holding a telephone, radio, a tiny bench-top fridge, a hot water jug, coffee, and cups covered with a tea towel to keep out the dog hair that infiltrated everything filled up the rest. Out back was a toilet she shared with the credit union shop next door.

Every cage was empty, and the room felt like a movie set after the actors had gone home for the night. She turned the radio on and a DJ shouldered his way into the empty room like an overly persistent party guest. After a minute, she switched the radio off again. She could handle alone.

She went back into reception and returned with the bundle of things she'd brought with her. She laid a foam squab on the floor to one side of the grooming table, then hugged Billy's old sleeping bag in her arms. He hadn't used it since his Boy Scout days, and it didn't feel like part of him any more. He'd been a good kid back then, and he would have matured into a good man if a burr on Lucky Del's genes hadn't hooked into him. She'd hoped he would outgrow it, but Tama hadn't given him time.

Wire grille doors blocked the dark, empty throats of the unoccupied cages and she cranked up one of the dryers another notch. Heather and Mo would be halfway back to Rotorua. Although The Dog House was normally like Piccadilly Circus with dogs and their owners coming and going, the radio blaring and people chattering, she was also used to being here alone. She usually spent at least one evening a week here preparing dogs for the next day's show.

Standing in the centre of the room she felt the whole world disintegrate as tears trickled slowly down her cheeks. Billy and Daphne were gone. Billy was only four when their mother left. Saffron had dropped him off at a crèche on her way to school on race days. She'd only been ten herself. And when Daddy died, she'd left school and started work at The Dog House, and two years later she bought the business and put all her sisters through their training without them having to take on a student loan. She would have done the same for Billy . . .

Ahh, Billy. She wiped at tears with her fingers.

Blood will out. Lucky Del's genes had taken over Billy's education. And now Daphne was gone. She hadn't needed time: she was perfect just the way she was.

Saffron felt torn between them in a way she never had when they were alive. How could you grieve for two people at once? Each time she thought of one of them, it seemed like an act of betrayal against the other. Her thoughts ricocheted from Billy to Daphne and back to Billy.

Both dead. How could the world change so much in the space of a day?

She picked up the telephone, but replaced it immediately.

She was trying to distance herself from her sisters to protect them. She fossicked among the cups and papers on the bench until she found a biscuit packet with one MallowPuff left. She took a bite, but it turned to sawdust in her mouth, her face twisting with tears that still wanted to fall. She forced the mouthful down, throwing the other half in the bin.

The walls of The Dog House felt as if they were folding in on top of her. Like a coffin, she thought, or a body bag. She winced, as if that could pull her back from the thoughts sliding into her mind.

She was alone, and she didn't want to be. OK, so she'd been the one to tell Heather to go, but Heather hadn't put up much resistance. She'd raced off with Mo without a second thought.

Saffron couldn't stay there. She grabbed her bag and keys and hurried out of The Dog House, as if at any moment she'd feel a heavy hand on her shoulder and find herself next on the list. And that would be better than Steve's idea — that Heather was the next skittle in Tama's lane. At least if he went for her, she'd know about it. With Heather and Mo in Rotorua, anything could happen and she wouldn't even know. How can you fight something you don't know is happening?

She walked aimlessly through town, turning corners randomly, and wasn't surprised when she found herself standing outside the house on Lake Terrace. But she couldn't go in now, not with a garden shed gift-wrapped in police tape.

Saffron crossed the road, feeling as if she was sinking into the black top, not walking on it, and stared out over the lake. There was a queue at the Great Lake Hole-in-One Challenge, laughing and chattering. People on holiday. People without a care in the world.

At the beginning of the weekend, Billy had taken the coins — by the end of it, he and Daphne were dead. It shouldn't have been possible.

Saffron's face crumpled, and the groundswell of loneliness rose up and engulfed her. She stood, eyes closed, hands gripping the wooden rail that ran along from the steps so hard her knuckles pointed white. Holding herself in place, until the swell subsided.

She opened her eyes. The golfers chattered on. Nothing had changed; everything had changed. How was she supposed to go on? She opened her mouth and drew in a deep breath that still carried the fresh taste of the mountains. This morning, the old woman had talked about getting Tama to forget them, and the sooner Tama had a major memory loss, the better. All she needed was someone else to steal the coins from his rock.

She felt her head wanting to turn to check out the possibilities. Was there an unsuspecting youngster she could drag down to Tama's Rock and point towards the coins?

They're coins, kid. Pick them up. If you don't, someone else will.

She couldn't do that. She couldn't hand someone else's child over to Tama. Not now she'd seen how roughly he played. But he was riding them hard — they couldn't take much more.

In a lull between golf shots, she ran down the steps and hurried along the shore. Ahead of her, the old woman was perched on the driftwood log chair with the banner of yellow and orange leaves fluttering above her like a standard.

'You've come back, girl?'

'You knew I would,' Saffron said.

'I thought perhaps I would not see you again. For your sake, that would have been best.'

'He's taken Daphne.' Her voice crawled over the words as if they were broken glass.

'I'm sorry. He's not a cruel man.'

'I'm having trouble believing that. Daphne had nothing to do with the coins. She didn't take them; she never touched them. She was one of the good guys, but he killed her. She didn't deserve that.'

'She was part of the boy's family. That is enough.'

'I want him to forget about us.'

The old woman pulled her shawl around her. 'This morning, Tama Ariki told me he had an idea.'

Saffron didn't speak. She watched the old woman intently.

'He thought perhaps he had punished your family enough. He wondered, and it was simply an idea that came to him, if you might be desperate enough to help us.'

'You asked the wind and the water to carry my voice to him.'

The old woman gave a deprecating wave. 'I am an old woman. I cannot command the wind and the waves. No, Tama Ariki had an idea. It is not for me to suggest anything to him.'

'OK. If you say so. What was his idea?'

'We lost many of our mokopuna that day. After they killed them, they threw the bodies into the lake. We never found four of the babies and because we never laid them to rest, their spirits are still restless.'

'So what is it you want from me?'

'Tama Ariki wants you to return them to us.'

'The babies? But they're dead.'

'Return their bones. If they are laid to rest, their spirits will be free to continue their journey to the Leaping Place.'

Saffron knew what she meant. An ancient pohutukawa grew high on a cliff at Cape Reinga, in the far north, where the spirits of the Maori leapt to the ocean below and travelled on into the afterlife.

'Why does Tama need anyone's help?'

The old woman shook her head. 'His hands are covered in blood and the spirits of the babies flee from him. He frightens them. They are too young to understand he did what he did to protect them.'

'Did you find everyone else killed that day?'

'Most of the women and children were lying on the beach. The others, the ones we could not find, Tama Ariki called their bones to him.'

'And they came?'

'Oh, yes, they were pleased to be found. It is a terrible thing to be separated from your family.'

'So why does Tama think I can find these babies if he can't?'

'He knows they want to be found and come home to their people. They will not be frightened of you.'

'Why don't *you* take them home? You're not frightening.'

There was a long pause. Finally, the old woman said, 'It's not quite so simple.'

Saffron's lips tightened in a humourless smile. 'I thought it might not be.' She waited. 'So how do I find them, after all this time.'

'Tama Ariki will ask them to sing. Follow the sound of their voices until you find them.'

'Why doesn't Tama get you to do this?' Saffron repeated.

'You lazy girl! You would have an old woman walk for miles to find the babies?'

'No, I mean why me?'

'Other women have tried and failed. But you are not of our people. Perhaps the spirits and demons that afflict us will not trouble you.'

'Spirits and demons.' Saffron repeated emotionlessly. 'Have you tried to get them back?'

'No. I am too old, it tires me even to sit and talk. But there have been others.'

'So what happened when they tried?'

The old woman shrugged and waved one hand vaguely.

'Specifically,' Saffron insisted. 'Tell me someone who tried.'

'There was Hine.' The old woman sounded reluctant.

'OK, Hine went to recover the bones of the babies. What happened to her?'

'I don't remember.'

'You do so.'

Saffron gave her the look that had always worked so well on Billy. The old woman looked annoyed.

'I am an old woman. My memory is no good.'

'So what happened to Hine? I take it she didn't retrieve the bones?'

'No.'

'Did she find them?'

'Yes. Tama Ariki made them sing for her.'

'Did she make it back?'

'Eventually.'

Now they were getting down to it. 'Eventually. What delayed her?'

'I don't know, I wasn't there. Why are you asking me these things? I thought you said you would do anything to help. Are you a sneaky girl who will not help an old woman after she promised?'

'I will help you. But the more I know about what I'm up against, the more chance I have of succeeding.'

'Hine told me she followed the sound of the bones singing back to the day of the massacre. She gathered up the bones, but the men who killed our people followed her and took them. She was lucky to escape with her life.'

'Doesn't sound good.'

'And she said there were demons, horrible black creatures that crept out of the earth and chased her. Hine thought the black creatures might have been the men that Tama burnt. He burnt them all—'

'And where do you think the bones are?' Saffron interrupted.

'Their bodies were thrown into the lake. Maybe they are still there.'

'Tama will make them sing so I know where to look, and when I return the bones, he'll leave us alone?'

The old woman nodded.

Saffron stuck out her hand. 'We have a deal.'

The old woman extended her hand; Saffron took it. It felt so frail, like the body of a tiny bird she could crush without knowing.

'I'll bring the bones back so you can lay your babies to rest.'

'You're a good girl.'

'When will Tama make the bones sing?'

'Come back here to his rock tonight, girl. The bones will sing for you then.'

Chapter Twenty

SAFFRON SET HER shoulders and walked down the grass slope between Lake Terrace and the steps. The street lighting yellowed the grass, and her shadow jutted out lean and black ahead of her. A necklace of lights curved away around the throat of the bay.

She stumbled as her foot landed in an unexpected hollow where the dirt had worn away at the top of the steps. She'd never noticed it in the daylight, but now it almost brought her to her knees. She clutched the railing and glanced about uneasily.

A few fallen leaves rustled in the Tolkien twilight that washed the cliff top. She hoped the old woman was down there. The wind blew ashore and waves washed noisily upon the beach. Would she be able to hear the sound of the bones singing above them?

And what did bones singing sound like? Would she recognize them when it happened? If it happened. For the hundredth time, she wondered if she was going mad. It sounded reasonable enough when she was talking with the old woman, but even she wasn't real.

She's as real as I am, petal.

But Daddy had been dead ten years. She heard his voice sometimes, but he wasn't real. She missed him, and sometimes it was better hearing his voice in her mind than being on her own. The moon was up, but the rocks didn't need moonlight to make them visible — they glowed under the reflected light from above. She reached the rocks and sat down on the driftwood log chair, her fingers tracing the skeletal hardness. She listened carefully, but could hear only the waves lapping the shore.

She didn't like the idea of waiting in the dark. The old woman had described demons and baby killers — dreadful black creatures Tama had burnt alive. Why hadn't she brought a torch? It was what any sane person would have done. But a sane person wouldn't be sitting in the dark waiting for an ancient Maori chief to conduct a choir of bones.

She pushed the gruesome thoughts from her mind. Feeling the damp chill through her jeans, she gazed out over the lake and waited.

She imagined Daddy telling her that she was the brave one, but he hadn't said much for a while. Perhaps he was busy with Billy and Daphne. The thought gave a spark of warmth; Billy, Daphne and Daddy together again. An illusion they were still a family.

She let her thoughts drift over the lake — noticing how at night the water seemed to smooth out until it became satin cloth rippling to shore. Ripples of water, ebbing and flowing as the lake breathed. Her own breath took up the pattern, air rippling in and out of her lungs. In and out, ebbing and flowing. Between the ripples, the lake pulled and distorted the shape of the water, and between the ripples she knew that all things could be explained. It was all in the ripples, in the gap between the ripples. She felt her head sag forward, then sat up with a start.

The air was damper, fresher. Goose bumps prickled her skin. She puckered her lips and began to whistle — it made her feel braver — then remembered she was supposed to be listening for the bones. She stopped. Silence. Nothing but the lake and the night.

And the ripples, petal.

Right. The ripples. Let's not forget the ripples.

Then she heard it. A note so pure, so flawless, the sound sparkled in the dark night like a jewel. Her mouth fell open as goose bumps swarmed up her arms and legs in a wave, reaching up to her throat and up the sides of her face.

She waited, mouth open, breath frozen.

A second note.

And a third. One perfect note after another. She whirled around.

There was nothing, except cascading, tumbling, soaring sound. The bones were singing to her, a song so beautiful it pulled her emotions out to the thinness of a single strand of hair and danced along it. Her eyes blurred with tears, but she didn't need to see as a feeling of unbearable sadness washed over her. She could feel their pain, the little lost souls. They wanted to be found, they wanted to be taken home to their people.

'Sing, little babies,' she whispered. 'Sing.'

She pushed herself up, feeling the bone-hard texture of the wood beneath her fingers giving up its strength, its hardness, to her. She would make things right, for the Delaneys, for Tama's people, for these lost babies. For all of them.

The singing came from the lake. The bones must still be out there, where they'd been thrown so many years ago. She walked into the water, but when she was knee-deep, the singing came from behind.

Uncertainly, she turned back as the singing now came from the shore. For a moment, she wondered if Tama was playing a cruel game. But she could hear the bones singing, not just with her ears but with her soul — nothing so beautiful and pure could be a game. There were some things even Tama Ariki couldn't alter.

Slowly she waded back to shore, the bottoms of her wet jeans stiff against her legs. And right where the water met the land, the singing rose up around her like an invisible fog. This was where the bones sang. This was where she would find them. The bones were singing up through the ripples.

She watched her feet carefully as the smooth black waves rolled to shore. At the last minute, each wave would break into a rush of foam, but the instant before they were smooth as oiled silk gliding towards her. Her legs were breaking the ripples. She began to lift each foot to let the slipping sliding black waves pass unbroken, and then quickly to replace that foot and raise the other. Slowly, she began to jump from one foot to the other, and those smooth black running things passed unbroken beneath her. It was just like being a child again when it had been so important not to tread on the cracks. Now, the danger zone was the ripples. But the ripples were getting further and further apart. It was getting harder and harder to reach the gap between each one.

She was running in place, bounding from leg to leg, leaping between ripple to ripple to ripple. Further and further. Reaching, straining, until finally she knew she was going to miss — she couldn't jump that far. She felt as if she was floating down from high up, her foot stretched, toes pointing, reaching for the space between the ripples, but she could tell she wasn't going to make it.

She floated down onto the ripple, and there was no solid shore to stop her. Her foot plunged into the water, and it rose up over her ankle, knee, and she was plunging down between the ripples, water or *something* surging up over her head. And once she was through — except she wasn't through so much as *in* the ripple — she could see it was a tunnel. A shimmering, shifting tunnel lined with silver and darkening grey streaks that ran along it in a random, ever-changing pattern.

A tunnel had to lead somewhere, so she moved forward — not sure if she was walking or swimming. The tunnel lightened, becoming more and more silver. It glinted, as if up ahead, someplace she couldn't see, it was lit by a light as big as the moon.

She was approaching a bright light. Great! I'm dead, she thought. She'd seen a programme about that on television where people had died and come back, and they all described approaching a bright light. And, yes, some of them were nutters, but some she had believed. Well, if she was dead, it hadn't hurt, and she was grateful for that. Maybe Tama had killed her quickly, which is more than he did for Billy and Daph. She walked — or swam — on through the bright silvered moon-lamp and it didn't hurt. But it did get noisier —

men shouted in a language she couldn't understand, women screamed. She understood that. Her legs became leaden, each step an act of will.

I'm walking, she thought, relieved to have decided something, then heard a scream that raised every hair on the back of her neck. The voices grew louder and louder, and the rippling moon-washed tunnel seemed to be — not thinning, so much as warming. The chill had gone. Whether this was good or bad she didn't know, but she forced herself on.

The moon-lamp was behind her — she'd walked right through whatever it was, and that had to mean she was in heaven — or hell. She sucked in her breath. The warmth took on an ominous aspect. Hell was warm.

A woman screamed close by and Saffron froze. She half-saw movement — a black shape that distorted, grew and shrank, as if seen in a funhouse mirror, and then it was gone. The ripple swallowed it. She wanted to turn and run, back to where she'd been standing on a familiar shore she knew . . .

Back through the Shining, petal. We all have to come through the Shining.

Right. Back through the Shining and through that smooth, black, running thing and back to the rock, back to where babies' bones didn't sing.

But she couldn't, not without the bones for Tama. If there was ever to be deliverance for the Delaneys, she had to continue.

The silver was flaking away from the ripple like scales from a fish, and as the black returned, it was no longer smooth and beautiful but thin and scratched. Voices became louder, and movements that a moment earlier had been hidden became clear. She realized she would soon be without the cover of the ripple; it was disintegrating around her.

And there were people here. She could hear them.

Then the tunnel had gone, and all that remained were scattered clusters of forgotten, wavering air. She backed into a patch of scrubby bushes and hunkered down, desperate to see what was happening before she revealed herself. One by one, the last patches of ripples disappeared.

Staring out between two rocks, she could saw an empty shore that shimmered before her eyes and heard the muffled tumble of the waves as if the sound was coming to her through cottonwool. A rock daubed with grey and orange lichen blocked her view, but past it, to her right, was a clear patch where the ripples were gone.

The sun shone. That was where the warmth came from. Not hell — daylight.

CHAPTER TWENTY-ONE

A MAN WEARING NOTHING but a piece of greenery around his waist stood with his bare feet planted firmly on the sand, his tattooed face a mask of black spirals and lines. He shouted and gestured at someone Saffron couldn't see and she shrank down further, trying to bury herself in the pumice stones scattered under the bushes, desperately praying she was hidden.

Brown legs trotted by and halted a metre in front of her. She could have reached out and touched them. She held her breath, her pulse thundering in her ears. A trickle of blood ran down the shin of one of the legs but not from any injury she could see. She watched as the blood caught on a hair, the red drop swelling until it could hold no more, broke free and continued down the leg. Then the legs walked on, revealing the body of a baby, lying in the sand as it flowered around him, bright, wet and crimson.

She wanted to look away but her eyes refused to move, as if by absorbing every last detail of this baby's death she could somehow save it. She felt the sun bake her skin, the wind move the hair against her neck. Her fingertips felt each individual grain of sand. Sweat trickled between her breasts. She wanted to gift-wrap each impression and give them to the dead child, but it was too late. Always, too late.

Ahead of her was the lake and she rested her eyes on the waves rolling ashore, feeling a wash of calm from something familiar. She breathed in and slowly felt the freshness, the *cleanness*, of her beloved lake giving her strength.

Her eyes swivelled back to the baby. She thrust out her chin, felt the way it wanted to dimple into tears, and swallowed them back. Someone would pay for this. Then she remembered they already had. Tama had taken his utu and burnt them alive. Right at this moment, she would happily have thrown the first match.

She breathed out forcefully, and looked cautiously around her, seeing where several women lay dead. She twisted her body slightly to peer around another rock and saw a line of smooth dark grey rocks stepping from near the base of the cliff out into the lake.

Tama's Rock.

Somehow — and she didn't know how — she had returned in time, arriving right in the middle of the killings. She prayed she would have better luck than Hine.

And these weren't bones; these were people. She was supposed to find bones, not this — she could handle ancient bones. She didn't think she could bear to find what was here.

She wanted to shut her eyes and cover her ears and bury her face in the sand. She wanted to lie hidden until it was over, but she knew she couldn't. She had seen how this day ended — every baby killed.

And there were still babies alive.

She forced herself to look out. A man stood in front of a woman sprawled on the sand. She was dead: with that head wound, she had to be. Saffron's breath froze, her body still, except for the blood that thundered like an express train through her veins. It was the man with the scar — the man she had seen in the vision. The scar ran down one side of his face, twisting the ordered lines of his tattoo into a tangled bird's nest. His mere was dark with blood, and he talked to it. Three steps in front of him was the smallest baby. Tama's newborn grandson.

A woman screamed as if she no longer needed to draw breath. The anguished cry went on and on, ripping into Saffron's mind like a knife. She wanted to clap her hands over her ears.

The man with the scar and the twisted tattoo strode up to the baby, whose tiny fists rose in the air. A woman ran along the beach towards them, but she was too far away. The man saw her and laughed. His teeth were large and brilliantly white against the ink-black tattoo on his face. He gave his mere an experimental slash through mid-air and laughed again at the woman's hoarse scream.

The woman would be too late. Everyone would be too late for this one little baby.

She'd closed her eyes last time. Not today. This time, she had to do something. Maybe, because she wasn't from their time, they couldn't kill her.

Maybe you'll disappear in a puff of smoke, Daddy chuckled. *You never were the bright one, petal — if they catch you, they'll kill you.*

Well, maybe I'm already dead, Daddy. I came through the Shining, remember, so maybe I have nothing to lose.

Somebody give me a fiver each way on that.

Scarface reached down with one hand and jerked the baby up, shaking it above his head in a gesture of triumph as his companions laughed. The baby's head snapped backwards and forwards with each shake. A bone tiki on a thong hung down, and the man wrenched it off. He showed it to the others — it seemed to mean something to them — then dropped it and spat on it.

He broke into a jog and headed out along the line of rocks to Tama's Rock. He bounded along, the baby dangling by one leg, its head only centimetres above the jutting rocks.

Saffron hunched in the shelter of the scrub, her hands half-raised, fingers splayed, upper body dipping, bobbing, psyching herself up like a long-distance runner awaiting the starter's gun.

She took a deep breath, blew it out in a rush of air and with a scream that seemed to hurl her body forward, she erupted out of the scrub and stones like explosive lava from a volcano. Her long legs ate up the distance between her and Scarface and she heard the men on the shore shouting, at her, at Scarface.

He spun around.

She froze.

For an eternity, they stared at each other. Her body shook with each hammer blow of her heart.

She took one gasp of air and advanced a step. Scarface took one step back. Scarcely able to believe it, Saffron took another step forward. Again, Scarface retreated a step.

He was afraid of *her*. That couldn't be right. Her mind raced, trying to find a reason why Scarface should be afraid of her. She couldn't find a solitary one.

He's afraid because he thinks you're a fairy — they all do. The old woman chuckled in Saffron's head.

A fairy? Saffron felt her mind give a sideways lurch. They thought she was a fairy? Fairies have gossamer wings and scatter sparkling dust as they grant wishes; they don't charge around screaming in dirty woollen jerseys.

Not our fairies — not patupaiarehe. They eat their meat raw and they only come out at night because the sun hurts their pale skin. These are ignorant men who have never seen a Pakeha woman. They think you're a fairy with your white skin, a crazy fairy because you're out in the sunlight. They think the pain of the sun on your skin will make you crazier still. Oh, yes, our fairies are not like your fairies. Don't your elders teach you these things?

OK, so her education was a little lacking, but now she had an edge. They thought she was something from another world. She almost laughed.

As she walked along the line of rocks, one step at a time, Scarface retreated ahead of her. He pulled his mere behind his body as if to protect it from her gaze. She breathed in deeply, her nostrils flaring as she sucked in air, more and more air, as if she could milk the hatred and death into her own body.

She must control this man through the strength of her will, the only weapon she had. That, and the fact that he thought she wasn't human. She must remember what these men had done to Tama's people, to the babies. She must see the blood;

feel the pain, pull the hatred from the air, and hold it all in her eyes. She stared at Scarface without blinking. The baby hung upside-down by one leg like a forgotten doll.

She must exude power, be invincible and wield the weapon she had so unexpectedly won. She must be a terrible, crazed, flesh-eating fairy. She must be the thing their mothers had warned them about when they were naughty, the thing that reaches out and rips them apart to eat their uncooked flesh.

She began to tread with soft menace towards Scarface; he had reached the end of the rocks. Desperately hoping the other men wouldn't fall in behind her, she kept her eyes firmly on the man in front of her. She must focus absolutely on him. She slapped at the skin on her face with her hands, as if in terrible pain, and rolled her eyes.

'Give me the child,' she demanded and winced when her voice came out thin and wobbly. He wouldn't understand her and she prayed he hadn't read the fear in her voice. She held out her hand and the man drew away from her, Tama's Rock a wall at his back. She wanted to take one quick glance over her shoulder to be sure the others weren't creeping up behind her, but knew that taking her eyes off Scarface for a second would be fatal. 'Give me the child.'

She pointed at the baby with a stabbing forefinger.

His eyes flitted from side to side of the narrow, rocky path as if he scarcely remembered he had the baby in his grasp.

'Mine!' Saffron demanded. She pointed to the baby again.

Then she bent double and charged towards him on her fingertips and feet, her back arched, her stomach tucked way up so that she must have looked like a crazed gibbon. She kept her head up, her eyes fixed on him in an unblinking stare, and she hurled at him every insult known to the Delaney girls.

With a cry of terror, Scarface dropped the baby and jumped.

Saffron's profanities turned to a scream as she watched the baby fall, an incoming wave breaking and swirling as it caught the wailing infant.

'Grab it!' she screamed. She scrambled across the rocks, slipping, sliding, grazing. 'Grab it!'

But Scarface waded frantically to the shore, glancing over his shoulder as he half-fell, recovered and lurched on.

Saffron threw herself into the water and floundered after the baby. When her hand touched a foot, she clamped down and pulled the coughing, spluttering baby towards her. She held it tight to her chest, her arms wrapped around it, rocking back and forward, lips muttering lines from a childhood prayer over and over.

With the child secure in her arms, she turned to watch Scarface's flight. He glanced back, and sprinted towards the yacht club — or at least where the yacht club would be in two hundred years' time — where the other marauders waited.

Slowly, Saffron waded ashore. She looked up at the cliff, but the women were gone. Far along the beach, she could see the rest of the women and children still running. She looked back: Scarface and company had gone.

A black shag sat on Tama's Rock, wings outstretched, drying in the sun. It seemed a long time since she had seen the white heron sitting there. That had been Tama Ariki, she was sure of it. So perhaps this was simply a shag. Surely if Tama was here, he would have helped.

You didn't look as if you needed help, petal. You even scared me with that scramble across the rocks.

Saffron stood ankle-deep in the swirling, gritty water and let out a huge, shuddering sigh. The baby was wet and naked. She laid it down on the beach while she pulled off her jersey, then made a nest and tucked it in.

Chapter Twenty-two

THE BEACH LOOKED like an abattoir. Blood glistened in the sun, coating the rocks and the dead babies, children, women. Saffron walked from body to body. Occasionally she knelt on the sand to feel for a pulse, but found none.

The air hung heavy, filled with a thick smell. Blood, she supposed. Blowflies were arriving already. She sank down upon her heels and looked around. She had saved one baby. It wasn't much.

And even that was an illusion, she reminded herself. She couldn't change history, and the truth was that every baby died. So Tama's grandson wasn't going to suffer from his dunking, he was already dead. However much she might think otherwise, the baby was already dead, she had seen him killed the first time. All she was doing was gathering up the bones.

Where was Tama? She wanted no more of this.

The world seemed to be coming and going around her, waves of air floating past as if the shore itself was breathing. She sat down and put her head between her knees and concentrated on her breathing for a moment, until the world steadied again.

She tried to think logically. The baby she had rescued

was the only one whose outcome seemed to have changed. Everyone else was dead. She had returned too late to save anyone else, but too early to find old, decently sanitized bones. These weren't bones, they were bodies, still bleeding.

What could she do? If she left the bodies here, would Tama find them? According to the old woman, he'd returned from his meeting with the people of the lake to find the bodies, buried them or whatever, and taken utu. But there were four babies missing.

She looked about her more carefully. Three other babies lay on the shore amidst the carnage. Tama's grandson made four. Somehow, she had arrived while the babies were still here, before they had disappeared. When the old woman had shown her the vision of this day, she had seen Scarface throw Tama's grandson in the lake. Perhaps they did the same with the other three babies. This time, because she was here, they'd been unable to throw the babies away. It sounded reasonable.

With the babies hidden in the lake Tama and his people couldn't lay them to rest. A double hit. And if Tama and his people had planned on gathering food from the lake, then the rahui or ban Maori traditionally placed on food-gathering at the site of such a tragedy would have made it a triple whammy.

If she was right, she needed to gather these four babies, and bring them back with her and hand them over to the old woman. Her part of this bargain done.

It made sense.

As she heaved herself to her feet she felt as though she had run a marathon, her muscles cramping. She walked slowly back, squatted beside the baby in its nest, gazed at it, touched its cheek. Tama Ariki's grandson, who had died two hundred years ago. She stroked his cheek again, and he blew a frothy bubble at her. She smiled, and her lips cracked with the movement. It seemed a long time since she had smiled.

She reached out and picked the baby up — he felt warm, real — there was comfort in the weight of him in her arms. For a moment she didn't feel quite so alone, and buried her face in his neck.

Somehow, when the old woman had described what she needed to do, it had sounded much more straightforward. The bones would sing, she would find and return them. What she needed was a sign, something to let her know she was doing the right thing. She looked around hopefully. There was nothing. The only certain thing was the baby in her arms. She had saved this baby, that was something to hold onto. She would return with him and somehow she would bring the three dead babies with her.

She looked down at the blood that darkened the knees of her jeans. There was a rip in them, and she didn't know if it was her blood or theirs. The dressing had fallen from her hand somewhere, sometime, the burn seemed so long ago. It wasn't important. She tucked the baby back into her jersey and focused on the bodies. Here was death as she had never known it. This time there was no one to wash away the blood. She dabbled her hands in the lake and watched as the blood made abstract patterns in the water before it swirled away. This time it was up to her to make things right.

She didn't know what to do about these people. She felt as if she should say something to someone, but her god wasn't theirs. Or maybe he was. But then she'd said some fairly harsh things to her god recently and she had a feeling he might have turned his back on her.

She went to each of the women and closed their eyes and folded their hands over their breasts, so they knew they hadn't been forgotten. It was nothing and everything. The bone tiki that had been around Tama's grandson's neck lay in the sand, so she wiped the dried spittle from it and slipped it in her pocket.

She picked the baby up, gave him a fierce hug and laid him on the beach, although it felt callous to place such a tiny child on cold, wet sand. She had to keep whispering to herself that he wasn't really alive. Like her, he was caught up in some in-between time, where life and death could merge and mingle. Again, she wondered if she might not be dead herself.

I hope not, petal, Daddy said anxiously. *I put a fiver on you — remember?*

'Yeah, I remember, Daddy. Each way. Alive or dead. You win either way.'

That shut Daddy up.

She picked up her jersey, pulled a lace from her sneaker and tied off the neck, then knotted the two sleeves together so they supported the tied-off end. The first dead baby had congealed blood in lumpy streaks on his head and she swatted at a blowfly.

The sun dimmed as dark clouds elbowed in front. Someone's god had his hand on the dimmer switch. Her shadow, which had been strong and sharp, faded and her energy went with it.

She took a deep breath, picked the baby up and placed it

in the jersey. Then she walked to the next baby, and the next, and did the same. It was a tight squeeze, but she set her jaw, stuck her emotions in neutral and carefully rearranged the babies until they fitted. Then, with a grunt, she swung the jersey sack onto her back.

When she staggered over to Tama's grandson, she realized she couldn't bend over to pick him up. Patiently, she put the sack on a rock, picked him up, pulled her T-shirt over him and tucked it in. Clamping it within her arms so both hands could reach up to her shoulder, she backed up to the rock. Finally, she had the four babies loaded and they were ready to roll.

Her knees buckled, but she stayed on her feet. She took three steps to one side as the weight dragged her sideways, but finally she balanced the load. She looked down at the baby clamped to her chest and hoped she wasn't squeezing him too tight with the weight over her shoulder. Then, she looked up and down the shore.

Where to now? Earlier, the bones had sung to her, calling her back through time. Their song had shown her the path. But where was she to go now? Was Tama somewhere, waiting for his precious babies? Or was she alone?

She leant forward and began to walk with the wind along the beach. She couldn't straighten her legs enough to lock her knees, but staggered along like a geriatric coolie. Ducks took flight as she approached, wheeling up to land into the wind behind her. She splashed in and out of the water as she zigzagged along. A straight course was impossible. Was she travelling forward in time, or was she simply walking along the foreshore? And how long could she walk like this?

After a hundred metres, she knew she had to rest. She

backed up to a rock and rested the weight of her load for a minute. Somewhere out on the lake she heard what might have been a goose shrieking its outrage. Her body ached and her T-shirt was drenched with blood. She stared down at it without expression, then picked up her load again.

Through it all, the baby smiled and gurgled and slept. Whether he really was alive, or dead and just looked alive, he was a *good* baby. That was all that seemed important now as great flocks of birds wheeled and cried overhead.

She made her way slowly for maybe half a kilometre along the shore. The bank became lower and lower, and when it ran out she turned, doubled up with her load, and looked back. Grey-green scrub and brown tussock covered where she would live — had once lived. Fantails manoeuvred in mid-air to catch insects, the colour of their tail feathers flashing from dark to light as they twisted and turned. Some drab brown birds dashed into the scrub, and the lake was grey. Above the horizon, a bank of dove-coloured clouds laced the earth to the sky. Heaven and earth connected. She hoped that was a good sign.

Mount Tauhara stood like a sentinel over the land, a rakishly angled beret of cloud covering its peak. For the first time, she realized the town she knew was nothing more than a squatter on the land. It didn't care for the land, not the way Tauhara did, and in a thousand years' time, or ten thousand years, the town would be gone and Tauhara would stand there just as he did now, looking out over the land that was his. There was something comforting in the thought.

'Come on, babies,' she murmured. 'We've got further to go than you can imagine.'

CHAPTER TWENTY-THREE

SAFFRON WAS SQUATTING beside her load catching her breath, when she heard a noise. She raised her head. A party of men was running along the beach at a fast dog-trot. Ducks fanned out ahead of them, quacking, taking flight. The men were maybe four, five hundred metres away. For a moment, she smiled apprehensively: Tama, come to claim what was his. But even as the thought entered her mind, her smile faded. This wasn't Tama. This was Scarface and his gang. They were returning, and they didn't look scared of her now.

She got to her feet. There was nowhere to hide and the lake bound her on one side. A tree stood in the water a few metres from the shore, but it was dead with no bushy green head to clamber into, just a skinny bole as if a giant had thrown a spear. On the other side, tussock and scrub carpeted the land, the manuka not much more than waist height. If she'd had more of a start, she could have hidden there, but with their eyes already on her, it offered nothing. Further inland, towering green forest stood on the horizon, but it was too far away.

Had someone told these men she was no fairy? The old woman had called them ignorant, but if one of their people had seen a pale-skinned colonial woman then her cover was blown.

She hadn't time to get the jersey sack onto her shoulder. She grabbed the baby up and began to drag the sack along the ground. There was no time for dignity. The sack left a lengthening bloody smear on the white pumice sand, but she tried to ignore it, feeling a whimper building in her chest.

Now the men were only two hundred metres behind and she could hear their shouts as they closed. Even jettisoning the sack wasn't going to save her. Should she leave the baby? Better she live than they both die — but she couldn't put him down, even though she knew he only seemed alive through some trick of time and place.

They're only bones, petal. Drop him and scarper.

But she'd carried him so far. She would leave the sack, she decided, and run with the baby.

'Sorry, little ones,' she whispered. She pulled the jersey sack behind a rock. It wasn't much camouflage, but it was the best she could do. And then, with the baby bumping up and down in her arms, she ran.

Her breath came in gasps as she splashed through the water at the lake edge and when she risked a glance over her shoulder she could make out the twisted tattoo on Scarface's cheek. They were running so much faster than her — she gritted her teeth into something like a snarl, sucking air into tortured lungs.

A large white bird flapped down the foreshore towards her, its long legs trailing just above the sand. It was going to collide with her. She moved to one side, but the bird changed course. She changed back, ducking. The bird flapped over her head, its black feet so close she felt her hair snag and pull. It circled around, landed on the tree in the lake and screeched.

Birds were crying, squawking, cawing, as the men charged towards them. The heron stood on top of the dead tree in the lake and screeched again and again.

Everywhere was confusion, panic. As the men grew closer, she glanced back, tripped and sprawled headfirst along the beach, the baby flying out of her arms. He landed in the shallow water and started screaming, as if remembering what had happened last time he flew from his mother's arms. The whole world was roaring.

She grabbed him, clambered to her feet and put her hands to her ears. As she swung around to face the oncoming men, a kaleidoscope of sand, lake and tree spun through her field of vision. Slowly, she turned back.

The white heron stood atop the tree, its wings extended, and from the tips of its wings, blood dripped into the lake. Below the tree, where the blood dripped, ripples would be spreading out into the lake. She wasn't close enough to see them, but she knew they were there.

Tama Ariki had come. He was taking her home.

She looked up again at the running men. Was there time to gather all the babies? If she was in Tama's team, then yes there was. If she could hand *all* the babies over, she could be finished with this. No more coming back. No more Delaneys dying.

She screamed out her terror as she sprinted back along the beach, grabbing the sack and dragging it to the water's edge, falling over the sleeves in her haste, stepping on them, stumbling. But she got them there.

The men slowed, talking, as if needing to reassure each other that this thing wasn't a fairy. She was drenched in blood and probably looked crazy enough to be anything their minds wanted to conjure up. She dashed a few steps towards them, screaming, and they stopped.

She felt a rush of air as the big white bird flew overhead and swooped in over the men. They screamed as loudly as she had herself as they twisted and jerked under this bleeding thing that flapped over them. Each time the bird raised its wings, drops of blood flew up into the air, sparkling before they fell, pelting the men with gore.

She backed along the shore through knee-deep water, her bloody load bobbing and bumping in her wake. The baby screamed, mouth gaping open in his red face. She didn't know where her strength was coming from, her face twisted into a grotesque mask, her hands locked on bits of jersey, arms, legs, hair, anything she could get a hold of, her legs pushing her back stride after stride after stride. Coherent thought had gone. The tree came into sight, and she changed course towards it. Her body rocked from side to side, as she pushed herself out, deeper and deeper. Grip with the hands, push with the legs. Grip with hands, push with legs.

Tama swooped over the men one final time and flapped his way back to the tree. She was going home, back through the ripples. The water deepened at each stride. It was up to her waist. She pushed on. Grip with the hands, push with the legs. The load was lighter now. Floating.

The sun was behind her. The tree threw a shadow upon

the water and the shadow rippled with sludge-grey water. She could hear splashing. The men were wading after her. Grip with the hands, push with the legs.

She was in the shadow of the tree, the water up to her neck. She turned her head as blood dripped from the heron down to the lake ahead of her, the ripples spreading in their eternal ring, one after another.

Everything was here for her return. The blood, the ripples — even Tama Ariki was helping this time. But the men were closing on her.

When she had come to this place, there had been time for the ripples to appear and pull the fabric of things so she could slip between. Now, the men were right behind her. She couldn't go any further out or she would drown.

Scarface was the first to come into her line of sight. She'd been staring at the blood dripping into the water, watching as the red at the centre of each drop faded and a rim of colour moved out, when suddenly he was there. A half-circle of dark faces, fiercely tattooed, splattered with blood, flanked him.

She forced her gaze back to the blood dripping from above. It was the hardest thing she'd ever done. Slowly, one drop at a time, and as each drop fell, rings spread from the centre. She watched as the concentric ripples moved out, until she knew she could wait no longer. Gripping her load she dived between two spreading ripples.

Down she went, although she didn't know where, because she'd been standing in shoulder-height water. Down and down, her lungs bursting, dragging the bodies with her. The baby clung around her neck, his skin the clammy grey of a waterlogged corpse. She kicked and sped down, and, when she couldn't hold her breath any longer, and knew she couldn't get back to the surface, she had to breathe.

She opened her mouth and sucked in a great lungful of water — and was back in the tunnel. Ahead was the Shining. The muscles in her arms were leaden, and every muscle in her legs was on fire, screaming their protest. She pushed herself on. Just a few more metres. Fingers touched her shoulder. She twisted and put everything she had into one last desperate run.

The Shining came in a great luminous cloud. She broke through, and everything darkened. For a moment, she thought the men must have speared or clubbed her and she was dying. She staggered, the darkness grew, and she stumbled on, wiping a hand over her eyes as if that might clear her vision.

When she glanced over her shoulder, the men were gone. She wiped her eyes again, trying to sweep away the darkness, and saw a moon shining in the sky. She rubbed both hands over her face and stood, head back, mouth open, dragging air into her lungs and staring up at the moon.

Then she remembered the baby. She lowered her hands slowly and looked at them, like a forgetful nanny in a comedy sketch. She looked about her. There was no baby. She'd been carrying a baby in her arms. Hadn't she? She turned in a small circle. She had. She knew she had.

She felt a weight on her back. Reaching behind, she pulled a flax kit from her shoulder, opened it and looked inside. It was full to the top with bones. Tiny bones. Silver-white with age, smoothed to a pearl-like sheen by two centuries of the motion of the lake, they looked too beautiful to be any part of death.

She let out a great shuddering sigh, emptying her lungs of air, then sank to her heels on the beach and stared at the kit. It smelt of newly cut hay, and she didn't know where it had come from.

Tama's Rock stood like a sentinel in the water. A white heron lifted off the rock and flew out over the lake into the dark with slowly flapping wings. Apart from that, she was alone.

Pale streaks edged the night sky aside in the east. Morning was almost here. She would return these bones to the old woman, then Tama would let them be. No more death. She stood up and swung the kit onto her shoulder. She was going home.

As she trudged flat-footedly towards the wooden step, a noise made her raise her head.

CHAPTER TWENTY-FOUR

FOR ONE HEART-JOLTING moment, Saffron thought Tama had come for the bones. Then the light from a torch exploded in front of her so that she squinted and turned her head away.

She set her jaw. Well, if it wasn't Tama, no one else was going to stop her. She hadn't gone through this bloody nightmare to be stopped by some pimply-faced youth. She began to climb the steps.

'Don't you come a step closer,' a voice said.

'Gilbert? Turn the torch off.' Relief surged through her.

'What have you been doing?' he demanded, his voice pitched high with agitation.

'Switch it off. I can't see.'

He aimed it at her feet. 'Don't you come any closer.'

With the light no longer directed at her face, Saffron continued to climb the steps. Gilbert backed up in front of her, one step at a time.

'I'm warning you: don't come any closer.' He thrust the torch forward, aiming the beam at her face again as if it were a weapon.

'Turn it off. What's got into you?' She was exhausted, confused. She didn't want to talk with Gilbert, she just wanted to get home — well, back to The Dog House. Home would come soon enough, once the bones were returned to Tama.

'What have you got there?'

'Mind your own business.'

He reached into a pocket and pulled out a mobile phone. 'I'm calling the police.'

Saffron stopped. 'What's the matter with you? I'm tired and I want to get home. Can't this wait?'

He gave a humourless laugh. 'I bet you're tired.'

She stood at the top of the steps, the kit over one shoulder, and looked at him, her head cocked to one side.

'Look at you,' he said, as if he couldn't believe he had to explain this to her.

Saffron glanced down, her eyes widening as she took in her appearance. Blood stained the front of her white T-shirt, her jeans were streaked red. Her hands looked as if she was wearing long red gloves.

She let out a long expulsion of air. 'Oh!' After a minute's silence, she added, 'I'd best get cleaned up.'

'I think the police are going to be extremely interested in what I have to tell them,' Gilbert said, nodding his head emphatically. 'Yes, indeed! They may have been sceptical when I told them my suspicions yesterday, but they'll listen to me today.'

'You're going to tell the police? What suspicions?'

'Yes, indeed! I owe it to Daphne.'

'What exactly are you going to tell them?' Saffron rested

the weight of the kit on the hand rail. She didn't want to lower it to the ground in case Gilbert saw the bones.

'That I met you sneaking home covered from head to toe in blood.'

She noticed he was keeping a respectful distance. 'There's a perfectly innocent explanation for it.'

'Yes?'

Which no doubt would come to her when she'd had long enough to think. At the moment her mind was wading through a dark swamp. 'Which is none of your business. I don't come around demanding you explain your every move.'

'I don't wander around drenched in blood.'

'Do whatever you think you have to,' she said tiredly. 'I'm going home.'

She hoisted the kit onto her shoulder again and began to walk up the grass slope towards Lake Terrace. An early morning convoy of ducks waddled past at right-angles, and she hesitated for a moment to let them pass. Gilbert kept pace, a dozen strides to her left. She walked across Lake Terrace and turned left.

'I thought you said you were going home?' Gilbert backed up in front of her.

'Get out of my way,' she said irritably. 'Go and do your morning crossword or whatever it is you do.'

The cat poked its head out of the azaleas at the entrance to Gilbert's drive and stared at her with enormous amber eyes. Gilbert circled her warily, she passed, and the cat dashed behind her and fell in behind Gilbert.

'You have a funeral to go to,' he shouted after her. 'Or have you forgotten?'

Saffron stopped in her tracks. 'Tomorrow. The funeral is tomorrow.'

Gilbert stopped. 'You don't even know what day your own sister is being buried.'

'Of course I know. Billy *and* Daphne's funeral,' she added pointedly because Gilbert seemed to have forgotten about Billy, 'is tomorrow. Tuesday.'

Gilbert looked at her pityingly. 'Daphne's funeral is on Tuesday,' he agreed. 'Today.'

'Today?'

She stared at him blankly.

'Today is Tuesday,' he repeated.

'I thought today was Monday.' She heard her voice, suddenly weak and unsure. It had been Sunday when she went through the ripples.

'Your sister's dead, and you don't even know when her funeral is.' He shook his head. 'I never had a very high opinion of you, but I thought even you—' He broke off. 'Don't you care? Did you love Daphne so little?'

For a brief moment, she closed her eyes. He'd gone too far. Slowly she turned. 'What did you say?' She lowered the kit to the pavement and began to walk towards him, feeling as if some essential part of her had broken loose and drifted away. Then she realized it wasn't some *part* of her. It was her. Herself. His words had hacked through the last fraying strands of the tether that anchored her to the world she knew. Now she was floating above that world, thinking, He can't say that. Somebody needs to stop him. Her fists clenched, loosened, clenched, rhythmically.

He retreated before her, one step at a time.

'Not just Daphne. Billy died too. Or have you forgotten him? Didn't he count?'

'It was Daphne who was my personal friend.'

'You stupid little man! Daphne was polite to you, the way she was polite to everyone. She wasn't your friend. You didn't know her.'

'You have no idea how far our friendship had developed.'

'Daphne liked your damn cat more than she liked you!' She was shouting, and couldn't seem to stop herself.

'You're a very cruel woman.' Gilbert retreated step by step up his drive. 'You didn't deserve a sister like Daphne. I don't know how she turned out so beautiful when you're so . . . so . . .' Gilbert's vocabulary didn't seem to have a word that adequately described her.

Saffron heard a car screech to a halt at the kerb, and Nick was calling to her before the engine had died. 'What the hell is going on? Where have you been?'

'You might well ask!' Gilbert yelled, from the safety of a dozen paces up his drive. He advanced a couple of steps as if Nick's presence gave him confidence.

'Saffron?' Nick stared at her.

'I'm going to The Dog House.' She turned and walked back out of Gilbert's drive, swinging the kit back onto her shoulder.

'Ask her what she's been doing!' Gilbert's voice yelled behind her. 'Ask her that.'

Nick was beside her. He grabbed her arm. 'Get in the car.'

'I'm OK.'

'You say that once more and I'll slap you. Get in the bloody car before anyone else sees you.'

His hand pinched into her arm as he marched her back, yanked the door open and said, 'In.'

She obeyed, the kit perched on her lap like something she was taking home to wrap for Christmas.

Nick looked at her. 'Where did the blood come from?'

'What?'

'You're covered in blood. What the hell have you been doing? Where have you been?'

So many questions.

'Been?' The word came out shakily. She'd been in control back there with Gilbert. Now her hands quivered like the wings of a captured bird. She clutched the kit to still them. Things were happening too fast. Only moments ago she had been dragging bloody bodies along the shore, and now Nick was worrying about a bit of blood on her clothes.

'Where have you been? Where did the blood come from?' Nick spoke slowly and clearly this time, as if he realized she was struggling to get her head around even the simplest statement. He pulled out, did a U-turn and headed back along the Terrace.

She didn't answer.

He tried again. 'What you got in there?' He nodded towards the kit.

'Bones.'

He swore. 'Damn it all, Saffron. Where do bones fit into this? Nobody said anything about bones.'

He sounded aggrieved, and she knew how he felt.

'I've been worried sick about you.'

To keep her hands steady she picked at the kit where a strand of flax had pulled free.

'And your sisters. We all have.'

'I'm sorry.'

He reached across and rubbed her arm. 'Don't be. I'm just relieved to have you back.'

'Gilbert wasn't quite the welcoming committee I wanted.'

'Would you have preferred me?' He sneaked a glance her way.

'Don't let's head down that road again.'

Nick snorted. 'Consider me chastised. Tell me about the bones.'

Saffron sighed. All she really wanted to do was sleep. 'After everyone was killed, Tama and his people couldn't find all the bodies. Seems as if Scarface and Co.—'

'Scarface and Co.?'

'It's what I call them — Tama's enemies, the men who killed his people. One of them had a terrible scar covering one side of his face.'

'And?'

'And they threw the bodies of the dead babies into the lake.'

'You went in the lake?'

'Not really. The bones were sort of . . .' Her voice faded away. How did you explain to someone about the ripples? Nick didn't seem to notice she hadn't finished.

'Where did the blood come from?'

He was still worried about the blood. She could have told him that this was nothing, she'd been up to her eyebrows in the stuff, but it didn't seem to matter. Nick had already moved on.

'Your sisters are frantic. They think Tama's got you too. Heather phoned me when she couldn't get you on your mobile. I've been looking for you for the last twenty-four hours.' He hesitated. 'Heather told me about Daphne. I'm sorry.'

She nodded and looked at him for a moment while Nick stared at the road. 'How has it all come to this?'

Nick didn't seem to have an answer for that.

The warmth from the car heater was making her feel drowsy. 'Is it really Tuesday?'

'The funeral's in a couple of hours,' Nick replied.

'I found all the babies.'

Nick looked across at her, then swore when a cyclist suddenly appeared in his path. He swerved, thumped the horn and said, 'Bones, you mean?'

'Bones, babies — it's all the same, I think.'

'Bones don't bleed.' He parked in front of The Dog House. A group of backpackers waiting for their tour bus outside the hostel next door stared at Saffron as she got out. Suddenly Nick was crowding her, using his body to shield her bloody clothes from their curious eyes.

Saffron fished in her back pocket and found the keys. Nick took them off her and let them in. They walked through to the back room where the sleeping bag sat, still laced, on the bench, and he steered Saffron towards the stool.

He took the kit from her, sat it on the grooming table, pulled the top open and peered inside. 'Shit!' He stared at her intently while Saffron picked at the rip in her jeans. Then he said, 'Coffee?'

She nodded. 'I need to phone Heather and Mo.'

'In a minute,' Nick said, holding up one hand. 'Tell me what happened first. Then we'll decide how much of this you're going to dump on them.'

Satisfied that the jug contained enough water, he switched it on. 'The blood. Tell me about the blood?'

Saffron opened her mouth and exhaled loudly. 'There's so much to tell and most of it isn't very believable.'

'Try me.'

As Nick put the coffee mugs down he frowned at the kit and removed it to one of the cages.

'When I talked with the old woman she said that this — the bad things happening — wouldn't go on forever. Evidently, at some point, something else will take Tama's attention, and he'll forget about us.'

'Sounds good,' Nick said.

Saffron took a sip of coffee. 'The old woman said that if I got tired of waiting for that, then maybe I could help them in some way.'

'But they're all dead,' Nick pointed out, rubbing at his chin.

'I know. I told you it was crazy.'

Outside, there was the sound of a bus pulling up and laughter and shouts.

'Tell me more.'

'So I went back to Tama's Rock and found the old woman — I suppose she found me — and she told me how four babies went missing. They never found the bodies to lay them to rest. Evidently, that's very important.'

'It is to the Maori. Bodies — even body parts — must all

be returned to the family for burial. They believe there can be no rest for the dead person until then.'

'That's what the old woman said. So I volunteered.'

'But they're all dead,' Nick said again, with more emphasis.

She ignored him this time. 'Tama made the bones sing for me so I could find them, and then I sort of slipped between the ripples on the lake—' She stopped and looked at him. His face was expressionless. 'That wouldn't have been what happened, of course, but that's what it felt like. And when I came out the other side, I was still at Tama's Rock, except I think I'd gone back in time.'

A frown creased Nick's brow.

'Don't tell me it's not possible. I'm well aware of that. Anyway, the bones were babies, and—'

'I think I need a cigarette.' Nick stuck his hand in his shirt pocket, then stopped and hesitated.

'Oh, go on,' she said. 'Give me lung cancer as well as yourself, why don't you.'

Taking that as permission, Nick lit up. When she finished telling him what had happened, her shoulders sagged. 'The babies all turned to bone. They were dead all along.'

Nick tapped ash from his cigarette into a saucer. 'You can't change history.'

'I guess. But I think I pulled them through the Shining,' she could see the expression on Nick's face, but she carried on, 'because when I got back here — present time — I found the flax kit full of bones. So, do they lock me up and throw away the key?'

'If you repeat a word to anyone, then yes they will.'

Saffron smiled. 'Best I don't say too much to Heather and Mo then.'

'Tell me more about the blood,' Nick said.

'What are you so het up about the blood?'

'Because you're covered in it; because that neighbour of yours has seen you covered in it, and now those kids outside. And the police get suspicious of people who wander about covered in blood, particularly when your brother and sister have just died and there's something strange about their deaths.'

Saffron froze with her coffee halfway to her mouth. 'You think — you think I . . .' She shook her head in disbelief.

'*I* know you didn't do anything to Billy and Daphne and so do Heather and Mo, but some people might wonder. Where did the blood come from?'

'I told you. I gathered up the bodies.'

'They were bleeding?'

'That's what people do when they've just been murdered.' For an ex-war photographer, Nick was being incredibly dense.

He shook his head as if he couldn't take it all in. 'Who killed them? This Scarface and Co.?'

'Yes. They were Tama's enemies who had followed them from the coast. I saw them once before when I had a vision of the massacre. This time I was there.' She slipped off her stool. 'I need to phone Heather. She must be out of her mind.'

'To put it mildly.'

'So I've been gone for over twenty-four hours? Have they contacted the police?'

'No. Heather wanted to, and so did Mo, but Steve convinced her you were off doing something crazy with the coins and calling in the police might rock the boat. I think he was worried it might somehow affect their daughter. They don't know about any bones, and I suggest you leave it like that. I've only talked to Heather on the phone, but I gather your brother-in-law isn't too happy with you.'

'He thinks we should leave it all alone.'

'He has a point,' Nick said.

'I can't. I have to return these bones to Tama, or every last Delaney will be down the gurgler. What will I say to Heather and Mo? Where will I say I've been?'

He gave a helpless shrug. 'I don't know. That you had to get off by yourself for a while?'

'They'll never believe that. Delaneys don't do alone.'

'Then lie, but don't say anything about the bones. Or the blood.'

The throaty sound of the tour bus pulled away, and Nick glanced at his watch. 'I'm going to have to go. I have to meet one of the reporters, the Mayor's doing something. Will you be all right? I'll be there for the funeral.'

She nodded.

'You need to get cleaned up. I heard that neighbour of yours talking about the police.'

'I haven't done anything wrong,' she said.

'I know, but right now you look like an axe murderer.' He stood with his hands in his pockets, staring at her. 'I don't like leaving you alone.'

'Have you really been searching for me?'

He stared steadily at her. 'Yup.'

'Why? We've only just met, we're hardly more than strangers.'

'We could be more.' His voice was quiet and even. When she didn't reply he pulled a wry face. 'Does there have to be a reason?'

'There's a reason for everything.'

'So call me the Good Samaritan.'

'You don't look like a Good Samaritan.'

'What do I look like?' he asked quietly.

Average everything, she thought, but she couldn't be that unkind, not when he'd been looking for her. Her father had been a handsome man — short, but handsome. Billy, with their mother's height and his James Dean forelock, had been a potential heartbreaker, although he didn't have much time for romance. Too busy with the horses.

But Nick was average everything. 'You look like a man trying to do the right thing,' she said slowly.

'So why not a Good Samaritan?'

'Because of the camera, Nick, it changes people.'

He didn't have a reply for that. 'I—' he started.

She held her hand up. 'Don't, Nick. Not now, not today.' She knew what he wanted to say, she could see it in his eyes — but she didn't want to hear it, not today. Probably never, but definitely not today. Time for a change of subject. 'Mo said yesterday — sorry, Sunday — that Lucy was getting better. Did Heather say anything to you?'

'Not quite so good this morning, I believe.' He had his back to her as he took the ash-filled saucer over to the wash sink.

'How do you mean?'

'Seems she might have picked up a bug. You're more likely to catch a bug in hospital than anywhere else,' he added, as if this made it more acceptable.

'But she was getting better. Heather said so, and she's a nurse.' Saffron felt her voice give a dangerous wobble. Damn it all, if Heather said Lucy was getting better then she should.

Nick glanced at his watch. 'I don't want to leave you by yourself.' He ran his fingers through his hair. 'Janey will have my guts for garters if I don't turn up.' He looked at his watch again.

'I'll be all right.'

'But Delaney girls don't do alone, remember?'

She smiled. 'I'm getting the hang of it.' She put on her bravest grin. 'Get on out of here. You're polluting the air.'

'Come with me.'

She shook her head. She'd seen enough blood and death to last a lifetime. The last thing she needed was him dragging her around whatever accidents and tragedies he had lined up for the morning.

He didn't persist. 'Get yourself cleaned up before anyone else sees you.'

'OK.'

'See you later, then, petal.'

She stared at him, feeling a rush of conflicting emotions rise up through her, and one second before they exploded, she threw herself into his arms. Nick staggered back but held her. She pushed her face against his shoulder, letting his shirt absorb the tears that spilled over. No one *ever* called her petal. Not now, not since Daddy had died. They'd all been his little flowers.

When she felt his lips against her hair, his hands moulding the shape of her body, she hauled herself off him. Because he wasn't Daddy, he wasn't a Delaney. Before he got ideas. Before he thought she liked him.

Nick looked surprised. 'What did I do?'

'Nothing.'

He shrugged. 'Then I'll do it again some time.'

She smiled at him because it was better than crying. 'Get going, Nick. You're a health hazard. A person could get lung cancer from your shirt.'

'That bad, is it? I haven't been home yet this morning, and that's your fault.' He fished in his pocket and pulled out a business card. 'You call me if you need anything. Or — anything. OK?'

Chapter Twenty-five

NICK WAS HEADING back to his flat when he saw Andy's car outside Big Wal's. He parked in the only available space and walked quickly across the road as grey clouds scudded overhead.

Big Wal wiped the counter in front of him and said, 'You coming here for breakfast, too, now? Might as well sleep here.'

'Naah, I'll get something later.' He yawned. 'Long night. I had a couple of jobs to do this morning.'

Nick had downloaded his pictures into the system and Janey would be captioning them now. He was on his way home, with the funeral only an hour away.

Andy looked him up and down critically. 'You look as if you've had a rough night.'

Nick shook his head. 'Believe it. Aren't you going out to the dig today?'

'Thought I'd go to the funeral of that Delaney boy. Somehow I feel should, especially as we found him.'

'Did you know it's a double funeral now?'

Andy stared at him.

'One of the sisters was killed Sunday morning.'

Andy whistled. 'How'd she die?'

Big Wal walked back towards the counter carrying a box of Coke, his face screwed into a worried frown. Nick guessed he was following the conversation.

'Went out to a garden shed and something fell off a shelf. Hit her on the head.'

Big Wal stuck a lethal-looking knife through the top of the carton and cut around the four sides until the top separated. He opened the door of the drinks cabinet, squatted beside it with a grunt and began to slide bottles into the lowest rack.

Nick stared down at Big Wal until he got a reaction, then raised his eyebrows questioningly when the other man looked up at him. 'What do you make of that?'

Big Wal chuckled grimly. 'Tama's showing his muscle.' He heaved himself back to his feet.

'But the sister didn't have anything to do with the coins being taken.'

'Don't matter.' Big Wal ran his thumb over the edge of the knife he'd used to open the box. He pulled a steel out of one of the drawers and began to sharpen the knife with long steady draws. 'You ever seen a shotgun in action?'

Nick nodded slowly.

Big Wal continued, perhaps for Andy's benefit. 'A flock of quail take off in front of you and you snap the gun into your shoulder and fire. You bring down a lot more than the bird you were aiming at. I think Tama's a bit the same.' He paused, then added, 'I'm glad it wasn't that other one. Saffron.'

'Yeah. Me too.'

Nick remembered how he'd felt on Sunday night when

the Delaney sisters had phoned to ask if Saffron was with him. He wondered why they might think that. Had she said something to them about him? About how she felt? He'd got the idea that if he were the last biscuit in the pack, she'd have bread, thanks.

When the sisters said she wasn't answering her mobile, or the phone at home or The Dog House, he'd thought then that Saffron was dead, and he'd wished he'd done a whole lot more. He'd wished he hadn't gone off and left her on her own. But he'd done it again this morning. Life didn't grind to a halt just because the woman you fancied was having a few troubles.

It had been two years since Fay had died and he hadn't really looked at another woman since. Well, he'd looked — men always look — but it hadn't meant anything, just male hormones rearing up and smiling. But Saffron, with her Jean Harlow mouth and enough trouble on her shoulders to stop a Sherpa in his tracks, had . . . ahh, stuff it, he didn't know what she'd done. He just knew he didn't want her dead, and last night had scared the shit out of him.

'It has to be a coincidence, doesn't it? The sister dying?' Andy was tucking into his second burger. A slice of tomato escaped, and he retrieved it from the counter and stuck it back in.

Nick slapped some money on the counter. 'I'll have a Coke,' he said to Wal. 'I don't know.'

'That family is going to have nothing but bad luck from now on,' Big Wal said.

'That's what Saffron says too.'

'So she's starting to listen, is she?'

'More than listen. She . . .' Nick hesitated. He wasn't

going to tell Andy that Saffron had been talking to an old woman who had to be at least two hundred years old. Big Wal would understand; Andy wouldn't. 'She's got a hunch that it's something to do with some bones, and she's found them. Going to take them—'

'Bones?' Big Wal said sharply.

Approximately a millisecond after which Andy echoed, 'Bones! Have you seen them?'

Typical, thought Nick. Tell Andy that Daphne's been killed and he almost falls asleep with boredom. Tell him about the bones and he's drooling like a college boy with his first *Playboy* centrefold. 'She's got them at The Dog House. Seems she has to return them to someone after the funeral.'

'She shouldn't get involved in bones,' Big Wal said. 'Best to stay well clear of things like that. Some things it's best to leave alone.'

'I'm with you, but you try convincing her of that.'

'Course it's different for her,' Wal continued. 'She's trying to save the others. But she'll get hurt if she's not careful.'

'Had you heard anything about bones?'

Big Wal nodded. 'Tama's people never found all the babies. But I don't know where she would have heard about it. Not many people know. It's private.'

'So these bones she has found are definitely old?' Andy asked.

'Seems so,' Nick said.

'She can't hang onto something like that, it's against the law. If the bones are pre-1900 they fall under the Historic Places Act. She's legally obligated to contact not just the police, but the Historic Places Trust, the iwi liaison officer, the—'

'I don't think she's planning on hanging onto them. She wants to get rid of them as fast as she can.'

'She could give them to me,' Andy said quickly. 'If these bones are tied to a well-known legend they could have historic value, despite being only a couple of hundred years old.'

'It's not a legend,' Big Wal snapped.

Andy ignored him. 'I'll make the necessary contacts. The first thing the Historic Places Trust will do is call in someone like me to assess the site.'

Big Wal scowled. 'It's nothing to do with the law.'

'She won't give them to you,' said Nick.

'Digging up historically significant bones is illegal. We get special dispensation, but the average person can't.'

'She's not hanging on to them,' Nick said, slightly louder this time. 'She's as anxious as the next person to get shot of them.'

'If anyone reported her—'

Nick eyeballed Andy. 'Who's going to do that?'

'I'm just saying. I didn't mean to imply I was, but I know the legal ramifications of digging up bones. It's what I do for a living.'

'She'll do the right thing,' Big Wal said stubbornly. 'I'm sure of that. But it doesn't alter the fact that it's best not to get mixed up with things like that.'

'And if she doesn't, Tama will soon change her mind,' Huamai added. 'Pity Tama don't have a go at some of these cunts who stole our land.'

'But you're starting to get compensation for that.' Nick stepped quickly and gratefully into the change of subject.

'Don't matter,' Huamai said. 'It was the land we wanted.

The trouble with you Pakeha—'

This conversation wasn't looking any safer. Nick liked stopping off each evening and chewing the fat with these two, but the alienation of Maori land, and how it should be resolved, depended on which side of the fence you were sitting.

'That'll do, boy,' Big Wal said. 'It's not Nick's fault, and I don't imagine he comes here to listen to you whinge about things.'

'I'm just letting him know that the history they taught him at school ain't the whole history. It's Pakeha history.'

'I hear what you're saying,' Big Wal said. 'But if Tama Ariki was going to get involved in our land claims, I figure he would have done it before now.'

'Huamai has a point, though,' Nick said. 'Why carry on a vendetta with some boy still growing bum fluff on his chin when there are still serious grievances to settle about land?'

Big Wal handed the knife to Huamai. 'Maybe he will one day.'

'Damn right,' Huamai said gleefully, and travelled the length of the counter in a series of lunges, swishing the knife through the air like a swashbuckler's sword.

'How about you go and cut some onions before you slice my ruddy ear off,' Big Wal said, hastily backing out of the way. 'We're getting low.'

'Low, my foot,' Huamai muttered, but he retreated to the back where Nick could hear him slamming drawers and cupboards.

A white Capri pulled into the kerb and the driver came across to order two burgers. Big Wal slapped four half-buns on the grill, then removed two patties from the fridge. 'He gets all fired up about land rights,' Big Wal said over his shoulder, flattening the patties with a fish slice.

Nick finished his Coke. 'Don't you?'

'I'm running a business. People — Pakeha, anyway — don't want to hear about land issues. It'll get sorted in the end. We've waited a hundred and fifty years, what's a few more?'

'You're a philosopher, Wal.'

'Naah, I'm a realist.' Big Wal placed two pieces of lettuce in front of him and topped each one with tomato, cheese, beetroot and mayonnaise.

Nick gave Andy a rueful smile. From being on opposite sides of the fence about the bones, they were back on the same side. Damned if Maori didn't make you feel guilty about things when you hadn't done a thing. He wasn't responsible for what the Crown did more than a century ago, so why did Maori always make him feel as if he was? They should put it behind them. Get on with things.

'But I'm worried about that girl,' Big Wal continued. 'She's getting mixed up in things she'd be better keeping clear of.' He handed the burgers to the Capri driver, who'd been following the conversation with interest.

'Time for a drink before the funeral?' Andy asked.

Nick sniffed at his armpit. 'I think I'd better go and have a shower and change. This shirt is one step away from attracting flies.' He wondered if he should go and see Saffron, check she was all right. He knew he probably hadn't said the right things about Daphne this morning: he was clumsy in those situations. And when someone died, words didn't mean diddly squat.

CHAPTER TWENTY-SIX

HEAVY GREY CLOUDS sulked in the sky, and thunder rumbled way off to the south, but the rain that had threatened all morning didn't come. Even the heavens refuse to cry for Billy, Saffron thought, glancing up as she and Heather got out of Steve's Capri at the cemetery. Ahead, two black hearses with flower-covered caskets were parked near two graves. The Delaney girls had decided to bury Billy and Daphne side by side.

Saffron looked around at the rows of squat, grey headstones set into concrete strips, most of them emblazoned with bright posies of artificial flowers and gaudy windmills that spun in the wind. She walked four rows over to where Lucky Del lay. A yellow silk flower had fallen out of its vase, its petals damp and dirty in the grass. He'd been wearing bright yellow silks the day he won the Melbourne Cup. She picked up the flower, wiped at it and poked it back into the vase. Today, she would give Billy and Daphne back into Daddy's care.

'What's happening to us all?' she whispered, but for once Lucky Del had nothing to say.

She wandered back to where the empty graves lay raw

and open like wounds in the earth. A grass mat covered the excavated soil, as if the mound was trying to pretend it was something more cheerful. Would a third grave be following? A fourth? How many before Tama said enough?

Room Four from Tauhara Primary School stood in a silent group. Mr Petrie and a teacher Saffron didn't know held several large black umbrellas, ready for instant climate control. She wondered if they'd been chosen for their colour. One of the boys had pulled two windmills off a grave and was racing up and down the drive pretending he was an aeroplane. Some of the girls were crying.

Billy's old Boy Scout leaders were there, and his teacher from the fifth form and the college rugby coach. There were probably other people who knew Billy, but she didn't recognize them. He'd stopped bringing his friends home right about the time he'd left school.

A young man with half a dozen rings through one ear and another through his nose ambled up and mumbled something at her. Saffron nodded her head and thanked him. She assumed they were words of condolence.

Aunt Sophia passed her as she walked over to Lucky Del's grave.

'Billy *and* Daph? What's happening?' she asked, dabbing at her cheeks with a crumpled handkerchief.

Saffron gave a helpless shrug. 'I don't know.'

'He was always unreliable,' Aunt Sophia said, jerking her head at Lucky Del's grave, as if she believed he was somehow responsible. 'Billy was the same.' Aunt Sophia removed her glasses so she could blot her eyes.

Mo and Steve, holding hands, stood close to the hearses on

the drive. Beside them, Heather, tall and pencil-slim in black, looked so alone. As Saffron walked back to them, Heather caught her eye and smiled. She looked worn out. Saffron knew she hadn't explained her absence very well. Heather had forgiven her regardless, but not Mo, not yet.

The minister walked over to the open graves. Four teachers from Tauhara Primary were pall-bearers for Daphne. There was momentary confusion when Saffron realized she hadn't organized pall-bearers for Billy and Uncle Frank was the only person who stepped forward; then Gus from the TAB, Nick and a bearded man Saffron didn't know came to the rescue. Gus had been at Lucky Del's funeral too, but there'd been no shortage of pall-bearers then.

Big Wal had come, dressed in a suit and tie so that Saffron almost didn't recognize him without his white apron.

She fell into step with Heather and Mo and they walked arm in arm behind the caskets. Mo's face was half-hidden behind a veil attached to a black hat. Steve walked alone behind them. Mount Tauhara rose in the distance, mist-covered, framed between two trees.

The minister began to speak. It had been easy for him to speak about Daphne at the service, and when he had asked if anyone wanted to say anything, it had seemed that the entire teaching staff of Tauhara Primary plus the cleaners and the groundsman needed to share their memories. When he'd come to Billy, he'd played safe and talked about his younger days. The rugby coach said Billy had been a talented player; one of the Scout leaders said he had shown initiative.

Saffron could see Gilbert in an overcoat with a closed umbrella clenched in his hand. He stood by Daphne's grave with his back to Billy and her, and she wondered if it was deliberate.

The pall-bearers positioned the two caskets over the graves and stepped back. Nick gave her shoulder a quick rub as he walked to the back of the crowd. He seemed to fade as he moved away, as if she was looking at him through a net curtain that rippled in the breeze. At first she thought it was her sleep-deprived brain smudging reality, but then she realized Nick was stepping into a mist. A tendril of mist slid along the ground between Uncle Frank's ankles. She noticed he was wearing one black and one pale green sock. Aunt Sophia wouldn't be happy if she noticed.

Saffron glanced at Mo. 'Mist,' she whispered, and inclined her head.

Mo looked at her blankly from behind her veil. 'What?'

She glanced at Heather, but she too seemed unaware of anything strange. Saffron swallowed, and hoped this was some local weather condition. 'Ashes to ashes, dust to dust.'

Saffron watched the mist ease in closer, glanced at the solemn faces around the two graves. No one was looking at the mist. Could no one see it but her?

The mist drew closer and closer, easing over the ground, twisting around ankles, slipping between legs, moving through the crowd like a curious sightseer. A tendril rose up, and it was like watching a time exposure of a plant growing. It curled almost lovingly around Aunt Sophia's head, then passed the minister, who tightened his grip on his prayer book. Aunt Sophia patted her hair as if a breeze had ruffled it.

Big Wal was staring at the mist with his head raised, almost cocked, his nostrils widening, as if his senses were straining to decipher some message. He must have felt Saffron's gaze because he glanced across at her briefly.

And when the mist had gathered at Billy's grave, Tama Ariki walked out of it, but it seemed no one else could see him. Aunt Sophia dabbed gently at her eyes, and the minister talked about Billy's final rest and the forgiveness of Christ. Tama Ariki didn't look forgiving. Even though she had never seen him, Saffron knew it was him. He wore a fur cloak that looked suspiciously like dog hair, with a long white feather in his topknot; and she thought of the white heron. He carried a mere, and the business end was stained black.

She watched as Tama stalked around Billy's grave, flicking each leg up behind him. He gestured and jabbed with the mere, rolled his eyes and shot out his tongue. Then he spat down into the grave, and Saffron winced as the spittle ran down the side of Billy's casket.

Tama turned and walked towards her. She wanted to scream, run, hide. Instead, she stood there beside her sisters while the minister droned on, her eyes growing bigger and bigger. This isn't happening, she told herself. Not really. I'm hallucinating. No one else can see him. This isn't real — not real — not real — not—

Tama Ariki stood in front of her. Her gaze fell and she felt as if she might die if she looked into his eyes. Instead she stared into the cloak he wore, and waited.

Slowly, he reached out one hand, but he didn't touch her. His fingers hovered a few centimetres away, and suddenly it wasn't a brown dog-hair cloak she was staring at but frightened, screaming women and blood on the sand. She cried out and fell back.

People stared at her, and a woman she didn't know crossed herself. Mo grabbed her arm roughly and pulled her back into line.

Heather slipped her arm through hers. 'Hang on, Saffy,' she whispered urgently. 'We're almost there.'

Nick moved forward, hesitant, unsure of what to do.

But it was Big Wal who stepped between her and Mo and enfolded both her hands in his.

The minister paused and glanced over, reassured himself she wasn't about to throw herself into the grave, and continued.

Big Wal squeezed her hands.

'I saw . . .' She stopped.

'I know what you saw, girl. Look to your brother and sister in the ground there. Hold to it. Sometimes it's best not to look too closely at what the shadows reveal. Look to what you know.'

She nodded, looking into his face with desperation, and for the first time seeing a kind man, a decent man.

He squeezed her hands again, 'Look to your brother and sister,' and he moved back. Heather looked confused but gripped her arm with steel fingers. Saffron was grateful.

After the final prayer people began to leave, many of them wandering away through the rows of graves looking for people they had buried themselves. Tama left, too, stalking back into the mist. She tried to follow Big Wal's advice, but Tama Ariki was a hard man to ignore. Her last view of him, from the corner of her eye, was just his face, eyes rolled, whites showing, staring straight at her. She flinched and half-raised a hand to shield herself, but he was gone.

Saffron's hands began to tremble so she crossed her arms and tucked them away. Heather's fingers softened and Saffron breathed again. Gilbert walked over to Steve and spoke to him. Saffron could feel their eyes on her every now and then, like punctuation marks, as the three sisters stood beside the open graves. It was time to go. Time to say their final goodbyes.

'What on earth did you think you were doing?' Mo demanded.

'I saw . . .' But what could she say? That Tama Ariki had been standing within a metre of Mo? Mo was still in the lucky position of actually believing the evidence of her own eyes.

'You saw what? God?'

Saffron shook her head. 'Not God. I don't think so, anyway.'

'You made a spectacle of yourself. You looked as if you were going to throw yourself in.'

'It's a funeral. You're allowed to act strangely at funerals.'

'We're all acting a little strangely today,' Heather said. Saffron suspected she was referring to Mo's behaviour as much as hers.

Mo thought so too. 'Do you mean me? Well, I'm sorry if I can't be quite as forgiving as you. But I thought she was dead. What else was I supposed to think? With Billy and Daphne . . .'

'But she's not,' Heather said quietly. 'She's here with us.'

'You could have phoned, Saf.' Mo raised the veil on her hat.

'I did as soon as I could.'

Mo shook her head. 'I thought you were dead. I was—'

248

'I'm sorry. I didn't mean to scare you. But I had to do something.'

During the short ride to the cemetery they'd been through every twist and turn of this conversation. Saffron felt as if she'd sullied their final moments with Billy and Daphne. 'So you said. Couldn't you have at least phoned and told us you were going away for a while?'

Going away. She hid the burst of hysterical laughter that bubbled up her throat in a cough. 'I should have, I know. I just didn't think.'

Steve wandered over. He stared into the open graves for a moment, as if he needed to organize his thoughts, and then said, 'Your neighbour has been talking to me.'

Saffron waited.

'He says you were up to something last night.' Steve turned his gaze on to Saffron, and she could see something in his eyes she'd never seen in the four years he'd been married to Mo. For the first time, Steve looked as if he'd just discovered a Delaney girl he didn't much like.

'Gilbert wants to try minding his own business,' Saffron said.

Mo was staring at her now. 'Is this something to do with Billy and Daphne?'

'Gilbert said you were covered in blood,' Steve said quietly. His eyes moved between Saffron and Mo.

'What?' Mo turned to her husband, but when all he did was shrug, she swung back and grabbed Saffron's arm. 'Is it true?' Mo demanded.

'Saffron?' Steve prompted.

She took a deep breath. 'I did have blood on me,' she

admitted. 'Do we have to have this conversation now?'

'Yes! Yes we do! Why did you have blood on you?' Mo asked. Her fingers dug in — there would be bruises later. When Saffron didn't say anything, little by little Mo's fingers loosened their grip. 'I have a right to know, Saf. They were my brother and sister too. But you're not going to tell us, are you?'

Mo took a step backward. She stared at Saffron with bleak, distant eyes. Saffron felt the chill and lowered her gaze. Mo was right: she wasn't going to say anything. Not to Mo, who'd miscarried twice before she had Lucy. Mo, whose own little girl lay in hospital with a broken arm, which now — surprise, surprise — was infected. Mo, who had confirmed only last week that she was pregnant again. Mo didn't need to hear about dead babies. She might tell Heather one day. But not Mo. Never.

'Or is this something else that you can't tell me?'

'I'd explain if I could. I'm trying to make things right. But it's difficult.'

'So you keep saying.'

'You're still meddling in this business.' Steve slipped an arm around his wife. 'We asked you to leave it alone, Saf.'

'I can't. It has to be made — right, before we can leave it.' Saffron tried to look into Mo's eyes but they were in shadow. 'There was a time when you would have accepted my word. Trusted me.' Heather understood. Why couldn't Mo?

'That was before her daughter was run over and two of her family killed,' Steve said. 'We don't feel very trusting right at this moment. I asked you to leave it alone and let me handle it. But you didn't.'

Saffron bit at her lip for a moment. 'I can't. I'm sorry.'

'If anything happens to Lucy,' Steve warned, 'we're going to hold you personally responsible.'

'How did you get blood on you?'

She shrugged.

'Whose blood was it, Saf?'

'I'm not sure.'

Mo stared at her as if she thought Saf was crazy. 'How can you not know?'

'Gilbert said you were covered in blood. Said you looked like you'd slaughtered a mob of sheep,' Steve added.

Saffron stared across the row of headstones at Gilbert who was now talking to the stranger who had stepped in as Billy's fourth pall-bearer. Somebody said he was an archaeologist.

Mo gripped her arm again. 'This has gone far enough, Saf. You stop whatever you're doing. You hear me? I don't like this. I'm scared.'

'So am I,' Saffron said. 'But you've got to understand. I'm doing it for you. For you and Heather and Lucy.'

CHAPTER TWENTY-SEVEN

THE DELANEY GIRL was stuck between a tall, blonde woman who had to be another sister and a man who'd be picking her nose if he jabbed his forefinger any closer to her face. She kept looking from one to the other as if she was watching a game of table tennis. Big Wal went over and tapped her on the arm.

'Let's go and visit your father,' he said. 'He's here, isn't he?'

Saffron looked at him gratefully.

The man glared at him, and Big Wal could feel his eyes upon their backs as he and Saffron walked across to Lucky Del's grave.

'You looked as if you were being interrogated.'

'I was. Steve — that's my brother-in-law — is convinced I'm making things worse. And now Mo thinks that too.'

'Sometimes you just have to do what you think is right, regardless.'

'But what if I'm not? What if I *am* making things worse?' She clasped her hands together and said, 'I don't want to be coming back to this place. Not ever again.'

'Sometimes it's good to come to where the ancestors lie and take advice from the old ones who have gone before.'

'Only advice my dad is likely to give is who to back in the sixth at Avondale.'

Big Wal smiled. 'I knew your father. Did I tell you?'

'No.'

'He used to come by every now and then, after he'd stopped riding, of course. Get a burger, have a yarn. He used to talk about you kids sometimes. I liked him.'

Saffron slipped her arm through Big Wal's. His assault upon Billy was starting to look like guidance from a caring teacher in comparison with Tama. 'When he died, some people acted as if it would be better for us kids, as if they didn't think he was much of a father. But we had fun. We laughed a lot.'

'You got good memories of him. That's the important thing.'

He reached across his stomach and gave her hand a pat. She was a brave little bugger going in to bat against Tama. He'd struck out tougher opposition than this.

'Did you see Tama in the mist?' she asked hesitantly.

He shook his head. 'I guessed he was about, but I didn't see him.' And he was perfectly happy for that state of affairs to continue. If he was lucky the winds of this disaster would do no more than whistle around the edges of his life. The Delaneys, though, were heading towards a Force Ten gale, with this slip of a girl at the helm.

'Do you know the old woman?'

Big Wal snorted. 'I know lots of old women, not all of them female.'

'This is a special one. She has a moko on her chin and lips.'

Big Wal stared at her. The night before, he'd dreamt about the old ones. There'd been a kuia with a moko.

'You know her?' Saffron said.

He wet his lips. 'She came to me in a dream, but her message didn't make any sense.'

'What did she say?' The girl had pulled away from him and was watching him intently, rubbing her hands up and down her arms.

'She said you should listen more closely to your elders. I thought she meant me, but perhaps she meant you. Then she said the strangest thing. I couldn't work it out. She said, "Patupaiarehe don't eat flesh."' He shook his head. 'It didn't make any sense to me.' He couldn't help a fleeting smile. 'I wondered if she was telling me I had to start selling vegetarian burgers or something.'

'Patu-pai . . .' The girl stumbled over the word. 'Fairies,' she finally got out. 'Someone thought I was a fairy.'

He didn't want to know who. He suddenly didn't like this conversation. Patupaiarehe belonged to the spirit world. They were tapu, and best left alone.

'Patupaiarehe don't eat flesh. That's what she wants you to know.' The old woman had spoken through him; it was his duty to hand the message on to where it belonged.

The girl shrugged as if it was no big deal.

'I must have heard her wrong. I thought she said they did.'

'What does it mean?' He could have kicked himself for asking.

'I was trying to think myself into something scary. I guess I just thought it was more scary if fairies ate people. I thought that was what she said.'

He tried not to flinch. Where had this girl been that she would want to pretend to be a patupaiarehe? 'No,' he said, his voice colourless as he held his emotions in check, 'patupaiarehe don't eat people.' He supposed in a loose way he was this girl's elder, and Lucky Del was gone. Someone needed to stand in. 'Patupaiarehe — fairies — are tapu which means they must eat their food raw,' he explained. 'They're frightened of cooked food. But they don't eat people.'

'Frightened of cooked food! Well, I'm glad I didn't think *that!* That's not very scary.'

He tried to smile, but it took a long time to reach his lips. What it was to be young and ignorant.

'The old woman said part of the reason Tama chose me to find the bones is because I'm not Maori. Hine tried to get the bones, and the demons chased her. He thought that as I'm not Maori perhaps some of the things won't affect me. I'm not sure he's got that right. Most of all, I think it's just that our paths crossed, because of Billy.'

'Tama has crossed paths with a lot of folk over the centuries. He must have seen something in you.'

'Maybe he just thought I'm expendable.'

He would like to have refuted that, but it struck him as being exactly how Tama might have viewed her, so he said nothing.

'He's going to let the Delaneys off the hook if I can get the bones back to him.'

'That's good.' Big Wal hoped it was good. Tama had been

a warrior, a master tactician. If he was in her shoes, he'd be wondering if Tama would keep his word. Not that Tama Ariki was dishonourable — on the contrary — but his priority would be, and always had been, his people. If lying to some young, modern-day Pakeha woman were needed, Tama would do it without hesitation.

'Excellent,' Big Wal said. 'Have you left a token for Tama?' He'd done so himself. Since Friday night, every morning before he opened the burger bar, he went down to the lakefront and left a gold coin. He would do that until this was over.

'No.' She looked surprised, as if she hadn't thought of that.

He could see her sisters beckoning for her and pointed them out.

'I'd better go,' she said, sounding as if she was off to the dentist.

'You leave something for Tama Ariki,' he called. He watched her walk away and decided he'd shout her a free burger or two if she came back to the shop. Her black skirt flapped around skinny legs and, although she was tall, she was starting to look as if she would blow away in the first puff of wind. And if he guessed right, Tama was puffing up his cheeks for the big blow.

Nick and Andy, that university fella who dug up bones for a living, wandered up.

'Is she coping?' Nick asked.

Big Wal wobbled his hand in a maybe gesture. 'Family's giving her a hard time.'

'She went missing, scared the crap out of everyone,' Nick said.

You most of all, thought Big Wal, if he was correctly interpreting the way Nick watched the girl. He looked on enviously while Nick lit up. He'd given up over ten years ago and he still missed the ruddy things.

'Is Tama finished?' Nick asked.

Big Wal shrugged. 'Your guess is as good as mine.' It wasn't, of course. He understood Tama in a way the Pakeha never could, but he had no intention of trying to second-guess Tama Ariki.

He looked across at Saffron and her sisters. From this distance they looked identical in their black. He was growing to like the Delaney girls and understand why Lucky Del had been so proud of them.

Saffron was heading towards the car park. Nick watched as Big Wal grabbed her by the arm and steered her over to the tap near the exit. He ran his hands under the water, then flicked a little over himself. Nick could see him explaining to Saffron to do the same. She did, looking a little nonplussed, and Nick felt a relief out of all proportion. Saffron Delaney had probably seen all the water she wanted to for a while, but if dabbling her hands like this freed her from any malign influence at the cemetery then it was a good idea. The Delaneys couldn't afford to take on any more trouble.

Nick stood under the trees for a moment, then self-consciously walked back and washed his own hands. It was a custom from a culture not his own, but right at this moment it fitted like a flak-jacket in battle. A man couldn't be too careful at a time like this. He'd been to war. He knew the dangers of friendly fire.

Mo and her husband walked straight past Saffron and Big Wal without pause. Heather wandered behind them and was collared by Big Wal and taken to the tap. Mo's neck and shoulders were stiff and unyielding, her head as still as a catwalk model's. There had clearly been words. Saffron watched them walk away as she waited for Heather.

Big Wal touched her arm, and they returned to the car park together.

'Are you coming with us?' Mo called. There was no invitation in her voice. The husband was already in the Capri, the engine ticking over.

'I might walk,' Saffron said, 'but Heather will come.' She turned her sister towards Mo.

'I'll go with you,' Heather said, digging her toes in.

'You can't, petal. We've been through all this. You go with Mo. Just for another day or two, just until we know.'

Mo shrugged and opened the car door. 'Come on, then,' she said to Heather. But then she stopped, hands resting on the top of the door, staring with hollow, haunted eyes across the cemetery towards the graves they'd just left. The hard lines of her body softened, and she turned back and walked across to Saffron. Blue eyes searched blue eyes. Questions, answers, all there. Acceptance? Maybe. But it didn't matter. Nick felt the loss of something that, as an only child, he had never owned. The sisters slipped arms around each other. Heather smiled, her arms going out to encircle them both, her lips touching the top of each head.

The husband was scowling and tapping the wheel rapidly with his fingers.

Heather and Mo got in, and the Capri purred off.

Nick called across to Saffron, 'Want a lift?'

'Please.' Nick quickly grabbed his camera bag from the front seat and put it in the back.

A man leaning against a black Commodore stood with his mouth slightly open. 'Hey,' he called to Nick. 'Didn't I see you at that accident with the little girl?'

'Lucy's accident?' Saffron had a strange expression on her face, as if she'd just discovered he skinned kittens as a hobby. 'What were you doing there?'

He suddenly realized the expressionless tone of her voice was dangerous.

'Were you taking photos?'

'The accident in town? Yes, why?'

'That little girl is Lucy, my niece. Thank God, Mo's gone — what do you think she's going to think when she hears that you took a photo of her baby about to be splattered all over the road.'

'But they didn't print it!' Nick protested. 'And I didn't know Little Miss Pink Shoes was your niece.'

'Little Miss Pink Shoes!'

'That's what I called her,' he said lamely. 'She had pink shoes.'

'I know what she was wearing,' Saffron said through gritted teeth. 'I bought them for her. They're ruined now.'

Was he supposed to say he was sorry? He wanted to light his cigarette but didn't like to move.

'Covered in blood.'

'Right,' he said. What the hell did he mean by that?

'Can you see the blood on her shoes in the photo?'

Was he supposed to answer that? 'I don't think so.' What

259

did she *want,* damn it? It hadn't been printed.

'And would it have made a difference if you'd known Lucy was my niece?'

'Of course,' he said.

It wouldn't have. At least he didn't lie to himself about that. He saw himself racing in to the restaurant with his camera snapping like crazy and Fay bleeding out in front of him. He wanted to tell Saffron about that and point out that her niece just had a broken arm and a little concussion — his wife had had her arm blown off.

'And I bet you were one of the ghouls who were there when Daddy died.'

He wanted to say, yeah, I was there, because he was getting pissed off with her attitude. He didn't. He loved her, even if he wanted to throttle her. Then his face froze. Where the hell had that thought come from?

She waited, as if she believed he might answer, then, with a snort, walked away from him.

How the hell was he supposed to know that Little Miss Pink Shoes was the Delaneys' pride and joy?

Chapter Twenty-eight

Mo, Steve and Andy stood outside The Dog House watching the street. Heather sat in the back of the Capri and stared resolutely in the opposite direction.

'Maybe we shouldn't be doing this,' Mo said, glancing at the back of Heather's head. She had a key in her hand, clutching it tight in her fist so that her knuckles showed white.

'Yes, we should,' Steve said firmly. He put his hands on Mo's shoulders and gently turned her to face the door. He'd been through it a dozen times. 'You agreed. What your sister is doing is hurting Lucy. She was mending well, the doctor said so. *Heather* said so.' He watched as Mo's face relaxed a little: she trusted Heather's judgement over a doctor's any day of the week. It was just a shame he hadn't been able to get Heather on-side for this. 'Saffron gets involved again, and Lucy picks up another bug. How many times can we let that happen before the doctors have to take her arm off?'

Mo didn't say anything, but her mouth opened and her face crumpled. That had been a low blow. 'Let's get on with this,' Andy said. 'I don't feel comfortable about breaking in.'

'Technically, we're not breaking in,' Steve said.

'I suppose not,' Andy said. 'Nick told me she's got some bones secreted away here. And if what that neighbour was saying at the funeral is right, she's done something at the very least illegal and at worst criminal.'

'Saf wouldn't do anything criminal,' Mo said.

'Since she got involved with this Tama business, who knows what your sister's crazy enough to do.'

'Don't say things like that.'

Steve could tell Mo wasn't far off crying. He kissed the top of her head. 'Give me the key, babe. Let me do it.'

Mo shook her fist a couple of times as if she was knocking on an invisible wall, then unclenched her fingers and stared into Steve's face as he took the key from her.

He poked the key into the lock and opened the door. All the Delaney girls had a key to The Dog House, same as the cars. He'd tried to put his foot down in the early days of their marriage and tell Mo she wasn't to give all her sisters a key to their home and their car. 'Just in case,' Mo had said. 'In case of what?' he had asked her. She just shrugged and repeated, 'You know, just in case they need it.' He'd said no, but he had a sneaking suspicion she'd done it anyway. Mo had to remember she had her own family now — it was time to loosen the ties with the girls.

He'd already searched the house on Lake Terrace, although he hadn't told Mo. There'd been nothing of interest there, so if Saffron had anything she shouldn't it would be at The Dog House.

They entered quickly and walked through into the back room.

'I don't think I've ever been here without Saf,' Mo said. Steve didn't like the tone of her voice.

It was an easy place to search. Quickly and methodically, he and Andy went through everything. Mo simply stood, gazing around her as if she'd never seen the place before. It took only minutes.

'There's nothing here,' Andy said, his voice laced with disappointment as he ran his fingers through his hair.

Damn!, thought Steve. He'd been sure they'd find something. There had to be some substance in what that neighbour said, especially with what Andy had heard at the burger bar. They returned to reception. There wasn't room out there to swing a cat, let alone hide anything.

'We'd better get out of here,' Andy said, looking anxiously out the window.

'I guess,' Steve said. As he pulled open the street door, his eyes wandered over the window display. A large furry toy pup sat in a silver cup, its front paws resting on the lip. Last week, the cup had been filled with big yellow flowers. The Harrison Challenge Cup, almost half a metre tall and lusted over by half the dog world — the New Zealand half, anyway. One of Saffron's clients had won it and enjoyed it being on public display.

'Was that how the window was on Friday night when I picked you and Lucy up?' he asked Mo.

She studied it, her head on one side. 'I think she had daisies in the cup last week.'

Steve scowled at the toy puppy, squatting as if it was doing its business in the cup, as his thoughts completed a circuit. He'd been married to Mo for four years and considered himself an expert on the Delaney girls. Mo had hardly been home since Saturday morning when Lucy had been hurt. Cups of half-drunk coffee left rings on the kitchen bench, three days' worth of dirty clothes draped their bed, and the bathroom had a musty smell of damp towels. He wasn't complaining. But there was no way that Saffron would have redone the window display when Billy and Daphne had just died. No way. Right from Friday night, some time after he'd picked up Mo and Lucy, Saffron had been up to her eyeballs in this Tama business. So no way would she have done it — unless it had something to do with what was happening.

He walked over and pulled the toy puppy out of the cup.

'Well, hel-lo, puppy,' he said with a smile. 'You've done little do-dos.'

'What's in there?' Andy asked.

'What you're looking for, mate,' Steve said. 'The bones.'

'Is there blood on them?'

'Clean as a whistle.' The stuffed puppy dangled from Steve's hand by a back leg.

'So where did the blood come from?'

'I don't know. Look, do you want these bones or not?'

Andy licked his lips. 'Yes. I want them.'

'What are you going to do with them?' Mo asked.

'I'm not sure exactly. I'll take them out to the dig. They won't attract any attention out there, until I can determine exactly where they came from.'

'Why not pretend you dug them up out there? Nobody would be any the wiser,' Steve said.

Andy looked shocked. 'I can't do that. They'd lose all their scientific validity if I fabricated their source.'

Steve didn't understand. It was OK to steal them from Saffron, but it wasn't OK to disguise where he'd found them?

Andy pulled a black plastic rubbish sack out of his pocket. 'Will they fit in this?'

'Heaps of room.'

Andy glanced at Steve. 'I'll hold the bag and you tip them in.'

'Sorry, mate. You're going to have to do this bit yourself.'

Andy frowned.

'I've seen some of the people Tama has dealt to. I've no intention of getting into his bad books.' Steve tossed the stuffed toy into the window and stuck his hands in his pockets.

Andy didn't look as if he was having any such concern. 'They're just bones, that story Big Wal tells is a legend.'

'Right.' Steve kept his hands in his pockets.

Andy gave him an irritated look, then placed the rubbish sack over the cup and tipped it onto its side. Something about the bones jostling inside gave Steve a bad feeling. Mo was edging towards the door. He kept his eyes on the toys and ribbons in the window, not wanting to look at the bones.

Andy peered into the sack, smiling. For one awful moment, Steve thought Andy was going to run his fingers through them. Then the archaeologist gave him a happy grin and swung the bag onto his back. 'Let's get out of here.'

CHAPTER TWENTY-NINE

AT THE DOG HOUSE, Saffron heard the street door push
open and then Nick's voice. She appeared at the half-
door, effectively barring his further progress.

'Get home all right?' he asked. Two cameras hung around
his neck. His jacket was dappled with dark splotches from
the rain.

'Haven't you got something more important to do? A road
smash to photograph or something?'

He ignored the barb. 'Did Gilbert go to the police? Have
they come around?'

'Left just a few minutes ago.' She paused, remembering
how Inspector Barker had looked around the reception area.
The cups and ribbons in the window; the toy ornamental
poodles that covered half the small counter in every colour
known to the breed, and a few that weren't; the April picture
on the calendar of a girl about Lucy's age in a blue bonnet
and sundress with a bichon puppy in her arms. Like a hawk
perched high up on a tree, he had taken it all in.

Saffron had invited them inside: she suspected she didn't
have much option, hoping they didn't have a search warrant.

They wouldn't find the bones without one, although Inspector Barker looked as if he might be good at sniffing out bones.

'And?' Nick queried, bringing her back.

'And nothing. They asked a few questions then left. They seemed satisfied with my answers.' Satisfied was probably overstating it, but they hadn't arrested her. Gilbert had told them about seeing her covered in blood and arrived two seconds after the police, as if he had been watching out for them, to enlarge upon the quantity of blood, the colour of the blood, the *wetness* of the blood. He had sounded so hysterical it made it easier to convince the police that what Gilbert had seen were black dye stains on her T-shirt — late at night, the street lighting, Gilbert half-crazed with grief. She believed it had been a convincing performance. 'Do you know what happened to my bloody clothes? I'm not swearing,' she asked Nick.

'I tossed them. I kept thinking about what the police would think if they turned up and found them so I came back this morning while you were asleep. Hope you don't mind.' He stuck his hand into one of the many pockets on his jacket and pulled out a bone tiki. 'I found this in your jeans.'

'Thanks,' she said reluctantly. She took it from him and ran her fingers over the smooth surface. The tiki had hung around the neck of Tama's grandson, and now his remains sat in the cup in the window. She shook her head and tightened her grip on the tiki, locking it in her hand. 'The police looked in the rubbish bin. I think I've convinced them the blood Gilbert thought he saw was black dye splashed on my T-shirt.'

'Did they buy that?' Nick looked unconvinced.

'Reluctantly. Some of my clients like their dog's natural

colour enhanced and I *do* have black dye on lots of my T-shirts. I showed them stains on some of the towels.'

'Where are the bones?' Nick asked.

She gave him a long, level look. 'Safely stashed away.'

'You don't trust me?'

'I don't trust anyone at the moment. I have to get the bones back to Tama before anything else happens. I can't return them until tonight and I daren't wander about with them in the daylight. If I'm spotted — Gilbert will have his nose pressed up against his front window for sure — and the police take the bones, then we're sunk. All of us.'

Nick pulled his cigarettes from his pocket and walked back out to the pavement. Saffron studiously didn't glance at the Harrison Challenge Cup in the window. That morning, before she had left for the funeral, she'd been convinced she could feel the bones, as if they were talking to her — even singing softly. But not now. Perhaps they didn't like Nick. She could understand that: she'd gone off him herself.

'Good turnout for the funeral,' Nick said as he lit up. 'Lucky the rain held off.'

'Mostly people who knew Daphne, she was well liked. A few of Billy's old ...'

She stopped and looked at the window display with a frown. The shar pei puppy sat in the Harrison Challenge Cup and everything looked the same ... but felt different. Was that crazy? Maybe. The bones had sung to her before and right at this moment there was total silence.

She leant over and picked up the puppy. The cup was empty.

Instant numbness, as if someone had shot her full of

novocaine. The toy fell from her hands, and when she bent to pick it up she almost fell. Nick grabbed her arm, steadied her.

The bones were gone. And if the bones were gone she couldn't return them. And if she couldn't return them, they were dead. All dead. Tama would strike out in his anger just as he had killed Billy and Daphne. Even now, Heather might be lying in some lonely ditch. Mo would be next. And then her. And Nick and Big Wal would get together and talk about the Delaney girls sometimes, say how sad it was. But only when they were alone. No one else would believe them.

Poof! said the old woman in her head. *Just like that — he'll snatch you off the water like moulting ducks. Poof! Poof! Poof!*

But I did my best, she wanted to cry out. I found the bones. I tried to get them back. It wasn't my fault you were all still fighting. That wasn't my fault. If you hadn't been fighting, you could have taken the bones last night.

'What's the matter?' Nick's voice sounded as if it was coming from some place far away. His hand still held her arm.

'The bones have gone.' Her throat was tight. She had to push the words out. Even saying the words gave them a finality she couldn't accept. She pulled away and hugged the toy puppy to her chest.

'They were in the cup?'

'Best place I could think of.'

'Have you been broken into?'

'No, I don't think so. The door was locked when I came back from the funeral. The police turned up a minute or two later, I haven't had a chance to check on the bones.'

Willing her legs to move, she clambered onto the stool. It was like climbing Mount Everest. Nick followed with his cigarette, hesitantly, like a pup who knows he's not really allowed inside. She didn't care. Lung cancer was just another way of dying. There were so many.

She had to think, had to reason it out. Maybe there was still something she could do.

She heard Daddy suck in his breath. *Oh dear, petal, this isn't looking good*.

This isn't an ordinary theft, she told herself. People don't steal bones. It had to be someone who knew about them and understood their importance. And the list of people who knew about them had grown by the day. She should have kept her mouth shut.

And she hadn't been broken into, so that implied someone with access. Someone with a key — well, her sisters all had a key, so that meant Steve. And Nick walked through reception that morning, and the police had just left, and Gilbert had been there, dancing and gloating when the police arrived. Too many possible culprits: half of Taupo had wandered through reception this morning.

'Who knew about the bones?' Nick asked.

'You for starters,' Saffron said tensely. Her hands gripped the puppy as if she wanted to squeeze the life out of it.

'It wasn't me. You don't really think I'd take them, do you?'

She should have pushed Nick away the moment she saw him with his camera. That camera had told her everything important she needed to know about him. Why had she thought he'd be different from any other press photographer? Somehow, in her grief, she'd let him get to her.

I'll get them back. Just give me time, she prayed. Please! Just give me time.

Somehow, she had to make someone tell her what had happened to the bones. Her instincts told her it was the men, chatting and whispering at the funeral, who knew the answers. And she had one of the offenders here.

Casually she picked up her trimming scissors, which lay on the grooming table. They were pointed and sharp — you can't trim a dog with blunt scissors. She wriggled off her stool and headed for the bench as if she was going to tidy things away.

Instead, she turned, her body between Nick and the stable door, the scissors gripped in one hand, the puppy in the other. She put the toy down. It sat on the car keys Nick had tossed on the bench and slowly wobbled over.

'What's going on?' he asked.

'Maybe you could tell me.'

He frowned. 'What do you mean?'

'I haven't got a lot of time, Nick, so stop playing games. You, or one of your mates, have the bones. I want them back. Now.'

'I haven't the faintest idea what you're talking about.' He tapped ash into a saucer.

'I haven't got time, Nick. The bones. Where are they?'

'I haven't seen them. You said you'd stashed them.'

'And now they're not there.'

She altered her grip on the scissors, and Nick's body tensed. He looked like a man who'd just seen his destiny.

'What are you playing at?' he asked.

'I'm not playing. Believe me, I haven't got time. Tell me where they are.'

The ash grew longer on his cigarette. 'I have no idea.'

'It has to be you, Nick. You knew about them. You told all your mates about them.'

'It wasn't me.'

'Why should I believe you?'

'Because I helped you return the coins. Remember? Doesn't that count for something?'

'If it isn't you, then it has to be one of your mates.'

'I doubt that.'

'Who else knows?'

'I'm hardly going to tell you if this is what you have in mind for them.'

'Did you tell Andy?'

'No.'

'Liar. Who else did you tell? Big Wal?'

'He wouldn't touch them if you paid him. Why don't you put those scissors down?'

'Who did you tell?'

'No one.'

'You talked to Andy. Right?' Nick's face was impassive, but she knew she was right. 'So maybe Andy told you how valuable they would be for his research. He could pretend he dug them up and get his picture on the wall at some university. So you decided to give them to Andy.'

The ash dropped to the floor. 'I didn't. Why would I?'

She shrugged. 'You tell me.' She could feel dampness under her arms. It had to be Nick and she had to make him confess what he'd done with them. She pushed the small voice of doubt aside and thrust the scissors out in front of her. 'Stop wasting time, Nick. Where are they?'

'Get a grip. I haven't got them.'

The skin around his eyes tightened. He positioned the grooming table between them, moving carefully. She took another step closer, not too far into the room — she had to cover the door.

'I don't know where the bones are,' he repeated. He placed both hands on the grooming table, as if he were a business man about to present a deal she couldn't refuse. A spiral of smoke rose from the cigarette clamped between his fingers. 'You need to find the person who does. Oh, fuck!' he yelped and dropped the butt. He shook his hand. 'Look what you made me do.'

'I already know who took them. You.'

Slowly, she circled a little to her right to let him think she intended to come around the grooming table — give Nick the opportunity to bolt. Then adrenaline would solve the problem. He would run and she would be forced to act. He'd feel the sharp point of her scissors, and then he'd talk and she'd have the bones again.

She edged closer. Nick backed slowly around the grooming table, then stopped. If she gave him too much space, he might get out the door before she reached him. She balanced her weight over her feet so she could spring either way.

Nick didn't leap for the door. He leapt at her. For the split second it took to realize what he was doing, she froze. Then her hand with the scissors arced around and up.

They stood toe to toe, Nick's head unnaturally high. She

was so close she could hear the pounding of his heart. The scissors were stuck in under his throat, and a single drop of blood beaded the tip.

'Put them down, Saffron.' He spoke in an unnatural tone that kept his Adam's apple still. His gaze twisted down as if he needed to see the scissors.

'Tell me where the bones are. Tell me!' she insisted.

'Don't you think I'd say if I knew?'

She met his eyes, and he must have seen something in hers. Slowly, he raised one hand, pulled the scissors out of her hand and put them down on the table.

He dabbed cautiously at his throat. 'What the hell do you think you're playing at?' He gave an experimental cough as if he thought blood might spray everywhere, then dabbed at his neck again and checked his fingers for blood.

'I . . .' She retreated to the stool, lowered her head to her hands for a moment and looked back up at him. 'Who's got the bones? If you didn't take them, then who did? Please tell me.'

Nick grappled in his pocket for his cigarettes. He clicked the lighter several times before the flame appeared, and the hand that raised it shook slightly. He gripped the cigarette cautiously between the tips of his thumb and burnt forefinger.

'I don't know.' He dragged in a lungful of smoke. 'It's time to go to the police with this. This is getting way out of hand.'

'Out of hand?' she repeated.

'You damn near slit my throat.'

'This has been *out of hand*, as you so neatly put it, for

days. You didn't feel any overwhelming need to go to the police when it was my family in danger. The minute your precious skin feels the point of Tama's club and it's a whole other story.'

'I'm more worried about your scissors than Tama's club. You damn near killed me.'

'To make you talk. I had to.'

'I can't tell you what I don't know.' He caught her arm gently. 'Don't you see that? You're running on nervous energy and you're going to hurt someone.'

'What about Billy and Daphne? They're not hurt. They're dead.'

'And this isn't going to bring them back.'

'Nick, I *have* to find the bones. Can't you understand? Tama will kill Heather if I don't. Steve is convinced she's next on his list. Maybe he's right.'

'And I haven't got them. I swear. Did your creepy neighbour get a look in the flax kit?'

'I don't know. I didn't think so, otherwise the police would have mentioned it. They mentioned blood, but not bones. But who else could it be?'

'So let's go to the police — I'll come with you — and tell them everything. Let them deal with it.'

'A few hours ago you were advising me not to say anything.'

'That was before you derailed. You're going to hurt someone.'

'Not unless I have to.' She picked up the scissors and examined the point. There wasn't much blood, and she wiped them on her jeans. 'I'm not the same person I was

275

yesterday, Nick. It was terrible on the beach with the dead babies. They weren't bones — they were real babies. There was so much blood! And I had to carry them — and there was blood everywhere — and—' She stopped and swallowed. She couldn't tell Nick about the crimson smear on the sand as she dragged the babies over the stones. 'I'm different. That's all.'

'You still have to live between the rules. I've . . .'

For a moment she thought Nick had said between the ripples. She knew all about that. Her mind drifted off.

'. . . and the one thing I've learnt is that when you return you have to change back. Soldiers have difficulty with that sometimes, and people in my line of business. But give yourself a bit of time and you'll come right.'

'Time!' She barked out the word. 'That's the one thing I don't have.' She slipped off the stool and backed towards the stable door.

'I'll take you to the hospital. To Mo,' Nick said.

She shook her head. 'I don't think Mo wants to see me.' She picked up the car keys he'd tossed on the bench.

'What are you doing?' Nick said, as he began to follow her.

'Sorry, Nick.' She spun around and raced for the street door.

276

CHAPTER THIRTY

BEHIND HER, SAFFRON heard Nick hit the stable door with a grunt, and then she was in the street and swinging the outside door shut. She thrust the key in, turned it, heard the lock snick and looked up at Nick's glaring face.

'What are you doing?' he yelled.

He didn't need to yell. She could hear him just fine as she turned and ran to his car. Her last sight of Nick was his mouth opening and closing like a goldfish. Bracketed in static, bits of one-sided conversations hissed off the car's scanner, which appeared to be set on an emergency channel. A stinking ashtray overflowed with cigarette butts. She crunched the gears as she circled the roundabout and went down Heu Heu Street.

She wasn't going to the hospital — there was nothing she could do for anyone there. If Nick didn't have the bones, then Gilbert was the next most likely person. He could have grabbed them out of the window while she was still in the grooming room being questioned by the police. The lights onto Tongariro Street changed to green just as she got there, and she turned in front of an oncoming vehicle.

What she'd said to Nick was true: she'd changed since gathering up the dead babies. A person couldn't wade through that much blood and not be changed, and Gilbert was about to find out just what big teeth she had. If anything happened to her sisters while she was trying to get the bones back, she'd kill him.

Whoa up, there, petal — steady now.

She remembered Big Wal's words: 'You'll be surprised what you'll do in the end.' Now she understood what he meant and hoped she wouldn't have to kill anyone.

She pulled into a parking space opposite Gilbert's antique shop and trotted across the road as chatter from the scanner followed her. There had been an accident out in the Spa Road industrial area and she laughed grimly to herself. Nick would be annoyed at missing it.

The window of Nantiques was an eclectic mix of china dolls, polished furniture with cabriole legs, and eastern rugs. Gilbert's mother, a tiny, fussy lady called Nan, had run the shop with her son until her death. A bell rang out back as Saffron entered. The shop was empty so she flipped the open/closed card over and snibbed the deadlock behind her.

'What are you doing here?' Gilbert appeared from the back, holding a curtain open at the far end of the long, narrow shop. His eyes were red-rimmed, his face gaunt. Around him dozens, hundreds, of dainty china figurines sat on shelves. For a moment, he looked like a forlorn king among his princesses.

'I've come to see you.' She walked towards him, stepping around a coffee table with an inlaid centre.

'I'll call the police,' he warned.

Saffron shrugged. 'You came to my shop with your nasty accusations. What's the difference?'

He didn't answer. His hand stretched out towards the phone, and he glanced to each side as if checking that the china doll troops were rallied.

'What have you done with the bones?'

'Bones?' He gave a gasp of high-pitched laughter. 'I don't know what you're talking about. What bones?'

'You were the one telling the police all about a sack I had on my shoulder. What did you think I had in the sack?'

'I haven't been well since Daphne passed on. I don't know what I said.'

'You told the police I'd hacked up a tourist and had them in the sack.'

'Did I? I don't remember. I was distraught.' He wiped at his face with one hand.

'And now you've stolen the bones from me. They aren't the bones of a tourist, they're old bones, little bones, and I want them back.'

'I haven't got them.'

'That's a pity. If you had them, you could give them to me, and no one would have to get hurt.'

'I'm not going to tolerate this! You can't break in here and threaten me,' Gilbert said. 'I'm warning you. I'm calling the police.'

Saffron stepped forward. 'Bollocks!' She ripped the phone cord from the wall. A feeling of power surged through her.

'You can't do that!'

'Just did.'

Gilbert didn't get it: she could do whatever she wanted.

This must be how Big Wal feels when he pulls out the softball bat, she thought.

'What do you want?'

'I've told you: I want the bones back.'

'I haven't got any bones. I don't know what you're talking about!'

'You're wasting time.'

Saffron picked up a figurine of a shepherdess who held a crook in one hand; her skin was ivory white with rose blossom cheeks. Her cupid lips looked as if they were puckering up to kiss someone. Saffron looked at her carefully, smiled and dropped her.

Gilbert howled.

'I want to know where the bones are.'

She picked up another shepherdess.

'Don't. Please don't.'

She dropped it.

'Please Saffron. Don't hurt them. I'll give you whatever you want, but don't hurt them.'

'I've told you what I want. The bones.'

She grabbed another figurine and threw it at Gilbert's legs. The head smashed against his knee.

'Stop it,' he cried, jerking down as if he thought he could catch it. 'I don't know about any bones. I'd give them to you if I did.'

Saffron fired another shepherdess at him. Trouble was, she believed him. He didn't know what she was talking about. She wiped a hand along a shelf and a whole family of shepherdesses crashed to the floor.

Gilbert dropped to his knees among the broken dolls. He

picked up a head and tried to find an unbroken body for it. 'Stop it. Please stop it.' Tears were running down his face.

'You haven't got the bones, have you?' she shouted.

He shook his head, looking up at her as if she'd disturbed him praying.

'You're wasting my time! Why didn't you say so?' She didn't know why she was screaming at him.

'I tried to—'

'Get up!' she yelled, grabbing him by the shoulder. Her feet crunched over broken china. 'Get up!'

He staggered to his feet.

'Come on.' She pushed him in front of her, and they brushed through the curtain that separated the back of the shop from the front. She believed him. He didn't have the bones. She'd lock him up somewhere, just like Nick, and carry on. It had to be Andy or Steve.

'What are you doing?'

He tried to look over his shoulder as he walked, but she kept pushing him so he stayed off balance.

'What's in here?' she asked, stopping in front of a closed door.

'The office. A safe — I could give you money.'

'I don't want money. I want the bones.' She reached around him and tried the door. It was locked.

'Open it.'

He pulled a key from his pocket and unlocked the door.

'Give me the key.'

She gave the little man a push and released his arm. The last thing she saw before she slammed the door shut was Gilbert flying across the room.

CHAPTER THIRTY-ONE

SAFFRON RAN BACK through the curtain to the front of the shop. Panic welled up inside as if someone had turned on a tap. All their lives, she'd been the Delaney girl who plotted their course, and now she didn't know what to do next. Was Tama watching her now, his club poised over Heather or Mo, waiting to see what she would do?

He wouldn't take her yet, she knew that. He was leaving her until last — to make her suffer. She had touched his bones and lost them. He would wring every last tear from her, and when she was all cried out turn his club towards her. And if he'd taken all her family, she'd welcome the blow.

She stumbled towards the door, her feet crushing the broken china figurines.

Such pretty little things, petal. Shame they've lost their heads. They're never going to get anywhere without their heads.

She stopped and looked down. Little headless china dolls. The thought played over and over, as if, once started, it took too much energy to stop. Nights without sleep, her grief for Billy and Daphne, and her fear for Lucy and her sisters were all taking their toll. The repetition continued but, out of the mindless chatter of her father's voice, she slowly found meaning.

She looked about her, half-expecting to see Lucky Del perched on the rocking horse in the corner, or grinning down at her from the spiralling horns of the goat's head on the wall.

'Thank you, Daddy,' she breathed.

She was racing around like a headless chicken, not knowing who had taken the bones, with no clear idea where to go or who to ask.

Never going to get anywhere like that, petal.

You're so right.

She could ask Tama to make the bones sing again. Once they sang, she could find them again. The bones liked her. They didn't run from *her* hands. And she was sure — *sure* — that any step she made towards returning the bones would meet with Tama's approval. He would hold his hand, wait to see how the cards played out.

She knelt down, shards of china biting into her knees, and picked up a headless shepherdess, searched around for a head that would fit.

Gilbert was shouting in the back room. She ignored him.

'You can be my good-luck Daphne doll. We need luck now, petal, buckets of it, because the bones are gone, and they're our one chance of getting out of this mess. We've got to find them. I know I was too late for you, petal, and I'm sorry, I'm so sorry for that. But if we find the bones, it's all going to work out for Heather and Mo. I just know it. I can . . . feel it in my bones,' she finished lamely.

She ran back to the car and laid the broken china doll on the passenger seat like the victim of a fatal road crash. She shuddered, then wrapped the pieces in her handkerchief and stuffed them in her pocket.

The air whipping in from the lake was clean and fresh after the stale smell of the car. The old woman will be there, she told herself as she walked across the grass slope to the wooden steps. She will be there. Saffron repeated the words over and over like a litany, walking slowly down the steps, trying not to look about too closely. She wanted to give the old woman time to arrive. She would know about this . . . hiccup. Somehow she would know. And she would come. She had to — everything depended on that.

To her left, the lake glinted silver, but past the pontoon, up towards the harbour entrance, the water darkened to gunmetal grey. Saffron sat on the driftwood seat, trying to hold her fear at bay. The old woman would come. She would.

Each wave crested and broke before the foam became a hundred white creatures racing for the shore. She remembered sitting here with Daddy and Billy and her sisters, watching these same little white-wave mice. 'Bet mine wins!' they'd scream, but of course nobody had any idea whose bit of foam was whose, so nobody won and nobody lost. Daddy had probably found it pretty boring, but he'd never let on.

'You need me, girl?' a voice said from beside her.

Saffron could have cried with relief. She jumped to her feet and hugged the old woman fiercely, then loosened her grip as she felt the frail bones beneath her hands.

'The bones have been stolen. Someone took them. I don't know where they are.' Words spilt out of her like water bursting through a floodgate.

'We know they're gone.' In contrast, the old woman's tone was calm and measured.

'Does Tama know where the bones are? I'll get them back again if he can show me where they are.'

'He'll make them sing.'

'Please.'

'He was angry when you lost them.'

'I didn't *lose* them, they were stolen from me. Tell him not to do anything more. Please tell him not to hurt Heather or Mo, or Lucy. I'll get the bones back if he'll just make them sing.'

'I cannot tell Tama Ariki what to do. He has offered to make them sing again. You should be grateful.'

'I am, I am! Tell him we're very grateful. But what if the bones are a long way away now? Will I be able to hear them? Will they get tired?'

The old woman smiled. 'They won't get tired. Bones can sing forever.'

Please, God, don't let it come to that, Saffron thought.

The old woman stood up. 'I must go now. You listen carefully.'

'Come with me,' Saffron begged, screwing her hands together. 'You understand all this . . . I'm out of my depth.'

'All you need to do is ask the ancestors, girl. The ancestors will help you.'

'I'd rather ask you. The only advice my daddy is likely to give is what to stick my money on.'

'Sometimes that is all you need to know.'

She walked away, leaving Saffron standing beside the

driftwood seat. The yellow and orange leaves flapped against the branches, but their brilliant colour had gone. There were fewer than there had been the other day, and fallen leaves lay limp and dull on the sand. Dying.

The waves changed as afternoon faded into evening. Further out, the lake smoothed as its colours drew towards night. Saffron watched the waves, letting her eyes half-close. As the waves rolled in, white foam became another shade of grey in the fading light. Slowly, the waves kept changing, as night came closer and the lake evened out into an endless grey prairie.

She opened her eyes. There was too much adrenaline zapping through her veins for this to work. She'd never felt less like slipping into a trance, or whatever it was she had done last time, when she heard the bones.

She tried to remember what they had sounded like. It seemed a long time ago now. This morning there had been a whispering murmur from the cup — now, there was silence.

She stood and turned in a circle, trying to use her mind as a receiver, tune into the right frequency. Somewhere out there the bones were singing, but not here beside Tama's Rock as they had before. This time, they could be anywhere.

Hesitantly, she took a step towards the wooden steps, then stopped. Despair pulled her in a dozen different directions. Where was the old woman? She heard the words in her head again. *All you need to do is ask the ancestors, girl.*

'Daddy?' she whispered. 'Daddy? I'm listening?'

You have to decide who to put your money on, petal.

She shook her head in frustration. That was the only thing

Daddy knew anything about. Who to back — who Lady Luck was about to smile upon.

Don't panic, she told herself. Tama made the bones sing once before. He'll do it again and she would hear them. There was no reason to think Tama would trick her. He said he would do it, and he desperately wanted the bones back.

Oh, but they were baby bones, and there might be a limit to what they could do. She stuck her hand into the pocket of her jeans and clutched the broken figurine. Talk to me, Daphne doll, she pleaded. You went to university. Did you ever hear about singing bones? And she could have sworn the figurine warmed in her hand. Ideas charged into her tired mind with the boundless energy Daphne had brought to any room.

She wasn't Tama Ariki, that was her problem. Tama would hear the bones whether he was standing next to them or whether they were a hundred kilometres away. But this wasn't her culture, she wasn't sensitive to the nuances. She needed an ally, someone Maori. Someone who knew about things like singing bones, someone who was already involved.

Someone like Big Wal.

CHAPTER THIRTY-TWO

BIG WAL STARED at the frightened girl standing on the other side of the counter. She looked much as she had that first night: pale face, enormous dark eyes. Still running around without a jersey, goose bumps roughening her skin.

'I'll help you if I can — so long as the fallout isn't going to blow in the direction of my family.'

'It won't, I'm sure. You'd be helping Tama.'

'Right,' he said doubtfully. That was the thing Pakeha never understood: whether you were working for the gods or against them didn't much matter. A man didn't want the likes of Tama Ariki noticing him for *any* reason.

But he'd watched her bury two of her family today. She'd picked up the coins from his counter. He owed her — something. He could listen, at least.

'Do you know about singing bones?' she asked.

It was the last thing he'd expected her to say. He nodded cautiously. 'When a person dies and their body can't be found, a chief of great power could make the bones sing — to reveal themselves.'

'You know I found the bones of the missing babies?'

'I heard.'

'The bones have been stolen before I could give them to Tama. He's going to make them sing, but I think they're far away, and I can't hear them.'

He nodded warily.

'Could you listen for me? Please. I heard them before, but I was standing right on top of them. I'll hear them when I get close enough but I need someone with a — a — connection to point me in the right direction.'

'You need a fool, you mean' he shot back.

'I think you're a man who would be sensitive to something like this,' she continued, ignoring him.

'It's one of the old beliefs. People don't believe in things like that now.'

'Do you?'

'I've never heard bones singing.'

'But you've heard *about* them?'

He shrugged. He had a wife and family to think of. He looked around at the confines of his burger bar — his world. He could lose all this.

The spirit world had always been a fearsome place — as much now as in the days of his ancestors — and yet, when a body was missing, they would call upon the bones to sing, so they could be found and, even in death, reunited with their people. And these mokopuna had been missing for two hundred years.

Big Wal found himself walking across Tongariro Street in the rain and into the park, holding the girl's hand. Lights sprang up along the main street as shadows strengthened. And here, in the relative quiet of the park, they stopped.

He dropped her hand. She watched, so much hope in her face it hurt to look at her. So he raised his face to the heavens. Rain stung his eyes, ran down his face. Slowly, he turned in a circle, listening with an ear he'd never used before.

They were out there in the twilight, watching him. His ancestors. They'd be proud of him, he reckoned. Probably figured an old burger man hadn't the guts for this sort of thing. And then he wasn't having rational thoughts any more, just feeling. Doing what his ancestors told him to do. He stretched his hands out, palms up, revolving slowly in the cool damp air. Listening.

He thought back to the mountain of his childhood, his father standing on the back porch, sniffing the air appreciatively: 'Pigs are over on your Uncle Tori's track' or 'Pigs are by the old whare.' And he'd be right. The boy would ask, 'Can you smell 'em?' and his father would smile and wink, tap the side of his nose, and say, 'I just knows, boy.'

And his mother, who rarely left the kitchen, saying, 'Boy, I want you to take the little kids over to the Far Burn and get me blackberries. And don't eat them all on the way home.' He used to wonder, as they trudged along with their billies, how his ma could know the blackberries were ripe when she hardly ever went outside.

And so he listened. And although he didn't hear them, he knew where the bones were. He knew. He pointed. 'Out there. Down the western shores of the lake. They're out there.'

'That must be where Andy's camp is.'

'That's where you'll find them.'

'Did you hear them?' she asked. 'They're beautiful, aren't they?'

But that wasn't how they'd talked to him. He'd just known with a surety that he'd never felt about anything before.

He took her hand again, and they walked back to Tongariro Street, but he felt this time as if *he* was leading *her* through the dark. Sometimes it did a man good to step out of his comfort zone.

The windscreen wipers clicked back and forth hypnotically as Saffron climbed the hill heading out of town and at the top turned left onto Poihipi Road. She put the lights onto full beam and pressed her foot down on the accelerator.

She was on the Whangamata Road, past Kinloch and heading across to the Western Bays when she heard her name on the scanner. The runabout lurched to one side as her gaze switched to the small black box built into the dashboard. For a moment, she thought Tama Ariki was talking to her.

'Yes,' she squeaked.

'Saffron? Can you hear me? Switch to transmit.'

She pulled over to the side of the road and stared at the scanner. It was Nick's voice.

'Saffron? Do you copy?'

Evidently he couldn't hear her. Her one petrified word hadn't travelled further than the car. But what did he want? Could he track her down? Hesitantly, she put her hand out, thumb and forefinger extended like tweezers, and in a moment of boldness turned one of the black knobs. Instant silence. The police were gone, the irritating static was gone and, best of all, Nick was gone.

She shrugged, gave a nervous laugh and drove on. She should have done that half an hour ago. But before she had got into high gear, there was a burst of static from the scanner. She frowned.

As she completed the final gear change, she heard a note — one crystal-clear note. She slammed her foot down on the brake pedal so that the car slid on the gravel. More static. Then another note.

The bones!

The bones were singing. Not the same beautifully pure notes she'd heard before, but it was them, and they were singing to her.

She laughed out loud, a gasping breathless laugh, and cupped her hands up over her mouth and nose for a moment. She put the handbrake on and leapt out. The headlights cut a swathe through the night and cold rain lashed her shoulders. Out here, she could hear nothing, and disappointment surged through her, swift and intense. She turned, staring out into the darkness. Nothing.

But the moment she sat down in the car, she heard them again. She felt the rain that had driven in through the open door, soaking into her damp clothes, making them wetter, and she laughed. The bones were out there. Static overrode them for an anxious moment, then she heard them again.

Cautiously, she put the runabout into gear. If she couldn't hear the bones singing outside, but she could hear them inside on the scanner, they must still be some distance away. Static hissed almost continuously, yet every now and then one, sometimes two, pure clean notes echoed into the car like butterflies alighting on a flower.

The miles passed, the wipers swished monotonously, she turned left again onto an even more obscure road. Slowly the static lessened, and the bones sang more clearly. They were guiding her in like a beam of radar, before a raucous grating of static filled the airwaves.

She frowned, braked, then reversed until the bones sang clearly to her again. She couldn't help but smile, despite everything. Hine was right: she could live out the rest of her days and never hear anything as lovely. In a way, she'd been blessed, and then she remembered why she was listening to the bones, and it didn't feel like a blessing at all.

When she got out she could hear nothing but the rain drumming on the roof of the car. It plastered her hair to her scalp, and ran from the ends down her face. She looked around but could see nothing. The night was black out here — not like in town, not like on Lake Terrace. She reached back into the car and switched the lights off. She stared up at the sky, but the rain hurt her eyes so she looked away, blinking out into the darkness until her eyes had adjusted.

On her left was a farm gate into a paddock that looked as if it had had more use recently than its middle-of-nowhere status warranted, so she walked across, feeling her sneakers sink into the mud, and opened the gate. Then she slipped and slithered her way back to the car and drove through. She vaguely remembered she should close the gate, but she didn't have time to stop and she might need to make a rapid exit. Hoping there wasn't some little harmless beast hidden in a corner that even now was galloping with lemming-like enthusiasm for the open gate and certain death on the road, she drove on, her wet clothes plastered against her. The bones sang as she hunched over the steering wheel, squinting through the driving rain, and slowly followed a faint track across the paddock. The track rounded a corner, and a single light up ahead made a tiny stand against the endless dark.

Andy's camp. She'd lay odds.

I'm in for a tenner on that, petal.

She smiled as she stopped in front of another closed gate. You and me both, Daddy.

Cautiously, she backed around into the paddock, shifted into low gear and eased her foot off the clutch. The wheels spun, and she felt the back end move faintly from side to side. Gritting her teeth she tried again, and slowly the car slithered back onto the track. She turned the engine off and breathed a sigh of relief. If she needed a quick getaway, she could jump over the gate, which would slow anyone following her.

She opened the door. Outside, the bones were singing their little hearts out, as if they thought they were the Vienna Boys' Choir. She quietly snicked the door closed. Maybe she could sneak in and steal the bones back right from under Andy's nose. Maybe he wouldn't even know.

And maybe pigs will fly, petal.

Yeah, yeah, Daddy. Don't you know you're supposed to be guiding me with your ancestral wisdom? Can't you come up with anything practical?

My Ancestor — isn't that running in the two-thirty at Hutt Park tomorrow?

She latched the gate and picked her away along the track towards the light, pausing to wipe some mud onto her face. She'd learnt that from all those war films Billy used to inflict on them when it was his turn to choose the Thursday night video.

Ahead of her, the bones were singing.

CHAPTER THIRTY-THREE

SAFFRON WALKED CAREFULLY down the track, every sense alert. She didn't have a plan: she'd see where Andy was, what he was doing, and make her mind up from there. She patted the back pocket of her jeans — keys at the ready. All she needed now was the bones. Out here in the dark, with a fresh wind blowing the sound to her, the sound was pure again, yet beneath their crystalline clarity lay a subtlety that led her emotions into unknown places. She couldn't understand how Andy couldn't hear the bones — or at least *feel* them.

Light shone out from a tent pitched in the middle of the paddock. The canvas rippled and snapped as the wind gusted in, making shadows lurch and stumble across the back wall. But the shadows were simply shapes, not human. A station-wagon was parked to the right of the tent.

When she stumbled on something and lurched forward, she looked down and saw a thatch of string-lines ahead. She moved cautiously around it and, as she approached the tent, got down on her hand and knees. After a moment's thought, and with a sigh of resignation, she lay down on her stomach.

She couldn't get any wetter, she told herself, but cold seeped up from the ground and into her and it felt like a taste of the grave.

She wriggled along until she came up against the canvas of the tent and lay there, listening to the sounds from within. The bones were singing quietly now, as if they understood she needed to be able to hear other sounds, a gentle chorus of little bones singing contentedly to themselves.

At the entrance, the canvas flap was laced back and rain was driving in. The beginning of a trestle table showed near the entrance. She waited just around the corner for what felt like forever, listening.

She could hear the bones, the wind, the rain, the canvas — each one singing its own tune, blending together into something no orchestra could duplicate. Finally, she edged her head around the corner and immediately jerked it back. Andy was sprawled in a beach chair, fast asleep.

Her heart raced. She wet her lips — as if they weren't wet enough — her elbows resting in the mud. She swallowed and peered around the corner.

An empty glass lay on the ground below Andy's outflung hand. A bottle of whisky sat on the trestle table running down the far side of the tent, alongside rocks, bones and artefacts. A black rubbish sack lay between Andy's legs. His lips were closed, and now she could see him, Saffron could hear a faint snore. His lower lip and bearded chin drew back slightly on each in-breath.

Her intent gaze lowered to the bag between his spread legs. She could have wept — the beautiful singing bones in a dingy rubbish sack. The old woman had woven a flax kit especially for them; she could imagine the ancestors singing as she worked, so that every fibre was steeped in magic. She had put them in a silver cup with a long and honourable history. Now, they were in a rubbish sack.

Slowly, with infinite care, she began to work her way around the corner of the tent, extending her left arm a couple of centimetres, waiting, repeating the movement and rolling her hips so that she moved ahead. Then she hitched her right elbow forward, her gaze glued to Andy's face. He moved slightly, and she froze, but he was simply stirring in his sleep.

Finally, she was at his feet. She reached out and grasped the rubbish sack by one corner at ground level, scared that if she grabbed the top of the bag it would topple over and bones would knock and scrape. Slowly, she manoeuvred backwards, easing the sack with her. It seemed to take forever, but at last her legs reached the entrance, and once her hips were there she began to bend herself around the corner.

She was almost out of the tent when the edge of the sack caught on the taut canvas and spilled away from her. She grabbed at it, rearing up and clutching the bones to her before they spilled into the mud. Quickly, she looked up. Andy sat there, staring at her as if she were a ghost; she scrambled to her feet, clutching the sack, and ran.

She got a decent enough start. Andy had been asleep, he was drunk, he was surprised. She flew back along the track, her feet slipping on the wet grass before she finally heard Andy clear the tent.

The bones were silent. All she could hear was the wind and rain and the occasional bellow from Andy. On the rain-soaked ground, the sound of his feet melted straight into the grass, but he was behind her, and probably gaining. He was tall — long strides — but she was tall too, and fit. She swung the sack from her chest up and over her shoulder so that one arm was free as she ran, the sack bouncing on her back.

She tried to keep her eyes on the path: if she lost it, she wouldn't find the gate. If she could just get there ahead of Andy and start the car, he would have to return for his own vehicle and stop for the gate. That would put her ahead for the run to Taupo. The car had seemed peppy on the trip out here: this time it would really get to show what it could do.

The gate suddenly loomed up. Saffron seized the top rail with one hand and flung one leg over it. The rail scraped her thigh and she winced. Her singlet top rode up, and she grazed her stomach as she got the other leg over and dropped on the other side.

As she landed, her free hand was already feeling in her back pocket for the key. Tossing the sack onto the passenger seat, she leapt into the car and jammed the key into the ignition. When she glanced quickly over her shoulder she wondered if what she could see was Andy's face or something from her imagination.

The growl of the engine shut out the wind and rain. Easing her foot off the clutch, she touched the accelerator and hissed 'Yessss' as the tyres bit into the soft dirt, and the car rolled forward. She hunched over the wheel, steering with one hand while she fumbled over the controls to find the wipers and the lights.

Rain sliced down through the beam of light as if trying to shred it. The track out onto the road showed ahead, and this time she was leaving the gate open again, little black beasts or no little black beasts. She gunned the engine and felt the wheels slip. Too soon, too soon. She lifted her foot, the wheels gripped, and she was through the gate and back up onto the metal road.

'Right,' she said out loud, as she watched the needle on the speedo rise, 'let's see what you can do.'

CHAPTER THIRTY-FOUR

ONLY A MINUTE passed before Saffron saw lights swing out behind her. She slammed her foot down on the accelerator. She tried to keep her eyes focused on the road ahead, but the lights that intermittently flared in the rear-vision mirror drew her gaze hypnotically. There was a T-junction coming up where this gravel road met the Whangamata Road, so she changed down to third and took the corner as fast as she dared. The back end of the car twitched on the loose gravel, but then she was on the tarmac and speeding back towards town.

When she reached the junction at Poihipi Road she dared to think she might have made it. Andy hadn't caught her. She saw his lights occasionally — well, by now there was more traffic around, and she could only guess it was him — but with each turnoff the road improved and she pushed the car faster. Once she hit Taupo, she would lose him in the traffic. The rain had stopped, and she switched off the dragging wipers. She glanced down at the sack on the passenger seat and smiled. 'I think we're going to make it, fellas.'

She climbed a small hill, swung out of a corner and saw

two vehicles parked up ahead. Three men stood beside them. As her lights picked them up, she saw that one of them held something long and narrow in his hand. They moved out onto the road and she swore in frustration. So close!

She hit the brakes. If she could turn . . . but she saw the lights around the corner behind her and knew it was Andy.

Trapped.

She slowed, changing down through the gears, trying to keep momentum and wondering about the moment when someone stepped in front of her.

She would stop, she knew that. With a despairing sinking feeling, she knew she couldn't run someone down. Oh, petals, I'm sorry. Her face twisted in pain as she thought of her sisters. That was the essential difference between her and Tama Ariki — he was a warrior. Once he had you in his headlights, you were nothing but a lumpy red smear on the road. She was a wimp.

She picked out Nick's tall frame and felt a bitter surge of disappointment that yanked the corners of her mouth down. She didn't expect much, *anything*, from the others, but she'd thought he cared. OK, so she hadn't given him any encouragement, but she would have — eventually. Yeah, she'd yelled at him, but she yelled at her sisters all the time. Didn't mean she didn't love them to bits. Nick should have understood that.

There was a short figure in an overcoat brandishing a stick whom she slowly realized was Gilbert. Her pesky but harmless neighbour was maybe not so harmless now.

And Steve was there. Once she knew Andy had the bones, she'd been sure that Steve would make an appearance. They'd had their heads together for far too long at the funeral.

She slowed.

The men moved across the road, patrolling it like highway bandits. Andy's headlights flashed in her rear-vision mirror. She flicked her own lights onto high beam to blind the men in front of her, and desperately hoped she looked like Mad Max bearing down on them. Their hands rose together to shield their eyes, so that it looked almost like a choreographed dance move.

Nick stood slightly behind the others as they barricaded the road. With one hand over his eyes, he was beckoning her with the other arm. Waving her on? What did he mean? Maybe he wasn't the turncoat she'd picked him for — or maybe this was all part of the trap.

She clutched the steering wheel and drove straight at Nick, desperately praying that their brains were both running the same program. Gilbert and Steve were looking down, their arms still raised to shield their eyes, neither able to see Nick beckoning her on. Andy in the car behind would.

She pointed to the passenger side as she drove straight at Nick, then realized he couldn't see because of the headlights. He stood on the driver's side, and for a heartbeat she feared again that it was a trap, then remembered the way he'd looked at her that morning, and knew she had to trust him.

One minute the men were stretched out in a hard black line ahead of her, the next, she was among them. Nick yanked the driver's door open and yelled at her. Steve shouted. A tremendous thud landed on the roof of the car as Gilbert wielded what turned out to be a bar.

Nick was half in the vehicle, bigger than she remembered,

and yelling at her to get over. She obeyed, scrambling over the handbrake and gearstick, trying not to sit on top of the bones as bits of broken china dug into her behind.

Loose gravel shot out the back as the tyres screamed. Someone yelped as if hit and the voices that had yelled at her were now aimed at Nick. As the car rocketed forward she slammed back in her seat, and a moment later they were hurtling towards Taupo.

'Nick?' His name came out in a gasp that used the last of the air she seemed to have left inside.

'It must be your lucky day,' he volunteered, glancing at her for one gas-guzzling second. He was grinning like the Cheshire cat, a neat little circular plaster on his neck. 'I don't usually help ladies who try to slit my throat.'

'I'm sorry. I was desperate.' She leant to one side and twisted around to fumble the rubbish sack of bones out from behind her.

They roared up the hill overlooking Taupo in third gear, the lights of the town flaring momentarily into vision and disappearing as quickly when they rounded a corner.

'Luckily for you, I have a forgiving nature.' He hesitated. 'Besides, I fancy you.'

She hitched herself back on the seat. 'Even after I—'

He touched his throat with the fingers of one hand, and she shrieked at him, 'Hold the wheel!'

'I've got it.' He put the hand back on the wheel and glanced in the rear-vision mirror. 'Even after that,' he said soberly, 'which proves it must be the real thing.'

'This isn't the time, Nick.'

'It never is with you, so I'm saying my piece anyway.'

'You're not my type.'

'So I'll come to your shop to get my nails trimmed until you change your mind.'

She shook her head desperately. The man's sense of timing was even worse than Daddy's.

'And what was it? Anal glands expressed? Would I like that?'

She shook her head even harder. 'You really wouldn't like that.'

'We'll skip that one, then.' He grinned at her again, then concentrated on his driving.

She stared across at his shadowed face, noticing how the skin on his cheek looked smooth and flawless.

They went through a dip, rounded another corner, and the glittering lights of Taupo exploded across the night sky. Intermittent clusters of sequins sparkled around the lake. Almost home.

'Heather let me out, if you're interested. I phoned her. Your sister has an altogether more accommodating nature than you. Did you know that?'

Saffron shrugged and watched him discreetly.

'I ran into Andy and Steve down at Big Wal's. Didn't take long to fill in the gaps in their conversation and work out what they'd done. Andy rang us when you grabbed the bones. I figured the best way of making sure you didn't get hurt was to join forces with them. Your neighbour's gone psycho. All he wants to do is break something — preferably you, I think — with that tyre jemmy. He's morphed into a mini Rambo.'

Saffron looked over her shoulder. The lights of two cars shone behind them.

'What are we going to do?' she asked Nick.

'Your call.'

'I have to get down the lakefront and return the bones.'

'How about I drop you off somewhere close, and then continue, and hopefully they'll follow me.'

'Sounds good.'

'Get down on the floor,' Nick said suddenly.

'Why?'

'They know you're in the car. But if you can't be seen now, then it won't be obvious when you get out.'

Saffron slipped down and scrunched herself into the leg space in front of the passenger seat. Her wet jeans clung, and she had to pull at the knees to let her legs bend so tightly. The stench from the ashtray was overpowering down here. Her face was beside the sack. Faintly, she could hear the bones trilling.

'Can you hear them?' she whispered.

'I can bloody see them,' said Nick.

'Not them. The bones.'

His gaze never left the road. 'Not a thing.'

'They're singing very softly.'

He shook his head. 'I never was musical.'

'They're very beautiful.'

'Hang on,' he called a moment later.

Saffron knew they must be at the intersection of Poihipi Road and the State Highway. She gritted her teeth and held her breath — they had to cross two double lanes and there was always traffic here — and stared blindly across at Nick's legs.

A horn blared, and the inside of the car darkened as a black monster rushed behind them. They were turning, a dab of the brakes, and she cried out. Another horn. Then they were pulling out, overtaking and swooping down the hill into Taupo.

'Watch out for merging cars at the control gate bridge,' she yelled.

'Nervous little thing, aren't you?' Nick had the effrontery to sound as if he was enjoying himself.

'No. I'm just not suicidal.'

They flattened out of their downhill race and crossed the narrow bridge. The engine screamed for a second as Nick changed down and swung through the tighter bends of the climb up to Tongariro Street.

'I've got a second or two on them—'

'I bet!'

'—so I'll turn up Spa Road and then head for the lake. Maybe they'll think we've gone down Tongariro. There's enough traffic around so they won't be able to tell.'

She didn't care how he did it so long as he didn't hit anything. More horns blared, and she heard the squeal of brakes — not theirs — as he barged onto the roundabout.

She saw his head duck as he checked the mirror. Lights flickered across his face and, with an electric jolt of surprise, she realized she wanted to reach out and touch him — touch his skin. He seemed larger than life, bigger than he'd been, more real and solid than any man she'd known. Is this what adrenaline did to you? When your subconscious decided you were one step away from being snuffed out and the family genes lost forever, did it lure you into enlarging the gene pool? Did it try to convince you that even a press photographer was a suitable mate?

'Hang on!' he shouted again.

She clutched the seat and the bones and shut her eyes this time. He spun the wheel to the right and the car began to turn, drifted, held again, and then he powered away.

'I've turned down Ruapehu. I'll get you as close to the lake as I can. You get ready to jump when I yell.'

She opened her eyes. 'OK.'

'Grab my camera bag off the back seat and put the rubbish sack inside. You won't be so conspicuous and Andy'll be looking for the sack.'

'Can I come up?'

'Yeah.'

She poked her head up, leant over the back of the passenger seat and grabbed the bag. She opened it, emptied all Nick's expensive-looking photographic gear onto the back seat and pulled the empty bag over to the front. Her body swayed as Nick dashed through the series of roundabouts that went all the way down to the lakefront.

'You ready?'

'OK.' She stuffed the rubbish sack into the camera bag and zipped it closed.

'A group of backpackers have just made their way up from that hostel beside The Dog House. They're walking down Ruapehu towards the lake. Get into the middle of them. Stick with them as long as you can and then make a run for it.'

'OK.'

'Right.' He glanced down at her and cried, 'Shit! You've got mud all over your face.'

She pawed desperately at her face.

The nose of the car dipped as Nick braked, flinging her

forward. She grunted as her arm hit the console.

'Go, go, go!' yelled Nick, like a demented drill sergeant. He leant across and flung her door open.

She grabbed the camera bag with one hand and the seat with the other and tried to pull herself upright as she clambered out. One foot caught, and she spilled out of the car and landed on her hands and knees.

She twisted and patted the door closed. Was there a cry of 'Good luck' as Nick sped off down the street? As she climbed to her feet she felt suddenly alone. It had been good having Nick beside her.

The backpackers stared but seemed more amused than concerned by her behaviour, so she tossed off the brightest smile she could muster and joined them in their procession towards the lake. She rubbed at her face as she walked, and a Japanese girl pulled out a packet of wet wipes. Someone else asked, in heavily accented English, if she was indisposing, so she nodded vigorously, waved her hand and said, 'Me, me' and kept nodding and smiling. Everyone nodded and smiled back, then left her to walk in silence.

They crossed over Lake Terrace as a flock. Tyres squealed and all heads swung to the corner where Tongariro turned into Lake Terrace. She saw Nick's car head off down towards the yacht club and the wharf, and two cars shot around the corner after it.

'Thank you, Nick,' she breathed. He was on her side, doing the best he could. He wasn't all bad. Maybe, deep down, he wasn't really a press photographer at all.

CHAPTER THIRTY-FIVE

SAFFRON SCRAMBLED DOWN the wooden steps, brushing against a broom bush, its dark wet fingers touching her clothes. It was never truly dark down on the shore — the lights from the Terrace above ensured that. She sprinted towards Tama's Rock. Now that she was so close, she couldn't bear not to succeed.

It might take Andy a little while to realize the one place she would have to return to was the rock. Steve, on the other hand, would guess straight away. And Steve was with Andy. So she hurdled the stormwater outlet, Nick's camera bag flopping against her back. The bones sang in her ear.

Ahead, she saw people running along the shore towards her. A hundred thoughts dashed through her mind. She had to relax. She couldn't force herself between the ripples. It was something that just happened, and she didn't know how, only that it had to be given time.

She could recognize the figures now. It was them — the gang of three. They had chosen to ignore Nick and concentrate on her. Trailing them she could see Nick, but he was too far away.

She reached the rocks that stretched out into the lake, Tama's own rock at the end like a fist on an arm. As she raced out angry waves swelled up and water swirled around her legs. All she could do was pray that Tama would help her in some way.

Andy and Steve reached the rocks a dozen strides ahead of Gilbert. They stood on the shore end and stared out at her. Gilbert joined them, the tyre jemmy clasped across his chest. She stared back. For a pulse beat, nobody said anything, and all she could hear was the blood pounding through her veins and the water against the rocks.

'Hand them over, Saffron!' yelled Steve.

She didn't reply.

'You've nowhere else to run.'

Still she said nothing.

Gilbert pushed up past the other two men.

'Give them back to me, Saffron,' called Andy. 'You know it's the best thing to do in the long run.'

'Best for who?' she yelled back. The wind was behind her and she felt as if it hurled her voice away, leaving her vulnerable. A weak little thing with a soft underbelly.

'Best for everyone, Saffron. It's illegal for you to have these bones in your possession. It's not for me.'

'But you stole them from me.'

'For your own good. Can't you see that?'

Nick had arrived and stood waiting on the shore, waiting to see how events would unfold. The others didn't seem to realize he was there.

'But I found them. They're mine until I give them back to the people they belong to.'

'They're part of the history of our country. They belong to everyone.'

'No. They're babies, and they belong to their people.'

Andy began to walk out along the rocks, Gilbert beside him. 'If they're as old as you say, then their people are all dead. Their rightful place now is with people like me, people who know how to preserve them and decipher the history they tell.'

The wind hurled Andy's voice at her.

'They belong to their people,' she repeated stubbornly.

'Whoever they belong to, you're not a fit person to have them. You destroy things,' shrieked Gilbert. He struck the jemmy against the rocks as he finished, as if to punctuate what he had said.

'Give them to me, Saffron. No one need get hurt over this,' Andy said.

'Listen to him, Saf,' Steve called.

'So why has he got a tyre jemmy in his hand?'

Gilbert held it in two hands across his body.

'No one needs to get hurt,' Andy repeated.

She wasn't sure if that was for her benefit or Gilbert's. It didn't matter much. Whatever Andy's intentions might be, she had no doubt that Gilbert wanted her blood.

Her gaze swung back to Steve and Nick on the shore. They waited together, but slightly apart.

Andy and Gilbert advanced. Tama's Rock felt rough and solid against her back. If he was going to help her, he'd better do it soon. She was running out of time.

She saw a sparkle of light, and for one moment thought Tama Ariki was racing down the rocks towards her, and then realized — and she didn't know whether to laugh or cry — it was the flash from Nick's camera.

And that flash ignited everything.

Gilbert leapt at her with the tyre jemmy over his head. She jerked sideways, too slowly, and the bar skimmed her arm. She cried out, her arm flopping to her side, and suddenly everyone was charging towards her. Andy grabbed at the bag. She screamed and tried to hang on, but her arm felt as if it was broken. Gilbert flailed about with the jemmy, whacking at everything that moved. Steve and Nick charged along the rocks towards them.

Saffron slipped to her knees, clinging desperately to the strap of the camera bag with one hand, and trying not to fall forward as Andy yanked and jerked. As Gilbert struck at her again, she pulled back to keep her face from the path of the jemmy and felt the strap slip through numb fingers.

She screamed.

Andy spun around and rushed back along the rocks. Nick ran towards him. Steve stopped, so that in an instant Nick was between the two men.

'Give them to me,' Nick demanded. 'They never were yours.'

Andy shook his head. 'You don't understand. She can't keep them. It's against the law.'

'So is stealing,' Saffron screamed. Tears ran down her face, lost among the drops flying off the waves.

'There's something weird going down,' Nick said calmly. 'She needs the bones to complete it.'

'Superstition.' Andy clutched the camera bag to his chest.

'You didn't think that when you saw Billy at the bottom of the cliff,' Nick said.

'That was different. I'd been drinking. The blood . . . It made me . . .' Andy shrugged, 'susceptible to a story like that. I've thought about it since then. It's a legend. Interesting, colourful, but just a legend. Nothing more.'

As Nick and Andy talked, Saffron saw Steve's gaze move to her. He smiled at her, regretfully she thought, and his lips moved. She fancied it might have been a 'Sorry, Saf' but the wind had no intention of bringing her the whispered apology. It tossed it away like trash. Nothing would ever be the same between Steve and her again — and they both knew that. But, like her, he'd reached the point when he would do whatever it took to look after those he loved. She understood, but he was wrong. That was all.

Steve's smile vanished and he began to tread softly along the rocks behind Nick.

'Look out!' she yelled, but it was too late.

Steve had grabbed Nick from behind in a bear hug and spun him off the rocks. Gilbert turned back to her, the look on his face almost gloating, the jemmy hanging loosely from one hand. He tightened his grip and jabbed at her with it. 'I'm going to break *you*.'

She didn't think he knew he'd spoken. Saffron dragged herself upright and stared him down. 'You do, little man, and I'll stick it up your arse.'

He jabbed again. She caught the end, feeling tendons pull in her wrist as the bar's momentum twisted it in her hand. She held on; her eyes never left his face. But it wasn't Gilbert she saw. She saw the faces of the other men she had fought on these rocks, and felt the strength flow back through her body. She'd fought warriors on this water-washed battleground, fought and won. This shopkeeper was fighting above his weight.

He couldn't hold her gaze. Something flickered across his face and he dropped the bar, took an uncertain step back, then turned and raced after the others.

Nick floundered ashore. 'You OK?' he yelled.

'No, I'm bloody not!' The jemmy dropped with a clatter from her hand.

She walked back along the rocks supporting her injured arm in her hand. She stopped midway, turned her head and looked out over the midnight lake, up at the dark sky. There was no help. The moon didn't care, and Tama Ariki hadn't come. He hadn't helped. All that power, and he did nothing.

Saffron shook her head. She wanted to just sit down and rest, maybe even cry, but she forced her legs into motion and walked off the rocks.

'Come on,' Nick yelled. He'd started along the shore after the others, but he stopped and turned when he saw she wasn't with him. 'Come *on!*'

She shook her head. 'They're gone. It's over.' She limped across and sat on the driftwood chair, rubbing her fingers over the hard, unforgiving wood.

'So we just wait while Tama lines up the next Delaney, do we?' Nick stared at her from a dozen paces. 'I wonder which of your sisters he'll take a swing at this time?'

She raised her head, sucked in her breath with a hiss. He was a cruel man. No wonder she didn't like him. But his words worked.

She took a deep breath and stood up. 'No, we don't wait. We get those bones back.'

Nick gave her a smile, lopsided and gentle. 'That's better. We can do it.' He paused. 'Have you thought any more about what I said?'

'No, I haven't,' she said insistently. 'When this is over, I'm joining a nunnery.'

'But you're not Catholic. Are you?'

She flapped a hand. 'Simply to get away from you.'

She was already jogging flat-footedly back towards the steps, 'I'll get the Mini in case they've sabotaged your car. You go that way, and I'll come down from the town.'

'Think about it sometime.' And then he was off, sprinting back along the foreshore like a hundred-metre dash man.

The run up the grass slope and across Lake Terrace felt like the longest of her life. She was desperately tired. Her arm tingled as feeling slowly returned. She was prepared to believe it wasn't actually broken and Gilbert had just caught a nerve in her arm, but how was she to find the strength to continue?

She batted the garden gate open and tore through. Into the house — keys — back out — and threw the car door open. Familiarity flooded through her as her body slipped down into the low-slung seat, and the snug confines of the little car pulled in around her. The engine caught on the first attempt, and she reversed around, then shot off down the Terrace, a cloud of blue smoke trailing in the yellow lamp-lit air.

There was no need to slow as Lake Terrace turned into Ferry Road and she rocketed down the slope towards the yacht club. She braked hard and changed down, and the Mini hugged the road as she whipped around the hard left, through the trees, hit the judder bar with a bone-jolting gasp that snapped her teeth closed with an audible click, and into the car park below the yacht club.

Three vehicles were parked facing the lake. Another car, young lovers perhaps, was just sneaking out. It was no longer a place for young lovers.

Andy's silhouette showed through the back window of the station-wagon. Nick and Steve were rolling on the ground pummelling each other. There was no sign of Gilbert. She suspected they'd seen the last of him for a while. By now he was probably cowering under his kitchen table with his cat.

Andy looked over his shoulder as if preparing to reverse out. Without thinking, Saffron flashed her headlights onto full beam, roared across the car park and stopped the Mini straight behind Andy. She leapt out of the car, engine still running, door open, and raced up to the station-wagon. The camera bag lay in the back. She yanked at the door. Locked. Her body froze as her mind slalomed from one desperate idea to the next, then she spun around and threw herself back into the Mini.

She backed up so that she was positioned only a couple of metres behind the station-wagon. Then she gritted her teeth and accelerated forward, her arms braced and her eyes narrowed as she awaited the micro-second before impact. The Mini hit the boot of the station-wagon with a shearing of metal and she whacked her ribs against the steering wheel. Andy jerked forward, then threw open his door.

Saffron reversed, hearing something pull off one of the vehicles, and quickly eased into first gear. Andy had one foot out of the station-wagon when she revved the engine and slipped the clutch. He quickly pulled his foot back in.

The station-wagon's boot snarled up like someone with a

hare lip. The bonnet of the Mini looked worse. The little car leapt forward like a hunting dog slipped the leash. At the last second, Saffron braced, closed her eyes, then grunted as the two vehicles collided. As she opened her eyes, the back of the station-wagon flew open.

Saffron leapt from the car. Andy was already on his feet. They both ran for the gaping mouth of the station-wagon. The camera bag was on the far side. Saffron flung herself across the warm bonnet of the Mini, her momentum shooting her into the back of the station-wagon so that her hand clamped down on the handle a moment before Andy's.

She grabbed the bag and crawled the length of the station-wagon, into the front seats. Andy swore and ran back. The driver's door was still open, and he jumped in. She felt his fingers rake down her back, but she was already clawing her way out the passenger door. She slammed it behind her and heard a bellow of pain as it closed on Andy's arm. She hurled the camera bag into the Mini.

Someone shouted at her, and she looked across the car park to see Steve and Nick struggling to their feet. Nick was calling something. He flung Steve aside and raced to his car. 'Give me the bag!' he yelled. 'I'll outrun them.'

He was in, and the runabout was hurtling towards her. She grabbed the camera bag, pulled the sack of bones out of it, dropped them on the floor of the Mini and spun around. As Nick neared, she raced towards him with his camera bag in her outstretched hands.

The driver's side window was down, and she thrust the bag in. Her eyes met Nick's. He felt the lightness of the empty camera bag and grinned. His bottom lip was split and bleeding, and his eyes danced with fire. He's enjoying himself, she thought in disbelief. This is just another one of his damn wars!

'Hold them up for as long as you can!' he yelled out the window. And then in a roar of engine and exploding gravel, he was gone.

The small car park suddenly seemed to stretch out to the size of a rugby field. The Mini looked a long way away. She was tired beyond belief, but she had to ensure they chased Nick. She had to make them believe he had the bones.

She flung herself towards the station-wagon, waving her arms and yelling, as if she thought she could stop them. Andy and Steve piled in. Doors slammed. She could see blood running from Steve's nose.

'Stop!' She made a last despairing dive and tripped. The fall made sure she didn't reach them before they roared out of the car park. It hadn't been hard to do. Her legs felt as if they'd wanted to let her down for a long while. She rested on her hands and knees on the gravel, watched them go and wondered if this really was the end. The darkness seemed to ebb and flow about her as if the night itself was breathing. Slowly, she crawled to her feet. Blood trickled from one hand as she walked slowly back to the Mini.

Its cheery red grille snarled in a toothless grin. The bonnet was up. She pushed it down, but it wouldn't catch. She sat on it, but it sprang ajar again as soon as she got off. It looked as if it would fly open at the first pothole. No matter. She'd walk if she had to. She slid behind the wheel and peered into the sack. The bones lay white and silent inside. Somewhere, she heard the sound of a police siren.

She turned the key in the ignition.

CHAPTER THIRTY-SIX

THE LAKE SLAPPED against her sneakers. Way off, she could hear the sound of the siren. Maybe it was following Nick, but sooner or later it would come here to Tama's Rock. They would all come here. She had to be gone before then.

The black water ran up and over her feet, gliding towards her, breaking against her legs. Breaking the ripples. That was how it began.

She swung the rubbish sack onto her back and began to lift each foot, tiredly at first, letting each wave pass unbroken, and then replacing that foot and raising the other. Slowly she remembered, and she began to jump from one foot to the other, the smooth, dark running waves moving beneath her.

One ankle felt a bit wobbly, but she pushed the thought from her mind. The only thing that mattered was jumping the ripples. So she ran, jumping further and further, the sack bouncing on her back, and at last the moment came. She floated down, her foot stretched, toes pointing, reaching for the space between the ripples.

The moment had come. She floated down onto the ripple and this time there was no solid shore beneath her foot.

Those smooth waves ran up her leg and pulled her down, water surged over her head, and she was through into the shimmering, silver-streaked tunnel. No time for mouth-gaping wonder this time. She landed on her feet and ran through the tunnel, feeling it shift and alter under her, the sack bouncing against her back. She thought she heard someone call out behind her, but she didn't stop. She doubted they could follow her. And then the ripples swallowed her up.

Ahead, she could see the bright light and hoped desperately that she wasn't returning to the same point in history. She couldn't bear to go through the killings and the blood again. There wasn't time. Until the bones were returned every Delaney was simply a fragile package of spillable blood.

The Shining came in a flood of warm soft light that pulsed through her veins and pushed her forward.

She skimmed through the ripple, her feet hardly seeming to touch the shimmering surface. It felt as if a giant hand gently pushed her from behind; ahead she could see the ripples beginning to waver. She heard the waves washing noisily on the shore and she glanced out to the lake, needing the reassurance of one familiar thing in a world gone mad.

Her body felt tired and sore beyond belief. Her arm still tingled and her ankle hurt — she listed to one side like a holed boat. As she hobbled forward she thought about the mothers waiting for the bones, ready to welcome them home. She heard a cry and stopped. Had she got it wrong again? Was she about to arrive in the middle of the killing? But this was a plaintive wail, in her ear. With a slowly dawning realization, she shifted the weight on her back experimentally, felt the way it pulled to one side. Awkwardly, she swung the rubbish sack of bones from her shoulder. But what reached the ground was her grey jersey holding four unhappy babies.

She knelt down beside them and saw her knees merge into the ripple, making her feel slightly queasy. She looked away, back to the babies. They were all alive, covered in blood, looking disgruntled, but alive. One of them gave a tentative smile. Maybe it was wind, but they hadn't been fed for so long, she thought it more likely to be a smile. She smiled back.

'Hi, guys,' she whispered. She stretched out one hand and touched warm silky skin, shaking her head in wonderment. 'That's one neat trick you've got there, fellas.'

She rocked back on her heels and looked at them carefully. Blood was crusted on their skin and hair, but none of the babies appeared to be bleeding. And it wouldn't matter if they were, she told herself. These babies were dead, she knew that. She was simply taking them home. These babies didn't need a doctor. They just needed to return to their people. She crouched for a moment longer, balanced in this place between life and death, now and then.

She clambered to her feet and arranged the babies in the jersey so that they looked more comfortable. She hesitated a moment, willing up the strength, then grabbed the top of the jersey sack and, with a grunt, lifted it to her chest. She wobbled on one leg as she stuck a knee under the weight, shifted her grip and got her foot back down before she toppled. She leant back, balancing the babies on her hip.

The moon wash was fading, and the ripple disintegrating. Saffron could hear birds twittering and singing. Hundreds of birds, and a stream gurgling. The ripple was disappearing. And this time, she knew, she had brought the babies home.

CHAPTER THIRTY-SEVEN

NICK REACHED THE wooden steps and almost cannoned into the senior sergeant, who was on his way up.

'Where is she?' Nick gasped. He hadn't run like this since he'd been back in Taupo. His heart pounded like a sledgehammer in his chest. He'd lost her again.

'Damned if I know. I could have sworn I saw her down there.' The sergeant pointed, then took off his cap and ran his fingers through thinning hair.

Nick turned and looked in the direction the sergeant had indicated. The foreshore stretched away in the strange half-light that the streetlamps allowed down there.

'Can't see her,' Nick said somewhat obviously.

'There were just a few bits of mist floating about.'

'Mist?' Nick jumped on the word and flung it back at the policeman like a soldier catching an incoming grenade.

'Strangest thing, like nothing I've ever seen down there before.' The sergeant shrugged. 'We'll take a look further along. Maybe she climbed up the bank.'

He manoeuvred past Nick and strode back up to the Terrace.

Big Wal had told Nick how he and Saffron had seen a mist at the funeral, and how she had watched Tama walk out of it. He reached for his cigarettes and found they were gone. Maybe Saffron would walk out of this mist. He narrowed his eyes and stared at the few scraps of vapour, trying to make them something they weren't.

He trotted down the steps, his footsteps echoing. The mist was heavier on the shore. Here, it was downtown Baghdad — after the Iraqis had lit the oil-filled trenches that ringed the city to confuse the US bombers, and the wind had whipped the desert sand and the black smoke into the city.

He tried to stare into the mist, but it hurt his eyes — burnt them, as if it wanted to keep him out. The searing sensation was as much mental as physical. His mind wanted to contract and close in snail-like protest, as he were forcing it to take in something unhealthy.

There was movement inside the vapour. He ran towards it and deep within — and it was as though he was looking into the sulphurous blast from a volcano — he could see a woman walking away from him. The fumes bit his eyes so that tears streamed. Heat radiated off his face and he threw his arms up for protection. He could scarcely see through the fumes and the tears, but he could swear there was a woman in jeans, leaning back and to one side as she trudged away from him, as if she carried a heavy load on one hip.

'Saffron!' he shouted. 'Saffron!'

The woman half-turned, slowly and laboriously. Her eyes were enormous in a face grey with fatigue. Heat bellowed out of the vapour. The stench of rotten corpses was thick and cloying. He felt his stomach rise in his throat. He took

323

a step, tried to edge forward, but the heat was blast-furnace hot, scorching his throat as he breathed in.

He raised his camera to his eye and shot. Sometimes, that was the only thing left to do.

The last of the ripple disappeared. Saffron stood at the edge of a large, flat clearing, bound on one side by the lake and on the other sides by manuka. Clumps of red-brown tussock were scattered among the white pumice stones tumbled across the land. Ahead, somewhere, she could hear the stream singing its way to the lake.

A group of woman clustered together on the far side of the clearing. As a figure tottered towards her Saffron remembered the first time she had seen the old woman in Ruapehu Street. She looked at Mount Ruapehu standing shoulder to shoulder with his brothers at the far end of the lake. The old woman's face looked as if it might split in two with her smile. 'You've got them.'

'I told you I would.'

'We've waited for so long, girl. So long.'

When Saffron glanced again at the group of women, she gasped with surprise and took a rapid step backwards, the weight of the babies on her hip almost causing her to fall. The clear stretch of tussock was now fenced with row after row of warriors, lines of tattooed men reaching out into the distance until they merged into the bush-clad horizon. Hundreds, thousands, of warriors waiting in total silence.

'Where did they come from? Who are they?'

'Don't be frightened,' the old woman said.

Saffron shut her mouth and stared at the men.

Some of them were magnificent — tall, muscular, bronzed. Others had limbs missing, dreadful wounds still wet with blood. Their dress covered the centuries: some were naked; others wore short flax skirts, or shirts and trousers. One warrior in a top hat stood next to a man with no head at all.

The old woman had not replied, but suddenly Saffron knew who these men were — these were the ancestors, stretching back through time.

'It is a great day. We have all come to welcome the mokopuna home.'

'You take them,' Saffron said suddenly. 'I've done what I said I would. Call one of those young fellas over to carry the babies. I'll just get on home now.'

'No, no. You must carry the mokopuna to their mothers. This is a great day. But don't be alarmed. Nobody will be watching you. It is the mokopuna they have come to welcome home.'

'My fifteen seconds of fame, and I turn out to be no more important than a pimple on a frog's arse,' Saffron said with a nervous smile.

The old woman chuckled. '*I* will always remember you, girl. And when we sit telling stories, I will tell the story about the ignorant white woman who brought the mokopuna home, and the people will cheer at your bravery and laugh at your foolishness. But it is the mokopuna who are important today.'

One of the women called a welcome, and the haunting cry flew down the path towards them, beckoning them forward.

Saffron staggered on beside the old woman. This is what it had all come to in the end: bringing the babies home. As they neared the women, Saffron eased the jersey sack from her hip, feeling her back scream in protest, and deposited it gently on the ground. The women swooped upon it with cries of delight. Babies were plucked from the sack. Fat, laughing babies.

Saffron squatted on the ground, breathing in deeply, and watched. Sweat dried on her back and she felt cold and naked. She had grown used to her load. The mothers were laughing and crying at the same time, and babies were hugged and held up for inspection and tickled. She felt in her back pocket for the bone tiki and held it out. The old woman took it and slipped it over a baby's head.

She heard a noise, a strange eerie sound, like wind playing through a shell. She looked up. The warriors had gone, simply disappeared. Confused, she looked around. Only the women and the babies remained.

Then a shadow fell over the group as a man approached, his footfalls echoing as if the ground were hollow.

The women became silent. Even the babies hushed.

Saffron didn't want to look up. It was Tama Ariki, and she didn't know if she could look upon him and not be harmed. She kept her eyes on the ground at her feet.

But he wasn't interested in her. He walked from one woman to the next inspecting the babies. Each was held up for his perusal. Each whimpered and squirmed in his mother's arms as if it wanted to escape.

Saffron remembered the old woman's words: *the babies flee from the blood that drips from his hands.*

For the first time, Saffron felt pity.

He spoke but Saffron couldn't understand him. He turned and walked away without a glance at her, and the women gathered the babies and moved off behind him. Even the old woman smiled briefly, then walked away.

CHAPTER THIRTY-EIGHT

SUDDENLY, SAFFRON WAS afraid. She scrambled to her feet. 'Hey!' she called, but no one turned. Maybe she was invisible to them now. She cried out again, and ran after them.

She stopped. She was running away from the Shining. What if she became lost? Then she heard a noise and looked down at her feet.

The ground was beginning to split. With each footfall, cracks raced out from Tama's feet, turning the tussock-covered clearing into crazy pavement. She watched in horror as a crack shot out, hit another and rebounded off in yet another direction. Pumice stones disappeared down gaps almost without sound. A crack raced between her legs, and suddenly one section sank or the other rose, so that while one leg remained straight, the other bent at the knee so quickly and forcefully she was thrown backwards.

Her head hit the ground hard enough to jar her teeth. She looked up, closing her eyes against the blinding glare of the sun. Points of light danced across her retinas. She rolled over onto her hands and knees. Just in front of her face rose a freshly cleft bank of dirt, crumbs of soil trickling down it. A clump of grass hung from the top, anchored by a few roots.

She climbed to her feet. The bank was waist-height. She looked behind her. The lake was now a long way away. Tama shooed the woman and babies ahead of him like an anxious shepherd. They still weren't that far away from her.

It wasn't just that the ground was breaking up — it was stretching. As Tama walked, the clearing was lengthening. She was being pulled further and further from where she had come.

Tama was taking the women and babies home, and she didn't want to think about where they had come from. They were dead, all of them dead, and they had what they had waited for for so long. Now they were returning, and she didn't want to go with them.

She had to return to her own time and she couldn't afford to wait. Already, it might be too late. She turned and began to run, but the land was distorting, lengthening. The ground she ran on was being sucked back, so that no matter how fast she ran, the blue of the lake retreated from her. And the lake was where the Shining would be. And the ripples.

A crack ripped across in front of her with a sound like a record being played at the wrong speed. She sprang for the other side, staring down into the abyss with horror-glazed eyes, feeling fingers of heat clutching for her flesh. She landed, stumbled, rolled into the fall and back onto her feet, and sprinted on. The lake was a spot of blue in the distance.

She glanced over her shoulder and almost fell. Tama and the women were still not far away. The broken ground tilted and tipped with each fall of his feet. The sound of the earth pulling apart was the sound of a heartbeat slowed down and stretched out until the sound was so distorted it became unrecognizable.

She recovered and ran on. The ground was a web of black lines, each one shooting out as if fired from a gun. She was losing her race.

And then she heard a sound. A note, and every other thing in this world was silent.

One bone sang out.

She stopped, every hair on her body raised, and a chill ran through her body.

The sound echoed out, and for as long as it did she stood motionless, frozen. The note ended, and the silence that followed seemed to echo around her too. She turned and cried out, hands flung up to her mouth. She could *see* the sound! A distant flickering firefly. Spun gold. Firelight. Dancing above the heads of the retreating group, and all the while she could hear the memory of that one note chiming out and out into a world without end.

And then another note.

The bones were singing to her, one last time.

And as each new voice joined in, another light joined the flickering group above the heads of the departing people. Colours merged and separated again and again, pulling through each other and apart. Threading through, twisting back, spiralling into and out of each other, and each time they came together, colour changed and reformed until it was as if every colour there had ever been danced above the land, and the voices of the bones rose in a crescendo.

But still their voices rose. The open-mouthed delight on

her face faltered and she clapped her hands to her ears. Their voices rang in her head, higher and higher, until she felt as if the sound was being driven in with a stake. And with each sledgehammer wallop, colours exploded like fireworks before her eyes, and she understood that her mind was short-circuiting. Her brain was exploding.

She should run, she knew that, but she stood and stared at the colours in the sky, shoulders hunched, hands over her ears.

The lights blinked out and the world dimmed. Hesitantly, she removed her hands from her ears. The bones were silent. And she didn't know whether to be relieved or cry. She knew she would never hear them again.

Something as soft as a summer breeze touched her shoulder. She turned. A gurgling laugh and then silence.

And galloping towards her across that broken land was a horse, a man in racing silks crouched low over its neck. Harlequin silks of every colour.

She lowered her hands and began to cry. The bones had done the only thing they could for her — they'd called out, bones speaking to bones, across the centuries. She was dead. And the bones had called for her daddy to come and get her. She gave a last look at the distant shore, then ran back towards him.

Between the gaps in the earth, a dreadful smell drifted up. The slab of earth she was on tipped, and she began to slide. She scrambled to hang on, grabbing at tussock and stones.

The horse leapt from slab to slab and she slithered her way towards it. The ground shook as it galloped towards her and she could see the light in its eyes and, just when she thought it would run her over, it flashed by and Daddy's hand grasped her and swung her up and they were galloping towards the lake.

Hang on, petal. She felt the power as the horse's muscles bunched and it sprang down over the final crack and onto the ground below. She looked down and the smell that rose out of that crack was terrible. And then they galloped on and the wind whipped her eyes until they were so blurred with tears she couldn't see. She buried her head against the bright silks and felt the wind sweep over her head.

When she looked up, the shore was only a few hundred metres away. She looked back. She could no longer see Tama or the women and the babies among the tumbled landscape behind them. Plates of earth lay tipped and tilted as if an earthquake had devastated the land.

She looked ahead to where a mist was forming on the shore.

'I don't—' she began to say.

And then in her head she heard Lucky Del say, *You can't come with me, petal, not yet*.

He was taking her back, but she didn't want to go. She wanted to gallop across this jigsaw puzzle land with the roar of the crowd in her ears and the wind blinding her eyes, on and on and on out into the furthest reaches of time.

CHAPTER THIRTY-NINE

NICK HAD NO IDEA how long he stood before the heat of that stinking vapour until it parted. When it did, he almost wished it hadn't.

Saffron stood there leaning against a chestnut horse much as she might have rested against a tree. She was smiling up at the man astride the horse. Tattered silks clung to his back; one hand held the reins, the fingers of the other caressed Saffron's cheek.

'Saffron,' Nick called gently.

Her eyes never left the rider.

Nick stepped forward, felt heat rush up from the ground as if it was a stove top, smelt the acridity of his shoe leather scorching and stopped. He spoke again and this time her eyes reluctantly turned his way. When he believed she saw him, he continued, 'I've come to take you home, petal.'

She smiled, lazy and dreamlike, and looked back to her father.

'No, Saffy, please.' Urgency raised the level of Nick's voice. 'You don't want to do that. You must come with me — now.'

Her feet were bare but she didn't seem to feel any pain.

Nick held out his hand and she laughed at him, glancing up at Lucky Del to see if he saw the joke.

When she didn't move, Nick resolutely picked his way across the cracked and uneven ground between them. 'Come home with me, Saffron. You don't want to stay here.'

He reached out and her skin quivered beneath his touch as if he'd hurt her. She pulled back, moving along the side of the horse, but he placed a hand either side of her against the animal's flank, imprisoning her within his arms. Finally, she looked up into his eyes.

Blood roared through his head; his body felt as if it shook. His head bent towards those beautiful Jean Harlow lips. He'd waited over twenty years for this fantasy to become real.

Her hand pressed against his chest and he paused.

She looked down the narrow gap between their bodies and he knew what she saw. He waited as she unlooped the camera from around his neck and all the time her eyes held his and he thought he might drown in what he found there. She extended her arm, but his eyes never left her face, and when she released the camera he hardly heard the rapidly distancing sound as it rattled and clunked down a crack in the ground.

Then his lips met hers, he tasted her sweetness, and he soared above the world, to some place he'd never been. He rode that current, feeling her warm breath as her lips responded, feeling her urgency match his.

When the horse jostled and moved, they reluctantly pulled apart. Her eyes shone with tears and he had to bend his head to hear her when she whispered, 'I want to go home, Nick. Take me home.'

He swept her up into his arms, feeling invincible, heroic,

like the sheriff in a goddamn western, and strode off across that broken landscape. Lucky Del and his steed had gone. So had any semblance of what looked like the shore. Nick's steps slowed, stopped, and he realized he might be just a bit player, the saloonkeeper, maybe, and not the hero at all.

He'd rescued her, but the cold hand of panic told him they were lost. He turned in a circle, looking for a bearing of some description, and saw what must be Tama Ariki and an old woman standing on an upturned edge of a slab of land. Tama held out his hand, and his mere shot forward and up like a missile from a gun until it hung in the grim, grey sky above him.

Tama Ariki's club. She'd told him about Tama's club. They weren't going to get back. Tama intended to finish them off.

Nick looked down at Saffron. They'd wasted so much time, and now their time was gone. He kissed her again, one last moment together.

She was looking upward, the expression in her eyes serene. Nick looked up and saw the club begin to descend. He could have run, but where was there to run to?

Tama's club seemed to come down at them from a very great height. It moved slowly at first, but the closer it got the faster it travelled and then there was a great rush of air that roared louder and louder and, with a drawn-out boom like a fighter plane breaking the sound barrier, the club hurtled past.

It was as if they'd been swatted with a giant blast of air. Nick was flung to one side; Saffron tumbled from his arms. He lunged to his feet, some part of his brain telling him Tama's club had fallen, but they still lived.

He grabbed at Saffron blindly, his head swivelling as he